INVINCIBLE NEMESIS

MEN OF VANGUARD BOOK 4

RYDER O'MALLEY

MEN OF VANGUARD SERIES

HEROES OF VANGUARD

Irresistible Power Prequel

(Patreon Exclusive Novella)

Infamous Heart

Infernal Justice

Iridescent Lust

Invincible Nemesis

VILLAINS OF VANGUARD

Corrupted Desire

ACKNOWLEDGMENTS

Thank you my Patreon Supporters
Jason Janes
Miranda Dal Zovo
James Holcomb
SLPrincess

1

"... AND THAT'S WHY THEY CALL IT A REVERSE ALEJANDRO Sandwich."

It's another morning at the HideOut. I'm on my second cup of coffee, and I still can't keep up with Alejandro's antics. The crowd is thinner than usual. It won't be dead for long. It had turned into the local hangout for folks needing an injection of pep, or a place to prepare for the struggles of the real world. Despite its popularity, Chad had maintained its coffee-shop charm, and the smell on its own was intoxicating.

"Liar," Xander said. "I'm Googling that."

The conversation at our table bordered on inappropriate on the best of days. If I hadn't helped Chad relaunch the coffee shop, I'm sure he'd ask us to leave and never come back. Thankfully, he repaid his debt with endless cups of coffee.

Either I looked more exhausted than usual, or Chad had telepathy as he appeared with another cup. There wasn't a man alive who made a cup of Joe as strong as this man, and lord knows I needed it.

"Holy crap!" Xander shoved his phone in Griffin's face. "He has a position named after him. I see why Theo keeps you around."

Griffin's face was a mixture of horror and confusion. One day at a time, Alejandro corrupted that poor boy. I had my suspicions Griffin's boyfriend was going to get himself a Reverse Alejandro Sandwich tonight. Or at least an attempt. I'd laugh when I got a call from the hospital with Griffin demanding I ask no questions.

"Hot sauce? Really?"

Alejandro is our resident trouble-making sexpert. Xander serves as the big brother, willing to clock anybody who messes with his friends. I referred to Griffin as the kid in the group, but after a year of being part of the Breakfast club, our starry-eyed geek was hardly new.

"Papi, you with us?"

Then there was me—the dad. Sure, it's partly because I'm the big burly man that needed a haircut and had a beard with more salt than pepper. Do the kids still say beefy? Alejandro liked to say I'm "thicc" with emphasis on the extra "c." I might be the father figure of this group, but I could teach these youngsters a thing or two.

"I prefer my Reverse Alejandro Sandwich with Sriracha."

The table froze.

Avoid eye contact, Bernard. It'll keep them guessing. If I could figure out how to work my phone, I'd pretend to be reading the news. But I didn't dare ask them for help. I'd never hear the end of it. It was bad enough I had to Google half the things they talked about. Man, even my inner monologue sounded old.

It took less than a second before activity resumed and Xander taunted Alejandro about his boyfriend. When Griffin joined in, they both gave him grief about his handsome live-in boyfriend. It would only be a matter of time before they turned on Xander. It was like this every morning, playful banter with an undercurrent of love. Cheesy, I know. But the Breakfast club had become a constant in our lives, and when their lives changed or relationships found trouble waters, we'd be here, ready to pick up the pieces.

"Earth to Bernard." Xander waved his hand in my face. "Are you having a stroke? Should we call somebody?"

"You're the paramedic," Griffin said. "Shouldn't you know the signs?"

"Are you going to give him mouth-to-mouth?" Asked Alejandro.

I hung my head while raising my hand. Chad doesn't

ask questions. I've known the coffee shop owner for years, longer than the actual Breakfast club. Like the truest of friends, he sat a fresh cup of coffee on the table, and like a telepath, he pulled a flask out of his apron and set it down, nudging it closer to the mug.

I chuckled at the gesture. "Do you remember the last time we started drinking at this hour?"

"Did it get sexy?" If I could shoot lasers from my eyes, Alejandro would be soot in his chair.

"I remember somebody woke up with a tattoo on their butt." Chad gave me a wink.

Bastard. They all conspired against me.

All three raised their hands as if they were school-children begging to be called on. They were insufferable. But I couldn't help but smile. Chad backed away, mouthing, "I'm sorry," while he made a heart with his hands.

"We're going to put a pin in that. Xander, buddy, pal, mi amigo." Xander leaned forward as if he were going to spill state secrets. Alejandro's line of questioning wouldn't end well. "When you were with Bernard, did you two ever, you know..."

"Were there gentlemanly relations?" Griffin added.

"Did you attend the bedroom rodeo?"

"See an optometrist about the one-eyed bandit?"

"Explored the hidden valley?"

"Gave a hot beef injection?"

"Boarded the beef bus?"

"Glazed his doughnut?"

"Played hide the sausage?"

"That's a lot of food," Griffin said.

I leaned forward to speak, and Alejandro held up his finger in my face. "Shhh. We'll get to your 'Slippery When Wet' tattoo in a moment."

Xander and I dated for two months. I had just arrived in Vanguard for a new job and, after leaving a relationship behind, we gave it a shot. As a couple, we had been awkward. But a series of uncomfortable dates had turned into a wonderful friendship. However, if he opened his mouth, I might kill him.

"He was a perfect gentleman."

Alejandro and Griffin whispered. It was Griffin who cleared his throat. "The council agrees. Xander has no knowledge of Bernard's penis."

That was not entirely correct, but some mysteries were best left undisturbed.

"Since we're talking about Bernard and his penis..." I brainstormed a dozen ways to murder Xander and hide his body. "When are you going to get back out there and start dating?"

I prided myself on doling out advice. But the moment attention turned to me and my life, I grew uncomfortable. It had been years since I went on a proper date. Other than Xander, I had dated nobody since arriving in Vanguard. It was hard to build a relationship when I continued focusing on the past and unresolved what-ifs.

Alejandro gripped my thigh under the table. Of the three, he was the only one who knew about the relationship I'd left behind. Circumstances had brought it crumbling to the ground and every day I thought about that decision. It haunted me every time I thought about my love life.

"You alright, Papi?"

I nodded. "With work being shut down until who knows when, I'd be a lousy, special someone."

For months, I had been working as the Director of Public Relations for one of the world's premiere superhero teams. Okay, that's a bit of a fib. Working for the Centurions served as my cover story for being one of the founding members. Yes, I'm a superhero, but other than Alejandro, nobody knew. I preferred compartmentalizing my life to protect my loved ones. Villains always wanted to kidnap somebody important to a hero. It's like they read the same play book. I couldn't imagine putting these three or Chad and the HideOut in danger.

A week ago, Eclipse broke into our headquarters and stole data from the computers. We still hadn't figured out what he'd stolen, and despite strong-arming him in prison, he laughed at my efforts. Until we figured it out, the team had been suspended. I don't want to admit it, but I missed heroing.

"Any idea when you'll be back to work?" Asked Griffin.

I shrugged as I gulped down another cup of coffee. "I have to go in today to talk to the leadership team. It's getting dangerous out there, and without the Centurions, it's only a matter of time before aliens attack."

"Or zombies," Griffen added.

"Mirror dimension doppelgängers," Alejandro said.

"Oh, I hate those people," Xander said. "They make my commute hellish."

"Yeah," I said, "so we'll see. Until we figure out what Eclipse stole, I think we'll have to rely on the other superheroes."

The room grew quiet to where my slurping of coffee filled the air. Everybody in the coffee shop had turned to the television hanging on the back wall. Chad kept it tuned to the Superhero News Network, and it appeared as if something big had occurred. I checked my phone, and the HeroApp™ hadn't sounded. It couldn't be a supervillain, or at least not one in Vanguard.

Xander patted my shoulder. "You'll be back to work in no time."

Chad turned up the television.

"... data leak has revealed the secret identities of the Centurions."

I ignored Alejandro's worried expression and stood. I knocked my coffee off the table, sending the cup to the floor.

"Looks like you're going to be busy at work today," Xander gave my back another pat. But he didn't know just how devastating this information could be. Not only could it upset the balance of power in Vanguard, but it could destroy...

"Among the identities, Bernard Castle, also known as the Centurion's founding member, Sentinel."

Shit.

G: *Finally! I can stop acting like I didn't know.*

    X: *You knew?*

    A: *See, I can keep a secret.*

    X: *You too?*

    G: *Xander, always last to the party.*

    A: *He wouldn't know if he were a superhero.*

    X: *Maybe I am!*

    A: *jajaja*

    G: *That'll be the day!*

I rolled my eyes as the three of them continued poking fun. They attempted to lighten the severity of the situation. I appreciated their efforts, but it didn't help. I was seconds away from a nervous breakdown, and the anxiety had me ready to scream. The elevator took forever, my foot rapidly tapping against the floor. With my secret out in the open, I could have stepped outside and flown to the helipad on the roof. That'd make the Director of Operations cry.

No, I wouldn't draw unnecessary attention to myself. There was no point in making a horrific situation any worse, right? With any luck, the other Centurions would already be there and we'd come up with a solution. Some of my teammates had families, and this meant villains would come out of the woodwork and threaten them just to get revenge.

We'd come up with a plan even if we had to enlist the Mystics and erase the memory of every person on the planet. But we'd still have to worry about the robots, or aliens immune to magic. People might think that being the Director of Public Relations served as my cover, but I worked my butt off for that title. The administration would need me to handle the world's perception of this disaster.

A: Papi, if you need to talk, I'm here.

The elevator dinged while I stared at the message. Despite my determination to keep my personal and hero life separate, Alejandro saw through the facade. Society thought that superheroes had secret lives for privacy, but the truth was, we did it for the people around us. Alejandro, knowing my secret, made him a target, and I didn't like the idea of some irate villain using him to get to me.

I squeezed through the door as it closed. The elevator didn't have buttons for the top nine stories. That required pressing my palm just above the panel. Lights flashed as they scanned my biometrics, confirming my identity.

"Designation Sentinel. Welcome."

"Morning, Gideon."

"Are you in distress? Your heart rate is 112 beats per minute."

"I'm fine."

"I beg to differ, sir."

The building had artificial intelligence, and I hated it. It would be one thing if it was just a computer reporting information, but Gideon came from alien technology. Not only could it learn at incredible speed, but it also had an attitude. Ever since I spilled coffee on an office keyboard, he made it his mission to rub me the wrong way.

"Are the other Centurions here?"

"Crimson, Iris, Lightyear, Valiant, and Synch have vacated the premise. Elixir is on the 99th floor with Director LaToya."

Director LaToya served as the woman behind the Centurions. She single-handedly took a ragtag group of heroes and turned us into the greatest superheroes on Earth. Whether it was funding, technology, or raw talent, she had a knack for making it happen. I teased she had powers of her own. No single person could have that level of tenacity. I'm sure she had a plan already unfolding.

The elevator stopped, and the doors opened. I expected to see a bustle of activity as the social media teams moved with purpose or the technicians prepared to reinforce the skyscraper for impending attacks. Apparently, I had missed a memo this morning as they reduced the lobby to a population of two.

"What do you mean there's nothing you can do?"

"We don't have the resources—"

"That's my family we're talking about."

Elixir functioned as our healer, and without her, I'd be dead. She might have an edgy look with her shaved head and an abundance of tattoos, but she was the most level-headed member of the team. She had her hand on LaToya's shoulders as if she might tear the tailored suit off the woman.

"What's going on?"

Both women turned. Elixir let go of Director LaToya and started pacing, as if she was about to explode. It appeared as if I wasn't the only one struggling with being outed. It was like high school all over again, except Billy Johns was a disgruntled supervillain.

"They know who we are," Elixir said. She pointed at LaToya, wagging her finger. "And they've pulled the plug."

"Wait. What? What does she mean, Director?"

"It's over," the director said, straightening her blazer. "The government has declared the team a risk."

"They can't shut us down," I growled. "They need us. How many times have we saved this planet?"

"They claim your identities are compromised, and they need to seek other options. I'm sorry. I fought for all seven of you."

"Other options? You mean other teams, don't you?"

Director LaToya's lowered eyes spoke volumes. It wouldn't take more than twenty minutes to fly to D.C. and speak with the President. With minimal shouting, I'm sure I could convince him to reverse the order. Public identity or not, we were still the planet's best line of defense.

"They know about us. Every villain out there knows. My family..." Elixir ran up to me, throwing her arms around my chest. Burying her face, she couldn't hold back the tears. "I have two kids in elementary school. If villains don't hurt them, then the fifth-grade bullies will."

I wrapped an arm around her while shooting daggers at LaToya. "Lix, I want you to go home and get your kids. You've been talking about going to a cabin in Vermont for years. Tell the kids it's an adventure. Stay out of town until the news outlets find a better story."

She nodded without saying a word. I locked eyes with Director LaToya. She maintained that annoying neutral face she used when breaking tough news. I'm sure she'd fought for us. I had no doubt she used every bit of influence to keep the Centurions together. But as the ship sank for the rest of us, I suspected she negotiated herself a life raft. After all, if she could build one team, then she'd be able to do it again.

"I'll have the intern deliver your personal effects."

"Thanks," I said, withholding a growl.

"Let's go, Lix. We might not be Centurions, but we're still family."

She wiped her eyes as we walked back to the elevator. If I had to drive her family to Vermont to keep them safe, I'd go without hesitation. Considering how many times she bandaged my wounds or healed a broken bone, it was the least I could do. I'd have to reach out to the others to see if they were doing any better. Synch lived with a sick father. It'd be harder to get him and his dad to safety, but I would not let them remain in harm's way. If the government wouldn't help us, we'd help ourselves.

We got into the elevator and as the doors closed, Director LaToya vanished. It would be difficult to recalibrate without the might of the Centurion brand behind us. It meant no high-tech gadgets, space ship, or fantastic snacks. Man, maybe without the snacks I'd be able to fit into my costume... Dang, even my suit belonged to the Centurions.

The doors closed and Lix leaned against me until I wrapped an arm around her shoulders. "Those jerks are going to ignore years of service?"

"Designate Unknown. You are in an unauthorized area."

"Well," I sighed, "didn't take long for them to toss us aside." I pressed the button to the lobby.

"Last week, we stopped an interstellar god from trying to turn Earth into slaves, and we don't even get a 'farewell' from them?" Lix kicked the elevator doors. I couldn't blame her.

Every time we donned the costume, we put our lives on the line. We risked orphaning children or widowing a spouse. It's the reason behind maintaining secret identities. More than that, it's the reason I'd kept everybody at arm's length. Now I had to worry about the guys, or even the HideOut being a target.

"Do you want me to go with you to Vermont? I can protect you."

She gave me a tight squeeze. "Thanks, Bernard. But we'll be okay. I hope. The family could use some bonding time. Maybe this is a blessing in disguise? I can go back to nursing and use my powers to help the sick?"

I envied Lix. Any hospital would be lucky to have her. A public relations guy with the ability to summon lightning? Not sure I'd have the same job prospects. Thankfully, I had been putting money away for years and didn't *need* a job.

"Maybe this is the worst of it?" Lix had a knack for bouncing back and keeping her chin up. Fired and furious one moment, but five minutes later, she was already trying to put a positive spin on the situation.

"Maybe." I wasn't convinced.

"Take care of yourself, B," she said with a kiss on the cheek. She let go, and with a wave, she headed to the front doors. I wished her the best and made a mental note to call her later and see how she was holding up. I'd be making a lot of those calls before hitting the sack.

Years of work thrown out the window. They disposed of us like leftovers. If I replayed all the things I sacrificed to be a hero, all the people I pushed away, it'd be staggering. Clenching my fists, I reminded myself to stay calm. I'd make this work and put a spin on it so the future looked a little brighter. That was my job, or at least it had been. But there remained a tightness in the pit of my stomach I couldn't ignore.

I exited headquarters as a Centurion for the last time.

"The worst has yet to come..."

2

I'D HAVE CALLED IT CLICHE AS MICK PUSHED ANOTHER BEER across the table. A superhero down on his luck, spending his day wandering the city lost in a fog. But instead of picking himself up off the ground and regrouping, he headed to the bar to slam back cheap booze. At least at Bottoms Up, Mick kept the lights dim enough that nobody asked for an autograph. I pulled the hood further down my face, being extra obvious in my attempt to be discreet.

"My day has been wonderful," Mick said as he popped the cap off a beer. "Thanks for asking. Call me crazy, but I have a feeling yours isn't going according to plan."

"I'll be fine." It was the truth. I needed a day or two to sort out my life. Now that the world knew I led the Centurions, getting a job wouldn't be easy. I couldn't add LaToya as a reference. But in truth, I didn't need a job. The Centurions received paychecks, and I lived like a pauper. My bank account would suffice for the next decade. But what about Sentinel?

"Let's skip being coy." Mick owned Bottoms Up, where he pretended to be a bartender. Most of his job was listening to customers as they poured out their hearts over a cocktail.

"What?"

"I ask how you're doing. You say fine. I prod a bit more. You resist. Ultimately, you realize I'm relentless, and you can either stop drinking and leave or answer my questions."

"Is that how this plays out?"

"Bernard, you're the smart one here. I'd have thought you'd know better."

True. The guys joked about how I dished out wisdom whenever they came to me with a problem. I'm pretty sure each of them had me as their number one on speed dial. But where do the wise go for advice? I need to look no further than my graying bartender.

"Sentinel, huh?" I appreciated his whispering.

"Yeah. No point in hiding it anymore. I'm a superhero."

"I have your action figure."

"Really?" I started downing my fifth beer. Me? Drunk? I wish. They never tell you about the downside of having superpowers. Alcohol didn't have the same effect as it did on a normal person. That was the biggest problem in my life right now.

"Sentinel is hot. If I were a few years younger, I'd have bagged and tagged that youngin.'"

I snorted. The beer burned the inside of my nose. Ever since I arrived in Vanguard, I had the luxury of listening to people speak about my alter ego. I could detach from the identity and treat it like a job. But now that they knew my big dark secret, every statement about Sentinel felt personal. I raised my eyebrow as Mick gave me a not-so-subtle wink.

"I'm pretty sure you'd ruin me for all men."

"Damn straight," he said, wiping down where I had sprayed beer. "But in all seriousness, how are you holding up?"

"Honestly, I'm doing okay. It's a lot of change at once. I have some tough choices to make. How do I go..." I paused as somebody nearby ordered an Old Fashion. Mick made the drink, exchanging pleasantries as the gentleman went back to his table. "I need to figure out how I'm going to carry on. I gave up everything to be Sentinel."

Bottoms Up was the Ward's low-key gay bar. There were no skinny guys standing on tables serving high-priced cocktails from their navels. After listening to one too many show tunes, Mick had ripped the cord out of the jukebox.

The men here knew when to give a guy space and when to drag them into the bathroom for a quickie. As Sentinel, I'd sip Hero Chasers with Alejandro at Midnight Alley. But as Bernard Castle? I always preferred to drain a beer with Mick.

At the end of the bar, two men poked one another, thinking they were being subtle. As they shimmied down the bar to get a better look at my face, I pulled the hood further over my head. It'd only take a text to their friends or a post on the HeroApp™, and trouble would find me. It seemed harmless enough, that is, until the wrong villain was scrolling while sitting on their couch. Minutes later and I'd be trading blows, wrecking Mick's bar.

"You two." Mick slung the towel over his shoulder. "Get out."

One man tried to protest, but Mick shooed them away. As they reached for their wallets, he told them the drinks were on the house and he saw them to the door. Did I mention Mick was good people?

He returned to the opposite side of the bar, shaking his head. "Damn kids and their need for validation on a damned app. You wouldn't catch me dead on those things. Back in my day—"

"Walked to school uphill both ways?"

He pulled the towel from his shoulder and snapped it against my forehead. "No. If you wanted to talk to a guy, you said hello. If you want to pound him, you took him into the bathroom. Now they woof at one another like pups in heat." He paused as he popped the cap off another beer and slid it in front of me. "And they best get off my lawn, too."

It reminded me of the conversation this morning with the guys and their determination to find me a man. Since moving to Vanguard, I hadn't so much as gone on a date, let alone thought about a relationship. I wouldn't know how to date anymore. If they knew how long it took me to send a text, they'd consider me hopeless. The idea of joining a dating app and perusing men like a meat market? It struck me as cold and impersonal.

I hadn't been willing to date when the world didn't know my secret identity. Now it'd be impossible. The fear of a supervillain swooping in and using the people in my life against me had always been a concern. Now it'd be inevitable. I already had the guys checking in every few hours to ensure a villain hadn't tied them up in a secret lair. It'd be Griffin. I'd wager a pretty penny he'd be the first kidnapped.

"You'll find a way." Mick snapped me back to reality. "You didn't wake up one morning and decide to be Sentinel. It's who you are. If you can't help people wielding a giant axe, there are other ways."

"You're right, Mi—"

"And can we discuss this axe? You wield lightning like a

god. Why are you carrying an axe like a vertically gifted dwarf?"

"Why do I wear a cape?" The public relations director in me would refer to the focus group data that said women 25-45 considered a hero wearing a cape to be more trustworthy. But men 18-35 liked a hero with a badass weapon. It was the price we paid for having corporate sponsorship.

"It's like you read too many comics."

"At least I don't wear my briefs outside my pants."

I pushed the empty bottle toward Mick and he replaced it with a full one. He snatched the bottle, never breaking eye contact. The intensity in his brown eyes made me shift. Just because I wielded one of the primal forces of nature didn't mean my bartender couldn't make me uncomfortable.

"Whatever it is, just say it," I said.

"All this time, I imagined you as a boxer guy."

I slammed back the beer until it ran dry. Pulling a fifty from my wallet, I dropped it on the bar. Mick politely pushed it back.

"Your money isn't good here, Mr. Castle. You've saved the Ward more times than I can count. It's me who owes you."

When I formed the Centurions, the world needed heroes to stop an alien race from invading. Vanguard City threw us a parade. Once we formalized our arrangement, it became an expectation that we'd protect Vanguard. I didn't need the praise, but I appreciated it. The pat on the back almost made the solitude worth it.

"Thanks, Mick." I paused, then walked up to the bar. I grabbed his shirt, pulling him closer before planting a kiss on his forehead. "And for the record, it's a jockstrap or nothing."

3

Heroes have to hero.

No wizard imbued me with powers, no freak chemical accident, no insect bite. According to the Centurion museum, I willed myself to have powers. What does that even mean? The public relations coordinator in me understood. It's hard to sell an epic-level tale when it starts, "Six years ago, I woke up hovering above my bed and could wield lightning."

Centurion headquarters hadn't texted me a hundred times informing me of disasters across the world. By this time of night, we'd have already stopped a giant lizard monster and defeated ancient gods. I checked my phone out of habit. Zero texts. The Centurions had run its course. I returned to being a free agent. I had attempted to squeeze into my original suit, but no luck. Tonight it was plain ol' Bernard watching over Vanguard.

I forgot the patience required by heroes without a threat assessment team. High above the city, it almost appeared tranquil. The roads were filled with the warm orange glow of street lamps. Cars made their way home from a late night at the office. Even the windows filled with light, peppering the darkness of the Vanguard. To the casual observer, the Ward appeared peaceful, untainted by crime. But alas, that'd be a lie.

"Fancy meeting you up here."

Cobalt, one of the Ward's newer heroes. Telekinesis. He had upgraded his uniform to rich blue leather with white gloves, boots, and a cape. His dossier made note of his efficiency and his tendency to follow up with the victims of supervillains to ensure they were okay. I had watched him abandon a fight with a lava monster to save a school bus of children. He went into the good people category.

"Centurions or not—"

"Once a hero, always a hero," he finished.

For the last hour, I had watched the flying protectors of Vanguard zipping out of the sky as they picked their targets. At first, I thought maybe they had hawk-like vision or super hearing, but it couldn't be *that* common. I wanted to ask him what I was missing, but my pride swallowed the question.

"Sorry about the reveal."

In the superhero community, a 'reveal' was one of the most heinous acts. With my face plastered on the television, every villain I ever locked behind bars itched at the chance to get their revenge. If they couldn't hurt me, they'd resort to seeking the unpowered people in my life. It's partially why, as Alejandro put it, my love life remained a barren wasteland.

"It's okay."

"How are the rest of the Centurions holding up?"

"We've disbanded."

"Whoa." I had all afternoon to dissect the monumental weight behind that statement. Without the Centurions, it meant heavy hitters like the Raiders and Cyber Squad were left to protect Earth from planetary threats. It forced me to understand all the good I had been doing. It warmed my heart, truly it did, but now I was back to six years ago as I relearned the trade.

"Hunting for a new team?"

"I don't think so."

"What about training the kiddos?"

I nearly laughed. The next generation of heroes? The girl at the store laughed at me when I traded in my flip phone. I could wrestle robots to the ground, but I couldn't set the clock on my microwave. As a mentor, I would never cut it.

"Not a chance in hell," he said.

"If you change your mind, let me know. There are

plenty of heroes who would love to play sidekick to the legendary Sentinel."

He reached for one of his utility belt's pouches and held up his phone. From this height, the light of the screen illuminated the stubble along his jawline. I tried to imagine him without the cowl. Who was the man behind the mask? My imagination raced until I pictured him naked. Okay, maybe Alejandro was right, and I needed to get laid.

"I'm going to take this one."

"This one what?"

He raised an eyebrow. "The HeroApp™. You..." Did my face give away my confusion? I guess there were more reasons to wear a mask than I thought. "I forgot you've been out of the solo game for a while."

"Stop pretending I'm old enough to be your father."

"Sure, daddy." If I wasn't angry at the situation, my jeans might have tightened. Was he flirting or mocking? Sometimes it was a fine line between the two. "The HeroApp™ has a subscription service for the average superhero. It uses your location and skill set to help prioritize rescues. It's that or..." He gestured at me.

"There's an app? What happened to the world?"

He showed the screen on his phone. "Saving the city calls. Good luck, Bernard. Think about what I said. If you ever need backup, let me know." Cobalt didn't wait for a reply as he fell from the sky.

I waited another twenty minutes for a building to

explode or sirens to fill the air. Nothing. I decided it was time to call it a night and head home. There was no point in staying perched above the city. Spinning around, I inspected the sky, just to make sure intergalactic overlords weren't lurking. Unfortunately, no.

Flying is hard to explain. It's not pushing off or even imagining a sense of weightlessness. It simply *is*. But falling, that is a chaotic sense of freedom. The streets come at such a speed it could spell certain disaster. Many superheroes describe it as letting go of all the stress in one ten-second descent. For me, it's as I change angles and speed through the streets of Vanguard that I feel most alive.

Weaving through the city, I spotted my apartment. A crowd of reporters huddled together by the front door. Alex, our doorman, held the line, refusing to let the harpies pass. Zipping past them, I wound my way around the block, ready to shoot upward and land on the roof.

A scream. A blood-curdling wail.

It was only a block away from my building when I spotted the lady on the sidewalk. Falling from the sky, I land a few feet away, fists clenched. She was well into her sixties, wearing a nightgown and slippers. Spinning about, I expected the shadows to come alive or the ground to shake. Her face held fast, terror in her raised eyebrows.

"Ma'am, where are they?"

Her arm extended until she pointed toward the sky. As I followed her finger, I couldn't see anybody above us. Had they already gotten away? Did she need medical help? There were a thousand assessments that needed addressing all at once. That's the real sign of a hero, making calls under pressure.

"Socks," she whimpered.

Socks?

It wasn't the sky she pointed at. I hovered off the ground near the branches of a tree planted in the sidewalk. Two tiny orange orbs, hidden amongst the branches, reflected the street light. Tonight's villainy came in the form of a black cat frantically meowing as it clung to a tree branch.

Heroes have to hero, but not all villains are powered.

"Here, kitty, kitty, kitty."

Autumn had rolled in and the leaves had all but fallen from the branches. Reaching for the cat, it hissed. Fine, I'm not a fan of moody furballs, either. It swiped at my fingers, nearly losing its grip on the branch. I grabbed the cat around the waist, peeling its claws from the wood. Once in my arms, he relaxed, but still tried to bite my finger.

"Aren't you a feisty critter?"

"Oh, thank you! Thank you!"

The woman's arms extended, waiting for the pet as I hovered toward the sidewalk. The cat didn't wait, jumping from my arms to hers. I swear it stuck its tongue out at me as it nuzzled against her chest.

"He's been going crazy since his misses had her litter."

She's sweet, kissing the top of the cat's head. It almost made up for the bandit chewing my finger.

"Socks, that's no way to behave," I said. Fine, I'll admit it. I'm a sucker for the little hell beasts. They're self-sufficient, arrogant, and more than capable of using their powers for evil. Package that all up in a cute bundle of fur and what is there not to love?

"I hope you have a good night, ma'am."

"I recognize you. Oh, you're him!" Was she one of the people I saved from a burning building? Liberated from mind control? At this point in the game, it was impossible to remember the face of every citizen I saved.

"You've probably seen me on the TV."

She shook her head. "No, that's not it. You're the guy always sitting in the park in the morning."

Vanguard was a large city. For her to recognize me from the park, of all places, she must have a mind like a steel trap. Depending on when the Breakfast club met, I'd spend time in the nearby park watching people. It helped remind me they weren't just victims waiting to be attacked. The people of Vanguard led rich, full lives. Oh, and there was, of course, some seriously sexy stroller meat getting a walk in before they headed to their jobs.

"That's me."

"Superpowers, huh?"

I nearly laughed. They were more common here than anywhere else in the world. But her lackluster acknowledgment made it sound as if she had led a life filled with excitement, and a man flying through the streets couldn't compare.

"Yeah, it's a thing."

"Well, you be careful out there. Vanguard isn't what it used to be. Streets can be dangerous."

I dared a scratch behind Socks's ear. The purring started and her face lit up in a smile. "I will. Both of you be careful, too."

"He likes you. Socks is an excellent judge of character."

"Take care, ma'am."

Lifting off, she gave me a wave. "The city needs more heroes like you."

Heroes like me? A man who saves fluffy balls of doom from trees? I mulled it over as I flew to the roof of my building. Had I become so obsessed with saving the planet that I forgot to save the people? I never scoffed at the street-level heroes. They were just as important as the Centurions. Heck, that's where I got my start. Maybe Socks had the right idea, stop worrying about the big threats and focus on the everyday. Did I just credit my epiphany to a cat?

More often than not, I used the door on the roof after coming home from a long day of work. It made sure that even the doorman didn't quite know my schedule or the frequency of my late nights.

In the door and down the stairs, I lived in one of two apartments on the top of the seven-story building. It might not be luxurious, but it was one of the tallest in the Ward and meant it was easy to find when coming back after slugging it out with a bad guy.

I stopped at my door, half expecting an eviction notice. I wouldn't be shocked if the management company asked me to leave for the safety of the other tenants. There were so many reasons heroes maintained their identities. It'd be months before I uncovered all the ramifications. But for now, I was glad to be home.

Opening the door, I hesitated. I loathed this moment. My apartment remained dark and empty. I didn't need to turn on the lights to know my coffee cup remained next to the pot. There'd still be a bowl in the sink from my cereal. And the silence... the signs mounted. After today, it was impossible to deny: I was lonely.

The steam poured out of the shower as I pushed back the curtain. I'd hoped the water pelting against my skin might bring a bit of clarity and help me unravel the conundrum I faced, but no such luck. Pulling the towel off the shower rod, I gave myself a pat down.

I hung it on the back of the door and wiped the fog from the mirror above the sink. Do people see their reflection and see the person they used to be? I always wondered because, after every shower, I swore the man staring back looked a little more exhausted. Feigning a smile, it looked awkward on my face, as if I had fallen out of practice. Did I smile anymore? The fact I had to ask couldn't be a good sign.

"You're handsome, Bernard."

But it wasn't my appearance that changed. Flexing my biceps, a sexy man stood in the mirror. Sure, I had a bit more of a gut than I did twenty years ago, but being forty, I remained a damned good-looking man. The beard, trimmed to highlight the angle of my jaw, lost its luster, and bits of white crept in. It was nothing compared to the white patch of chest hair that steadily darkened as it pointed to my package. No, Bernard Castle remained a handsome man.

The fire behind the eyes, that's what changed. I traded life for a sense of duty. My sacrifices ensured the people of Vanguard, heck, the world, slept soundly in their beds. Somewhere along the way, the cost grew, and I continued paying.

I pulled on a pair of flannel PJs and grabbed my phone. Sitting on the couch, I dimmed the lights as if I didn't want to be caught doing something inappropriate. I flipped through the screens until I reached the apps.

"Heaven help me." The list of dating apps went on for twenty pages. There were apps for singles looking for dates, more than one that promised a night of wild sex, and did circus performers really need their own? I did not know there were so many folks looking to be dominated. And another for pup owners? Did dog walkers struggle to date?

"Deep breath, Bernard. It's not like you're facing off against Cerberus again."

WoofR. For bears, husky men, and their admirers. Okay, at least those words, I understood. And based on the spare tire I sported, I'm pretty sure I qualified. Okay, downloaded. A short five-minute questionnaire seemed easy enough.

"Why was I so scared of online dating? This is easy."

I scrolled through the fifty pages worth of terms and services and, like every other person in the universe, clicked accept. Photo? Scrolling through my albums, I realized that there were plenty of other people, but almost none of me. I looked handsome at the moment. Could take one now, I guess.

Twenty minutes later, I had a photo I didn't hate. Who knew having your identity shrunk into a thumbnail made you look too skinny and not skinny enough. Shirtless came off too desperate. Of course, I had to try on half a dozen t-shirts before I found one that made my eyes stand out but didn't make my arms bulge like I lived at the gym.

"Never getting those twenty minutes back. Okay, what next?"

Gay. Hairy. Few extra pounds. How vain were the bears? Ten questions so far, and all of them had to do with my appearance. Why on Earth did they need to know my shoe size? Were guys into that? I stared at my feet. Suddenly, they were both too big and not big enough. I hadn't even received a message, and already I hated myself.

"Top or bottom? Are we really reducing ourselves to labels?" I was about to click versatile, then changed it back to top. No point in lying, right? "Single. Wait, dom or sub? Cub, otter, werewolf? They're just making it up at this point."

The questions continued. How hard was it to find somebody to have coffee with? Feet licker or feet licked? Spanker or spanked... Okay, at least for that one, I had a preference.

The welcome screen appeared, thanking me for filling out the brief survey. "Brief? I just went through the olympics of questionnaires. They should buy me dinner."

I scrolled through the photos, surprised by how many men lived within a mile of my apartment. This is why Alejandro recommended it. It'd have taken sitting at the bar every night for a month before I came across this many beefy men. I hadn't reached the end of the list when the phone dinged. Somebody woof'd at me? I never understood why bears woofed.

I clicked the message and woof'd back. "What the heck does that mean? Is this one of those dog walker things? Does he think I'm a pup now?"

Another message came in.

Looking4U: Hey

DaddyBear: Hey, how's it going?

Looking4U: Bored. Horny.

Well, that went from casual to intimate a bit quickly. How do I reply to that? Do I just ignore it and ask about their favorite novel? Before I could respond, a slew of photos popped up in the message. Naked from every angle imaginable. His cock might be impressive, but... This is not exactly what I was looking for.

DaddyBear: Handsome.

Looking4U: Need your load in my hole

I stared at the words, blinking in disbelief. Wait, what? Did men use these lines on each other? Did it work?

Looking4U: Big cock?

I flicked the phone, shutting off the app. What happened to having a coffee and shamelessly flirting, hoping to get a number? It might be nerve-wracking, but there was something wonderful about getting groped by a hopeful suitor. This... This was like the Uber Eats of cock.

"Nope. Nope. Nope. Alejandro, I'm going to slap the grin off your face next time I see you."

After that, how bad could the HeroApp™ be? Every citizen in Vanguard had it on their phone, but I had never considered signing up for it as a hero. When a team of analysts dolled out mission assignments, an app on my phone didn't seem useful. But now that I was an expert in online dating, why not give it a shot?

Every phone came with it pre-installed, a sign of how

many heroes and villains were running around the streets. Unlike WoofR, the HeroApp™ only took a minute before I had the screen asking for my powers. I half expected them to ask how hard I liked to spank a guy.

"Lightning. Strength. Flying. Speed." Easy enough. With a few more questions, I signed up. Did they vet the heroes? Would I have to show off my skills for a team to prove that I—

"Approved? Well, that seems suspicious."

I could see the alerts popping up all over the city. Bank robberies, kidnappings, and... jaywalkers? I guess crime was crime, no matter the severity. My heart swelled as I spotted dozens of heroes zipping through the city, answering the call. Photos from bystanders showed them in action, doing their best to keep Vanguard safe.

"Impressive." As I searched for bigger-caliber villains, I considered my ego. Had I gotten used to saving the planet? Did I think myself above these petty crimes? I needed to do some soul-searching and check myself before I went into the streets. As the leader of the Centurions, I might have once led the most powerful team in the world, but by myself, I was just another blip on the HeroApp™. Socks had made sure I knew my place.

"Depressing." Admitting my new role made my stomach uneasy. I needed to be done with this day. After a good night's sleep, I'd start regrouping and carve out a place for this new version of myself.

I headed to the bedroom, but like entering my apartment, I paused at the door. I loved my bed and the softness of the pillows. But the king-size mattress had grown more and more spacious. Try as I might to sleep in the middle, there was a comfortable groove on the right side where I dreamed away the night. I swallowed my feelings and ignored the loneliness.

Tomorrow would be a better day.

4

THE SUN BROKE THE HORIZON, FLOODING MY BEDROOM WITH light when I woke to the dinging of my cell phone. I had thirty text messages, which is exactly thirty more than I expected to receive. Those could wait until I was out of bed and had a cup of coffee in my head.

Dozens of alerts flashed about the Centurions and the impending announcement of the new director. They had wasted no time replacing us, and after my pity party yesterday, I'd decided I didn't care. I'd be interested to see which heroes they recruited, but it wasn't news I needed while still in bed.

Click. I deleted them all.

I wasn't prepared for all the messages from WoofR. The number of dick pics and shots of men bent over were more than enough to get my cock hard. To my surprise, there were dozens of pictures and no words. How did you respond to a stiff cock? Did you compliment it? Send one in return? I hated to admit it, but I'd have to ask Alejandro to be my virtual wingman. The amount of attention was flattering, but I thought it'd be difficult to invite a cock to dinner. Or is that how this went?

"I'm too old for this."

I was about to toss the phone on the nightstand when another message came in. Would it be another glistening erection, or a guy on all fours waiting to be mounted? Text.

SeekingBeefy: Handsome man. You've got a nice smile. Hope you have plenty of reasons to show it off today.

I clicked on the photo, saddened when I found it only contained a silhouette of a chubby man standing in front of a window. The curves of a belly, slightly thicker than his shoulders, got my attention. When I zoomed in, I could tell he was naked, but the light made it impossible to make out his features. I didn't know how to respond to a dick pic, but this I could handle.

I slid my finger to hit the chat box when the camera went off. The flash made me cringe. Before I could respond, I heard the whoosh of a sent message. To my horror, my sleepy face shielding from the light had been sent right along.

"What the hell!"

I went to send an apology and my fat fingers punched at the keys. Another whooshing sound. This time, "I'm so…"

and, dear God, an eggplant emoji. I might be old, but even I knew the disaster unfolding in front of me.

SeekingBeefy: Either that's the worst pickup line ever, or you're not a morning person.

I let out a sigh of relief. I expected little from the app. Human sympathy? I'd take it. It made me even more excited. But before I replied, I sat up, wiping the sleep from my eyes. I gave my fingers a good flex to prevent another misfire.

DaddyBear: Lesson learned. Don't answer texts while in bed.

SeekingBeefy: That's a nice eggplant you have there.

DaddyBear: Nothing compared to my cucumber.

SeekingBeefy: Lol. There's a tossed salad joke in there.

DaddyBear: What I mean to say... Reading that left a smile on my face. It's a good start to the day.

Maybe putting myself out there wouldn't be a horrible experience? I might have to wade through waves of horny men looking to get their rocks off, but how was that any different from a Saturday night at Bottoms Up? At least their photos would serve as some inspiration.

I eyed the tent rising under the blanket. It was early enough that I had time to kill before heading to the Hide-Out. A little self-care was in order after the last twenty-four hours. The day might as well start with giving my cock some attention. Throwing back the comforter, it smacked against my belly, leaving a wet spot.

"Doesn't take much these days, huh?"

Precum had already coated the head of my cock. Wiping the bead of clear liquid from the tip, I licked my finger. Salty with a hint of sweetness. After this week, playing with myself was well overdue. Running my fingers along the underside, I trace a line from my balls to the tip. I shuddered at the sensation. Maybe I needed this more than I thought.

Wrapping my hand around the base, I give it one long slow squeeze, letting the skin gather over the head. I was never one to brag, but I had been told it was thicker than normal, and barely able to touch my thumb to my middle finger. I guess I understood why. With just about two fists worth of length, it was a fun toy, and other than causing some much-needed whimpering, I never had a complaint.

I started a slow up-and-down motion. Each time I reached the tip, I held still, savoring the sensation. The precum drizzled down the shaft, proving it had been too long since I last came. It could be a speedy affair, a maintenance come, but I wanted to start my day relaxed.

My phone vibrated. The plight of the modern gay man, answering with a precum-free hand. It was another message from WoofR. Since I already had my cock in hand, I might as well scroll through another wave of dick pics.

SeekingBeefy: I'll consider that my good deed for the day. Now I can go back to being a deviant. And here I thought I'd have to wait until I had coffee.

"Oh." Yes, it made me smile. Any man who put coffee on his priority list couldn't be half bad. I couldn't think of something witty when I was halfway to firing a load across my chest. I should probably have waited until I finished, but I couldn't let him get away without responding.

DaddyBear: I usually wait to be a deviant until after my first cup. That way, I'm thinking clearly when I get into trouble.

Was this flirting? Without body language or the husky voice, I had no idea. I'm sure once I showed the texts to Alejandro, he'd give me a lecture about how I wasn't being subtle enough, or that I was being too subtle. If Griffin and Xander joined in, I'd flip the table before Chad brought us coffee.

I dropped the phone and returned to the important matter at hand, or *in* hand. With a steady motion, I continued moving up and down, tightening my grip until I couldn't resist moaning. Changing tactics, I held my hand steady and started rocking my hips, fucking my hand. Gripping tightly, I could imagine a guy straddling my lap, riding my cock.

"God, I need this."

After a week of ignoring my cock, it wouldn't take much before I exploded. I closed my eyes and imagined the man in that photo bent over the back of my couch as I eased my way inside him. Holding his thick hips, I'd take it nice and slow until he was ready to get railed.

I spread my legs and held my hand a few inches from my sack. Electricity jumped from my fingers to my balls, and I moaned loud enough for the neighbors to hear. Wrapping my hand around them caused the skin of my cock to go taut. It made every stroke feel as if I might lose control. I edged for the next twenty minutes. Every time the tingling started in my groin, I let go, watching my dick sway back and forth, the head coated with precum. I'd wipe the tip with my finger, licking the sweet fluid.

Bucking my hips, I let go, letting the lightning go from my palm to my shaft. After years of practicing, I had perfected the voltage necessary to make my cock twitch.

I thought of resting a hand on SeekingBeefy's back while the other ran along the curves of his stomach... I grunted. Letting go of my cock, I grit my teeth as the orgasm forced my toes to curl. My balls tried to pull tight, but I held them in place. I opened my eyes in time to watch a rope of white shoot from my cock.

I turned my head, closing my eyes just before it splashed across my cheek. The next couple coated my chest hair and stomach. It might have been a week, but I didn't expect to cover my upper body. Tremors worked their way through my muscles, and I had to hold my hands away from the bed as sparks showered from the tips of my fingers.

"Damn." I opened my cum-free eye. Licking my lips, I tasted the cum covering my beard. My phone vibrated.

Holding my palms together, I let the electricity arc from one to the other, burning away the remnants of a satisfying morning. I smiled at the sight of another message. If only SeekingBeefy knew he was the inspiration behind this mess.

SeekingBeefy: I guess that means we'll have to get coffee first.

Did he just invite me to coffee? Okay, maybe I didn't hate online dating as much as I thought. At least the morning started off with a smile. Maybe this was the start of a new chapter?

"First, a shower." I dragged my finger through a puddle of cum running down my chest. "Then we can think about this fresh start."

With the hood pulled over my head, I turned, scanning the street for any reporters that might be following. It was bad enough they camped out at the entrance to the building, but to call in the news choppers? They really wanted an exclusive interview. Until I figured out what I was going to do, I wanted to avoid the press.

I ducked into the HideOut. The regulars were used to seeing Cobalt or Zipper come in and grab their coffee. It had become common to see supers. Sentinel in street clothes? They'd hardly bat an eye. I just hoped the patrons were too busy writing their novels to be bothered by the likes of me.

By the time I reached my seat, Chad was already bringing over a cup of coffee. Nowhere in Vanguard did a barista know my order like Chad. Mmm, coffee strong enough to kill a man. He always had it behind the counter, waiting for me to arrive. There were plenty of reasons we treated this as our home away from home.

"Bernard," Griffin started, "settle a bet for us."

I prepared for a conversation about sex, possibly bondage, depending on how their previous nights had gone. Their goal every morning—get a rise out of the old guy. These youngins would have to get up pretty early to shock me. If they hadn't figured out that I played the prude as part of the alter ego, I would not ruin my image.

"Why do heroes that fly all have jets?" Griffin's question didn't have to do with sex. Had I slipped into a mirror universe? Were they being possessed by ancient magicians? Cause something seemed off.

"Why does somebody have a driver's license and take a taxi?"

They all nodded as if it satisfied their curiosity. But it was Xander who leaned across the table. "Can you join the mile-high club without a plane?" This was more in line with the typical breakfast conversation.

"Good question," Griffin added.

"Yes." Alejandro and I answered at the same time. We

locked eyes as we sipped our coffees. I'm sure he was busy trying to think of who I shagged to warrant that answer. I was busy trying to figure out who he hadn't. Neither of us would spill our secrets, so we drank in silence.

"So, Mr. Big Shot Hero, what did you find out at work?" Only Xander hadn't known about my secret identity. I appreciated him skipping the questions about Sentinel. We might give each other a hard time, but he knew when I needed a friend.

"We disbanded. Let me correct myself. They *informed* me we had disbanded. They'll have a new team in place soon enough. They'll have to recruit—"

"You haven't heard, have you?" Griffin raised an eyebrow. "They announced the new director late last night. It's not good, not in the least."

"Who?"

"Damien Vex. A guy Sebastian used to work with at Revelations mentioned it."

Revelations had become a thorn in the side of every hard-working hero in Vanguard. Vex used his magazine to create suspicion and discredit the good intentions of Vanguard's protectors. I rejoiced when Sebastian quit and took a position with Griffin at the Beacon. At least they did an excellent job of showing the humanity behind the heroics.

"So Revelations is sponsoring the new Centurions?" Asked Xander.

Griffin shook his head. "I don't know what qualifies him, but he *is* the new director of the Centurions."

I didn't know whether to laugh at the absurdity of Director LaToya being cast out with the rest of the riffraff or cry. It was hard to not think of it as years of my life thrown out the window. It had all come crashing down because one villain got his hands on a few files. New day, new life. I needed to move on.

"Let him have it."

"It doesn't make you mad?" Xander's clenched fist made it clear that he was mad enough for the both of us. "Want me to clock him for you?"

The phone vibrated in my pocket. If I reached for it too quickly, Alejandro would sense a disturbance in the force. I might have taken the long way to the coffee shop this morning so I could continue chatting with this mysterious SeekingBeefy. We'd progressed from roundabout flirting to complimenting one another's physique. It wasn't a date, but considering it had been years since I went on one, it was moving at a brisk pace.

"How long before you think he answers it?" Asked Griffin.

"He's trying to play it cool," Xander said.

"Leave him alone," Alejandro said. The smile spread. "Or DaddyBear will spank you."

I threw my hands up in the air. Why did I try to keep anything a secret from them? "How did you know?" Had they bugged my apartment? It wouldn't surprise me if Alejandro had cameras in there. If one of them had found me on the app, they, of course, would have texted the others. Hiding my superhero identity—easy. Hiding my dating life from them—impossible.

They all turned their phones in my direction. My profile was on all three screens. "Papi, it shows who's nearby."

"You're all taken. Why are you on there?"

Even Griffin rolled his eyes at the statement. "We're taken, not dead. Besides, looking is fair game."

"So, who is he?" Xander wasn't one to pry, but the way he leaned forward on the table meant he wanted details. "Look, we just told you that the biggest jerk in Vanguard has your old job. And here you are fighting to keep a goofy-ass grin off your face."

"Spill it, Papi" said Alejandro.

I grabbed my phone, and before I could read the message, Alejandro plucked the device from my hand. "SeekingBeefy." He eyed me. "Yup, that checks out. Tasteful nude photo. He's coy, but a freak in the bedroom."

"You got that from his photo?"

Alejandro handed it to Xander while staring at me. "Do I question *your* superpowers?"

"Oh, he's chubby. I'd tap that." Xander leaned in closer to the screen. "Okay, just checking I hadn't already tapped it. But if you don't want him, let me know."

Finally, Griffin took the phone. At this point, Chad joined in. Peeking over Griffin's shoulder, he gave me a thumbs up. "Cute, but let's check the rejects." With the swipe of a finger, he started scrolling.

"Wow, that's impressive," Chad said. "Need extra lube."

"Damn. That's a lot of dicks. Apparently, Bernard has got game," Griffin said. His eyes lit up. "Oh look, another message from SeekingBeefy. Two in a row? Somebody's thirsty."

"What's he saying?" Chad knelt next to Griffin. The HideOut's owner considered himself a dating guru. I couldn't argue with the title. He had a knack for inserting himself at just the right moment. Between him and Alejandro, I'm sure they'd gladly dictate my dating life.

"SeekingBeefy." Griffin cleared his throat, dropping it an octave. "No work today? Consider me jealous." The voice was ridiculous. I forced my face to remain neutral, but even *I* wanted to grin. "What are you going to do with your handsome self?"

Chad jumped in on the next line. "SeekingBeefy." His voice matched Griffin's. "I'm new in town. Is there a good place to grab a drink?"

All four men leaned back, disbelief on their faces. "What did I miss?"

Alejandro put his hand on mine, batting his eyelashes. "Papi, that's an invitation. He gave you the opening to say something like, 'I could show you around' or something."

Griffin started typing. "If you want, I'd be happy to grab a drink and show you the city." He eyed me before returning to the keyboard. "I'd be happy to show a stud like you around the city."

"What have I done? Shouldn't I talk to him first? Give him my phone number?"

It was Griffin's turn to reach across the table and pat my hand. It had gone from sincere to patronizing. Was I this bad at dating? "Bernard, I love you, really I do. But you're hopeless." With that, his other hand clicked the button. The whoosh of a sent message had everybody holding their breath.

Maybe if I was lucky, a reporter would show up, and I'd have to run. Was it bad I hoped a supervillain busted into the coffee shop threatening to kill us with a death ray? Not kill anybody, just maim them. I'd settle for a good maiming right now.

Ding.

I held my breath. When Griffin said nothing, I thought they had ruined my chances with SeekingBeefy. I should have kept my mouth shut and stuck with being a hero. *That* I knew how to do. Dating? That was already more—

"Who's calling who a stud?" Chad said before biting his lower lip. Based on the expression, you'd think he had won the lottery.

Griffin cleared his throat, continuing in his best baritone. "An offer for arm candy? I won't say no. What did you have in mind?"

The table cheered. They held coffee cups high as they saluted my victory in dating. I thought they had been giving me a hard time, but as they started talking about their online dating experiences, I realized they were genuinely excited. Even as Chad refilled my cup, he gave me a kiss on the cheek.

"That man doesn't know how lucky he is."

I blushed. Now, to get life in order so I could enjoy showing SeekingBeefy around town. I didn't realize how nervous I had been about meeting a new guy. While yesterday had been a disaster and sent my life spinning out of control. Today offered a different type of chaos. Maybe the Centurions falling apart meant out with the old and in with the new?

I clicked on SeekingBeefy's photo again. No matter how the night went, at least I'd have the chance to drool over him. My pants grew tighter, imagining my hands running along his sides. Now I just had to make it to tonight without blowing it.

5

AFTER A LONG DAY OF CLOTHES SHOPPING FOR TOMORROW and catching up on Game of Crowns, it felt good to be sky bound. Unlike the previous night, I couldn't find any other heroes. It must be a busy night on the streets. Not good for the people of Vanguard, but at least I'd be able to get in a little clobbering before my shift ended.

I never thought I'd miss wearing my uniform, but something about hovering above the city in jeans felt wrong. Without the weight of the axe between my shoulder blades, it created an imbalance. I noticed I drifted while hovering. Eventually, I'd need to get another super suit. But maybe this time, I'd skip the axe.

"So we meet again."

I spun about, pulling my fist back. Lightning fell from

the sky, coating my arm as I prepared to wail on— "Oh. Cobalt. Stop sneaking up on a guy."

He pointed to the electricity wrapping around my hand. "Are you going to put that away?"

I shook it off. "Where is everybody?"

"Crime is out of control. Without the Centurions, even purse nabbers have gotten brave. Dozens of heroes are off planet brokering peace with the Shalayians."

"Good luck with that. Shalayians really love their wars."

"A lot of the heroes are scouring the city to see if the rumors are true."

"Rumors?"

"A new villain league. The Centurions are missed. If nobody has said it, you guys made it possible for us to do our jobs."

I gave him a nod. I appreciated the sentiment. But he had it backwards. As I returned to my roots as a street-level hero, it was them that made the Centurions possible. They let us focus on the bigger threats. Now all I did was save kittens from trees. All of this power at my disposal, and nowhere to wield it.

When I realized he wasn't rushing off to save a gaggle of Girl Scouts, I swallowed my pride. Years in the business and I needed help from a rookie. "Hey." I fished my phone out of my pocket. "Can you do an old man a favor? I'm useless if I can't find the villains."

His cape caught the wind as he drifted closer. Patting

me on the shoulder, he gave me a slight nod. "I'd be honored. It's not as easy as it used to be. As the crimes have gotten more high-tech, we've had to play catch up. Let me show you."

Taking my phone, he moved to the map. There were several dozen crimes happening throughout Vanguard. He pointed to a cluster of dots. "Seems the west side of town is hopping tonight. You could start there."

I shook my head. "Zipper is near there. He'll have it cleaned up before I reach them."

"What about—"

"That's the Magician's territory. He'll have his golem's policing."

"I see why you led the Centurions. You could organize the heroes."

"Here?" I poked at the screen. Unlike the others, this blip had a name. A supervillain tore up the street in front of city hall. I wanted to punch something, and it looked like I'd get my chance.

"Titan? Only vigilantes are nearby. This has your name on it, big fella."

He handed me my phone and flew to the side. I dove toward the city, heading straight to city hall. I had put away Titan before. Twice, actually. How did supervillains always escape prison? You'd think the penal system let them go as long as they attended anger management sessions. I'd need to talk to the mayor about this in the future.

Titan came into view. Built like a tank and just as durable. It had been more than a year since I stopped him from demolishing the bridge into Vanguard. He had a car ready to throw at city hall. Pushing my top speed, I landed just in time to catch the vehicle.

"Who are you?"

"Don't recognize the guy who put you away?"

"Sentinel? They told me you were..." He trailed off. Villains had a notorious habit of not keeping secrets, launching into monologues, and revealing their plans. At least some things never changed.

"Whose plans?"

"Your mom's plans."

Yup, still childish as ever. I threw the car at the behemoth. He swatted it away. Flying at him, he couldn't say the same thing about my fist. He hammered both fists onto my back, slamming me into the street. The crater I created would have construction crews busy for days. It hurt, not bad, but to even feel the blow meant the brute was strong.

"Guess I'll have to finish the job for them."

Did he mean the villain who released my identity? Had it all been part of a master plan to eliminate the Centurions? If so, it had worked. But it didn't mean Sentinel planned on retiring.

Titan tried to drive his heel into my face. I caught his massive foot. I summoned the lightning. The bolt of feverish white light crashed down from the sky, striking

Titan as it pooled around my hand. If electrocuting him wasn't enough, I flew upward, delivering an uppercut to his chin.

For a second, the world flashed white.

Titan launched into the air. I followed, outracing him. With a fist out, I drilled him in the back, speeding toward the street. I'd have to leave a note for the construction workers. Maybe I'd buy them lunch for the disaster about to occur. I pointed Titan toward the crater, hoping to minimize the damage.

Asphalt exploded. When he tried to push himself up, I called the lightning again. This time, I stepped out of the way and let it strike the villain. Titan collapsed.

"Not too shabby." I held a foot in the middle of his back. As he tried to move, I held him in place. His arms wobbled as he attempted to push me off. My phone dinged. It's poor form to text while heroing, but I didn't want to miss a message from a certain stud.

SeekingBeefy: Up to anything fun this evening?

I stomped on Titan, pushing him onto the asphalt.

DaddyBear: Just wrapping up some work.

SeekingBeefy: At this hour? You must be somebody pretty important.

"I'm going to kill you."

"Please, my grandmother could take you. Now stop moving."

Sirens sounded in the distance. I'd stay long enough to

make sure they apprehended Titan, but then I'd be off for the night.

DaddyBear: Workaholic.

SeekingBeefy: My ex was the same way.

The ex? Did he mention it as a potential warning? Good news, with my identity revealed, I needed to make some changes to my life. Working less had reached the top of the priority list. Being a hero had ruined one relationship... A relationship? The thought had crossed my mind, but I dismissed it. I couldn't put somebody in jeopardy just because I wanted a warm body in my bed.

Titan tried to move, and I slammed my foot down again. "Told you, I'm trying to talk to someone."

DaddyBear: It's a bad habit I'm trying to break.

The police arrived, prepared to take custody of Titan. I bent down and patted the lug on the cheek. "Thanks for being understanding." Pushing off, I flew away. I hadn't lost my touch, and only at the cost of some minor property damage.

SeekingBeefy: Off to bed for me. Looking forward to seeing you tomorrow.

DaddyBear: First round is on me.

I just pummeled a giant with hardly any effort. And yet, when a man I'd never met responded with a winky face, my palms grew sweaty. I didn't want villains chasing after people I cared about, but one night of flirting should be fine? Right?

The city had a song. Sitting on the ledge of my rooftop, the hum of electricity and the honking of distant horns came as a comfort. Not everybody appreciated the hustle, but after settling in, Vanguard had become home. No matter how many curveballs life threw in my direction, admiring the city from high up brought a sense of peace.

It also brought solitude. Most of the time.

"Hellcat." I didn't turn to acknowledge the vigilante. If she wanted the element of surprise, I wouldn't have heard her coming. Unlike Cobalt, she knew the dangers of surprising a man who wielded lightning.

"Sentinel," she said. "Care if I join you?"

"Since when do you ask permission?"

"Consider me a wiser woman these days."

The Centurions kept files on all superpowered people. But vigilantes came and went with such speed our analysts never kept them up-to-date. I knew her from the world-wide depowering. It had been an honor to fight alongside a woman with her fighting prowess. But short of her amazing skills in hand-to-hand combat, little was known about the woman.

"What do I owe this pleasure?"

"You've heard rumors about the new villain group?"

"Cobalt mentioned it."

"They're more than rumors. We think the Centurions disbanding was part of their mission."

While superheroes banded together, it was rare that villains formed organizations. When every member wanted to stab the next in the back, it made for trust issues. But when they managed, they created havoc on a global scale.

"Evidence?"

"Three shadow-related villains. One of them releasing your identity. We think they were henchmen for somebody much bigger."

"Tonight, Titan mentioned somebody calling the shots."

"They're organizing. I hate to admit it, but I think they've been under our noses for a while. We can't—"

"Leave it for the new Centurions."

"I don't trust them. Even if they recruit top-tier supers, they're not ready to take on this threat."

I inhaled and the air held a crisp dampness. It'd start raining at any moment. While I appreciated Hellcat trusting me with this intel, I had no idea why she told me. Did she believe I had inside information about this threat?

"I've put together a team."

I've heard the sentence a dozen times. In times of crisis, heroes frequently joined forces. This hadn't been a casual house call. She came as a recruitment officer.

"I appreciate it. But Sentinel doesn't need a team. We saw how that ended. It's time for him to be a solo act."

She patted me on the shoulder as she stood. "You don't have to do this alone. We're stronger together."

Being part of a team meant constantly worrying that you'd make a wrong move, and they'd suffer the consequences. It might be impressive to have teammates capable of amazing feats, but as I thought of Lix and her family, I decided it was best to distance myself. At least alone, nobody would get hurt.

She nodded her head as I came to my conclusion. "When you're ready, we'll be there. In the meantime, get yourself a suit. You're a hot mess."

With the last piece of sage advice, she leapt from the building. Swinging from a grappling hook, she disappeared into the streets below. Hellcat's brand of tough love had struck a nerve.

The life of a hero is a lonely one.

6

"YOU'RE A LITTLE OVERDRESSED FOR JOCK NIGHT."

I leaned over the bar to see Mick wearing nothing more than a jockstrap. It wasn't unusual for the men in Bottoms Up to be clad in leather harnesses or rubber suits. I should have suspected something when the doorman asked if he could help take off my pants.

"Consider me embarrassed."

"It's okay. Just get down to your skivvies and I'll let it slide."

He overemphasized the wink. I spent the better part of the afternoon trying on clothes to prepare for this date. The dress shirt clung to my body, just tight enough to pull at the buttons and give a peek at chest hair. I even bought jeans that showed off my calves and gave my package a little extra fluff. But as another bear leaned over the bar to order a drink, his ass exposed to the world, I realized nobody would give my biceps a second look.

I should warn SeekingBeefy. The bar made for a suitable spot to meet with no commitment or stuffiness of a date. But I didn't want the guy to think I brought him here to show off all the—

I eyed the guy's ass as he wiggled it in my direction. With a smile, he made it clear he was looking for a good time. I gave it a light slap. He growled and leaned over further. "Harder, daddy."

Instant hard-on.

"Leave the man alone. He's overdressed for a date."

Mick handed him a beer as I texted SeekingBeefy to see if he'd rather meet at the HideOut. "For what it's worth, you're looking more handsome than usual. But I'm still sad I don't get to see you in a jock."

"There are a hundred guys here for you to gawk at."

"But none that could toss me against the wall."

I laughed. "You hero chasers..." Guys like him and Alejandro loved the idea of bagging a superhero. It had nothing to do with the mask, but how often could a guy get railed while flying above the city? Contrary to popular belief, sex while flying was a logistical nightmare.

SeekingBeefy: I'm down for coffee, but I'd hate for this jock to go to waste.

DaddyBear: That *would* be a shame.

SeekingBeefy: Be there in a few.

Dammit. Now I felt overdressed. Stripping down to my briefs didn't feel any better. I'd have to rely on charm. Were my hands getting sweaty? Nervous? I single-handedly defeated a brute yesterday, and here I was, nervous about meeting a guy. Maybe this was a bad idea. Between being outed as Sentinel and—

"You'll be fine."

Mick pushed a shot across the bar. The pungent smell of vodka halted my downward spiral. He eyed the shot and then me. I took the cue. Downing the alcohol, it lit a fire in my stomach, warming my chest.

"Meeting people is hard. Meeting special people in your life, that's even harder. Be nervous. But from where I'm sitting, there's nothing but an amazing, sexy bear that would make any man happy."

I didn't know if it was the vodka or the kind words, but my cheeks warmed. Reaching across the counter, I put my hand on his. "I'm still not stripping for you."

He threw his hands in the air. Mumbling, he stormed off to take drink orders from two patrons also wearing jocks. One of them had a belly hanging just low enough to hide the band of his underwear. I chuckled as Mick gave a sign for them to turn around. Both men spun, showing off their furry backsides. If this date turned out horrible, at least I'd enjoy the eye candy.

God, I hoped it didn't turn out horribly.

I finished my beer, staring at my phone, waiting for

another text message. The guys warned me about ghosting and how common it was with internet dating. They were trying to be helpful and keep my expectations in line. But all it did was reinforce how out of practice I had become. It had been years since I went on a *proper* date, and even longer since I've been in a relationship.

"Are you that guy on tv?" A young man in a red jock saddled up to me on the adjacent barstool.

The last thing I wanted was to be recognized as Sentinel. There was no point in lying. My face continued to be a topic for talk show hosts to debate. The number of death threats circulating had almost tripled. I only came to Bottoms Up because of the anonymity. But perhaps I should have gone to Midnight Alley with the rest of the superhero elite.

"Yeah, I'm that guy."

"Wow." He scooted closer. "Looking for some fun?"

"I'm waiting for somebody."

"We could make it quick." His hand rested on my thigh.

I scooted off the barstool, towering above him. It was flattering to be hit on, but manners seemed lost on the man.

"No." I made sure the tone made it clear there was no discussion to be had.

He backed up and, without another word, turned around and vanished into a crowd of men. I assumed he was telling others that there was a superhero in the bar. It wouldn't be long before another tried the same, hopeful they'd score with Sentinel.

"This was a bad idea."

I finished my beer and left money on the counter for Mick. My alter ego had become a hot topic, and coming out in public had been a mistake. It would only take somebody snapping a photo and posting it on their social media for a villain to find me. Simply existing put the bar in jeopardy. And to think, I considered bringing a guy into this disaster. At worst, the date turned out horrible. At best? I... what? Dated a guy and put him in the line of fire? My occupation didn't make it easy. I had kept Sentinel and Bernard mutually exclusive for a reason.

"A very bad—"

My phone vibrated.

SeekingBeefy: Handsome as ever.

"Huh?" Had he arrived before I could make my escape?

"It's been a long time, DaddyBear."

That voice. I hadn't heard it in years, but I'd never forget the warm tenor laced with a bit of teasing.

Spinning around, I spotted a familiar, devilish smile.

"Jason."

7

Jason Jaynes.

How do I describe the sensation of my stomach tying itself into knots and, at the same time, wanting to thank a divine being? As I slid off my stool, I froze, unsure if I should run toward him or away. Did I apologize or beg for forgiveness? I spent years wondering what I would say if I mustered the courage to see him again. I drew a blank.

Much like the rest of the patrons at Bottoms Up, he only wore sneakers, socks, and a jock. I went from nervous to terrified, so much so that I couldn't appreciate the thickness of his thighs and how they rounded to the pouch of his jock. His belly reminded me of the many nights I spent using it as a pillow as he forced me to watch avant-garde science fiction films. The pierced nipples were new, as was the tattoo across his left peck. I focused on his devilish grin. It was the same one I thought about as I fell asleep.

Jason Jaynes, the one who got away, walked toward me.

I braced for the slap across the face. I waited for the furious tongue-lashing. I deserved nothing less. If he started—

Jason's arms wrapped around my waist and he gave me a kiss on the cheek. The slap would be next, followed by insults detailing my shortcomings as a boyfriend. He wouldn't be wrong, and I carried that fact with me for six years.

"I don't know what to say." I lied. Sorry. Sorry for vanishing in the middle of the night and never explaining myself. No, not vanishing, that's too kind. Erasing. I had abandoned Jason, wiping any evidence that I ever existed. Only Jason knew what had happened, and even then, I had robbed him of any chance of closure.

"First, DaddyBear, buy me a drink."

Was it a trap? If I turned my back, would he sink a literal dagger between my shoulder blades? Did he lure me here to exact his revenge? Did he create SeekingBeefy just to tear down my self-esteem? I wanted to make no assumptions. Was the Jason I once knew the man standing before me?

"Mick," I shouted over my shoulder.

"Ahead of you."

I turned to see two beers and a shot each. Mick had

already moved on to his next customer. I handed Jason a beer and held the shot up in a salute. It would be the second of many if I hoped to survive this evening.

"What should we—" I downed the shot. "You haven't liked vodka since the Jell-O shots at Veronica's party."

In one statement, he tore open a gaping wound. Few men knew me as well as Jason, and he was absolutely right. I hated vodka. I never suffered a hangover since we threw Veronica's going away party. It wasn't just the reminder that he knew me well, but that he served as a relic from a time long since passed.

"Have you stayed in touch?" I reached into the wound, ready to tear my heart from my chest. I waded into dangerous waters that'd require Hallmark movies and ice cream. Every question served as a reminder of the life I abruptly left behind.

"She still lives in France. She has two kids. Two! The girl who swore she'd never get married and couldn't keep a cactus alive..."

He trailed off. Which was more uncomfortable? The awkward silence or missing my former life? Jason shifted back and forth, taking another sip of his beer as he looked about the bar.

"Maybe this was a mistake." He set the bottle on the table. "I didn't know what to—"

"Don't go."

"I didn't mean to catfish you."

Like cajun catfish? I dared a raised eyebrow.

Jason laughed. "Still scared of the internet, huh? It's when somebody impersonates a person hoping to lure them into a trap."

"Is this a trap?"

"No, nothing like that. I just—" He signaled to Mick, who didn't need words to pour two shots. Handing me one, he quickly emptied the small glass. Shaking his head, he stuck his tongue out. Jason liked vodka even less than me.

"I saw you on the news."

I swallowed the pungent alcohol. "Surprise, I'm a superhero."

Two guys in jocks moved closer as they flagged down Mick for another round of drinks. If Jason thought I didn't notice him checking out their bare asses, he was sorely mistaken.

"Let's find a corner to talk," I said. In my imagination, this conversation had been carefully scripted. I admitted my wrongdoings, gave him my reasons, and... Even in my imagination, Jason's hurt crept into his eyes. I never dared to think beyond that moment, to the conclusion of my apology.

We found a corner table away from the crowd. He yelped as his exposed backside touched the wood of the seat. "If he's going to have jock night, man needs to turn up the heat."

"I think it's forcing men to huddle. Mick is diabolical."

"I'm sorry," he said.

"For what? You have nothing to apologize for."

"Bernard, I closed the door on us a long time ago."

The statement stung. No, it burned. I walked out of his life without an explanation.

"I moved on. But, when I saw your picture on the news, it was like I was waking up that morning all over again. I guess I needed closure."

"You have every right to be angry. I—"

"I'm not angry, Bernard, just confused. Bernard Castle, the most loyal man I've ever known, and in the dark of night, he vanished. You destroyed me, Bernard. At my graduation, there was an empty seat with your name on it. When my mom got sick, she..." Jason wiped the tears from his eyes. "She asked for you."

I hung my head. I hadn't abandoned just Jason. My actions rippled outward.

"But when I saw you on TV, things clicked into place. The late nights? The wandering off? I thought you might have left me for another man."

"Never."

"The fire in the apartment wasn't from the toaster, was it?"

I shook my head. "I had my powers for a week when that happened. There was no controlling them at that point."

"The conference the next day?"

"I went upstate to learn to control them. I didn't want to set the apartment on fire again. God, I was terrified of hurting you those first few months."

"The late nights at the office?"

"Looking for trouble on the streets. At the beginning, I wasn't good at much, but I was a pro at finding criminals."

"And then..."

"Do you want the entire story? It's a little... odd."

He leaned on the table, resting his chin in his hands. He didn't need to urge me forward. Jason had a gift for softening his eyes that invited a story. I forgot how he listened to me spin the most mundane days at the office into epic tales. It was he who suggested I seek a career in public relations. If I dissected my life, much of it originated with the man beckoning me to provide the answers I denied him years ago.

"New heroes start with street criminals. I saved more stolen purses than I can recall. For a while, the biggest success was stopping a robbery at that bodega around the corner from our apartment." Our. I hadn't used that word to speak about another man since.

"I made my first enemy by stopping a shipment of drugs at the pier. When I dropped them off at the police station, one of the dealers said his boss would get his revenge. But what did I care? I can stop bullets and hurl lightning. He didn't stand a chance. But one night, when I got home, I found a man across the street with a rocket launcher. He wasn't waiting for me. He couldn't hurt me. But he could hurt somebody close to me."

Jason's eyes went wide as he realized he had nearly died. It's shocking the first time you discover somebody wants you wiped off the face of the planet.

"The kingpin ordered his men to kill you."

"Oh."

"Yeah. I stopped him. I never thought they'd trace my actions back to you. But I had been careless. At that point, I was just running around doing heroics as Bernard Castle. Nobody taught me to be a hero."

It was enough to scare a man, but Jason didn't make any move to interrupt my story.

"The kingpin had powers. He swore he'd kill you to teach me a lesson. I nearly killed him. I stopped myself, but after being electrocuted by a lightning bolt, he'd spend the rest of his life drooling into his Jell-O."

"So you stopped him. What changed?"

"There were a hundred more kingpins. Every one of them was plotting their revenge. They couldn't hurt me..."

"But they *could* hurt me."

I nodded. It wasn't as clean a story as I had imagined. I prepared for him to turn around and walk out of the bar. He got his closure, or at least I hope he had. I didn't want him to leave. I wanted to hear about the life I missed out on, but now it was up to him.

"You left to protect me?"

"I didn't know how else to do it. Then, as time passed, I didn't want to barge into your life like a whirlwind. I was ashamed. I had done enough damage."

He mulled it over. If he had questions, I'd answer them. It was the least I could do. But part of me hunkered down and expected him to hate me for what I did.

"I teach fourth grade."

Not what I expected. "What?"

"You gave me so much grief about not picking a major." At last count, he had switched four times. I'll admit, I gave him plenty of grief. "I took an education class. Then another. And what do you know, I enjoy working with kids."

"And here I thought you never wanted kids."

"Oh, please. No. Never. Not in a million years. But other people's kids, that's a different story. I'm like the fun uncle that teaches multiplication. And I'm pretty good at it. Last year I received the Teacher of the Year Award."

My heart swelled. He applied to college without telling me. I knew he was up to something as the college letters came in the mail. When he got his first acceptance, he left it on the table. When he got home from work that night, there was a cake with a misspelled "congradulations" on it. I could still hear the music playing as he lured me into a dance party for two.

Without thinking, I reached out, cupping his hand. "A teacher, huh? I'm so damned proud."

"I would have understood." It was sweet, but it didn't change the fact that somebody had attempted to kill him. My actions put Jason in danger. I'd never been able to live with myself if he got hurt. The decision to leave had less to do with his acceptance and more to do with my... what? Duty? Loyalty to the mask? Seeing those hazel eyes, I wondered if I had made the wrong decision.

"We have a lot of catching up to do," he said.

When he returned the gesture, holding my oversized paws, I nearly lost it. I had prepared for him to turn his back and walk out the door. But as his finger ran along the tops of my knuckles, I found he kept the door open.

"I don't even know where to begin." Did I tell him about the Centurions? About the small group of friends I had made? Or did I—

"It might be the alcohol speaking, but I'm sitting in a strange bar with a handsome bear and my ass exposed for all to see."

"I noticed. It's looking better than I remember."

"I'm sure it feels better, too."

Wait. What?

The latch echoed as Jason locked it into place. No doubt, a dozen guys grinned from ear to ear as I followed him into the private bathroom in Bottoms Up. When I suggested we walk to my apartment, Jason replied it was a waste of a perfectly good jock. It appeared age hadn't diminished his wild streak. In response, my cock pressed against my zipper.

"Somebody's excited," he said, eyeing my groin. It was impossible not to notice. I could say the same about the tent in his jock. I leaned against the wall as I admired the man. The thick thighs and the way the fabric pressed into his skin, all pointed to his package. I didn't know if I wanted to tear it off him or stare.

"Are you sure?" I could lead a team of superheroes against denizens of the underworld, but the idea of rekindling my past left me sheepish.

"I can't count the times I've jerked off to the thought of you."

He pressed against me, his belly pushing against mine. When he cupped the front of my jeans, I shoved my hips forward. There had been lovers since Jason, but none *like* him. I had heard of couples settling into a routine with their sex lives. But Jason... he only got more adventurous. As he closed the distance between our faces, pinning me to a bathroom wall in a gay bar, I had some catching up to do.

Unlike him, I needed coaxing to awaken the inner animal. Jason didn't require any encouragement. The man nestling my testicles, thought getting me in the mood counted as foreplay. When he bit my bottom lip, the beast came out roaring.

I returned the kiss, tasting like vodka and excitement. But it was my turn to push him back. His ass cheeks pressed against the cold tile, forcing out a yelp. He fumbled with the button of my jeans and I grabbed his wrists. Pinning his arms above his head, he tried to kiss me, but I pulled back, just inches out of reach. He feigned struggling to be free, but unlike our previous romps, he couldn't budge against the strength of Sentinel.

While he tried to wiggle free, I gawked. The goatee was new, but damn, did it make his lips look inviting. With a final touch of his lips, I decided there were other places I needed them to go. But before I watched him swallow my cock, I needed to test out his new hardware.

I kissed down his chest, following the dusting of hair until it nearly vanished. Each nipple held a small silver loop. I stopped close, teasing him with the heat from my breath. Before, they were like electric currents that connected to his cock, and all it would take was a slight touch of the tongue. But now...

The spark jumped from my tongue to his nipple.

"Holy shit," he yelped. I paused, worried I had misjudged the intensity of the spark. He let out a groan. "Don't stop."

"Wasn't planning on it."

I dragged my tongue across the nipple. I held the tip between my teeth as he tried to push forward, forcing more into my mouth. He wanted me to bite, to make him squirm before he tapped out. Instead, I moved to the other, repeating the same move.

"Harder," he begged.

"No."

I waited until the disappointment crept into his hungry eyes. Letting go of his wrists, he raised a confused eyebrow. Perhaps our rediscovery was too fresh to pull a stunt like this, but he'd understand.

Holding my pointer finger and thumb against his nipples, he closed his eyes, hoping for a firm grip. When the sparks arced between my fingers, he bit his lower lip to stifle the moan. The sound amplified in the tight space. An entire bar knew somebody in this bathroom was receiving exactly what they craved.

"Don't stop." He whimpered as his hands grabbed the waistband of my jeans. Pulling me closer, he reached past my dress shirt into my briefs and wrapped his hand around my cock. Jason hated to come without the feel of cock against his body.

"Fuck," he yelled. "I'm close." I had done this with my mouth a thousand times. But there were some techniques that only came with the benefit of having powers. I didn't need to touch his cock as he humped the air. His tempo picked up speed, and the fabric pulled away from his body as he went from hard to rigid. It wouldn't be long before—

His entire body shook. I reached up, pulling his head forward. My lips pressed against his, as if I'd swallow his excitement. I had never met a better kisser, and I wanted to live in this moment as long as he'd allow. I slid my hand down his torso, running my fingers along the underside of his belly, savoring my favorite spot on his body. Finally, I journeyed south to find the front of his jock dripping. Giving the underside of his testicles a slow, gentle touch, he gasped.

"You remember what comes next?"

He muttered under his breath as he nodded. Hooking my finger inside the fabric of his jock, I dragged it to the side as he leaned against the wall. The glisten of white covered the head of his softening cock. I'll admit it might be sadistic, but there was something hot about knowing his load wouldn't go to waste.

I knelt on the bathroom floor, tongue touching the tip of his cock. As my free hand roamed his belly, I paused as he shivered. This had been our custom. Every mess he made, I ensured he walked away clean as he started.

I held the base, taking time to admire the sizable amount of cum. I swallowed the length of him, burying my forehead against his stomach. Salt. I forgot just how salty. But as I gently ran my tongue along the underside of his cock, tasting the cum, I considered sucking him until he shot again.

I considered it. But I had something else in mind.

"Thank you, sir."

Sir. One word, and I knew he was ready for the next

event. When I finished, I stood, leaning in for a kiss. I savored the taste of his lips mixed with his load. I could have spent the next hour kissing the man, leaving his lips chapped. But the chaffing of my zipper needed a remedy. And it'd be cruel if I didn't give him a finale.

"Turn around," I said. Jason spent his days as an assertive, strong-headed man. In the bedroom, only one of us could be in charge. I left no room for negotiation. He needed somebody to take charge. I gladly accepted the role.

"Need to be fucked?" I whispered in his ear. He arched his back as he whimpered out a 'yes.'

I squeeze the cheeks of his ass hard enough to leave fingerprints. I walked the line between pleasure and pain. But this was different. These hands could bend steel. And he trusted that I'd control myself. I pulled back, admiring the way his ass jiggled. I brought my hand down fast. The slap echoed in the bathroom. His moaning grew louder.

I repeated the gesture to the other cheek. When we walked through the bar, every patron would know two men had fucked. But I wanted them to see the signature of my hand. There'd be no doubt who got railed. The red print wouldn't last for long, but as I traced it with my finger, my cock begged for freedom.

With a quick pull at the button and drop of the zipper, my pants fell. The white fabric of my briefs turned translucent from the steady flow of precum. Seeing Jason braced against the wall, ready for my cock, was almost as intoxicating as the taste of him. Normally I'd tease and make him beg, but it'd have to wait for next time.

Pulling down the front of my briefs, my cock slid along the underside of his ass. My moan drowned out his whimpering. I lazily rocked my hips, the tip of my cock pressing against the back of his testicles. Did I take the time to bury my face between those soft mounds of flesh, or did I—

"Fuck me." I'd make him wait. "Sir."

Grr.

I pretended I called the shots, but Jason knew how to manipulate me. I licked the length of my fingers and pressed them against his ass, sliding one inside to prepare.

"I need your cock," he whimpered.

With a hand between his shoulder blades, I pinned him to the wall as I slid a second finger in. It didn't compare to the thickness of my cock, but it'd get him primed before I shoved inside. He pushed back until he reached the base of my fingers.

"Somebody's greedy tonight," I said.

I slid my fingers from his ass and positioned the head of my cock at his hole. It was a beautiful sight. My cock pressed against an eager bottom. The head vanished inside him.

"Fuck," he yelped. "I forgot... so big..."

I gripped his hips, controlling the motion. Slow, steady, persistent. Jason whimpered, reaching down, gripping my fingers as I started with short strokes. I might be aggressive with my bottoms, but I never wanted to break them. Only a few inches deep, Jason tightened, reminding me who was *really* in charge. I groaned my approval.

"I missed this ass," I whispered.

As I rocked back and forth, it was like jerking my cock. Only better. So. Much. Better. If I wanted, I could come like this, but then I'd have to listen to Jason tease me about being fast to finish. Baseball. Quadratic functions. Did I need to buy milk? It was all I could do not to explode inside him.

"Fuck me." It wasn't a request.

I pulled at his hips, burying the length of my cock. As my balls pressed against his ass, I held still. Now it was his moans filling the bathroom. Anybody within earshot would have a stiff cock from the soundtrack of our session.

When I retreated, removing all but the head, I marveled at how he took the thickness. I sank all the way in and repeated the maneuver until he pushed back. It wouldn't take long before the tingling started in my groin and threatened to curl my toes.

I leaned across his back, reaching around his stomach and chest. Holding him tight, I kissed the space between his shoulder blades. At this angle, it was impossible to get my cock all the way in him, but it also meant I rubbed across that magical spot in his ass.

"I'm going to come," he hissed.

With short, rapid strokes, I ensured he'd come without

touching himself. He held my hands, nails digging into my palms as he came for a second time that night. His body shivered as his ass tightened. I'd only have a few seconds before he tapped out...

"Ready for it?"

He nodded. "Yes, sir."

He accentuated the sir. I growled. My cock thickened, and I stood upright so I could bury the entire length. He squeezed down as my cock pulsed, unloading. I might have come earlier in the day, but it didn't diminish the load I pumped inside him.

"Fuck," he moaned. "I'm going to drip," he said.

"Good." I mustered through clenched teeth.

I held still, refusing to part ways with his ass. He'd have to wait until I went soft and slid out. I wouldn't willingly end this perfect moment. In the meantime, I caressed his belly, continuing to kiss his back.

"Damn," he said.

"Damn," I echoed.

"I'm already looking forward to next time."

Next time? I froze as my brain caught up to my cock. I had gotten carried away with the memory of Jason. Ghosts from the past pulled me along, promising a happily-ever-after. I shook my head, dismissing the what-ifs. Despite the best sex I had since I saw him last, it didn't change the fact there was a target painted on my back.

He turned around, sliding his jock back into place. "I guess we should head out?"

Sliding on my underwear and pulling up my jeans, the awkward aftermath of what had occurred settled in. Did him knowing my alter ego change our situation? Did Jason understand being in my presence put him in danger? I kept the thoughts to myself. I needed to process these questions before I opened my mouth.

But first, we needed to survive the gauntlet outside the bathroom.

8

STARING AT MY PHONE, I SMILED. JASON HAD DEMANDED I hand it over so he could add his contact information. He even snapped a photograph to add to the listing.

That smile.

"Bernard, what are you doing?" I asked nobody.

It only took an evening and my heart ached. I had never forgotten the man, or the way he averted his gaze when I stared for too long. He still spoke quickly when he got excited and then paused as his train of thought outran him. I couldn't place my finger on it, but he had changed. He was still the adorable man I remembered, but that youth had been tempered. As I walked him back to his hotel, he'd eagerly shared stories about his students.

"I'm proud of you." There were still a thousand stories between us that lacked a conclusion. But I smiled, thinking of him receiving his degree. Did he throw his cap in the air with the other graduates?

"I've missed you."

The wind carried away the words. The night remained turbulent, powerful gusts threatening to push me around as I hovered above Vanguard. In the distance, the clouds turned dark. Small bursts of light gave away the impending storm heading toward the city. It meant many of the fliers were grounded, and a wave of crime would sweep the city tonight.

My phone vibrated. In my zeal to see if the text came from Jason, I dropped it. Flying downward, I snatched it out of the sky. Rookie mistake. I'd scoff at myself later, but—

J: You haven't changed. I missed that smile.

I hadn't changed. Mulling it over, I wasn't sure that was the compliment. Was I the same Bernard who vanished from our apartment in the middle of the night? The memory of plowing my fists into the face of the kingpin who threatened Jason remained as vivid as the day it happened. Would I nearly kill a villain to keep him safe?

My head hung.

"Same ol' Bernard."

I didn't want to ghost him again. This time I'd at least be man enough to stare him in the face when I said... said what? I missed him, but couldn't have him in my life? That

I'd always choose duty over him? That every night I saved the city I put his life on the line?

"I hate feelings."

My phone shook again, and I expected a follow up.

*: Yellow Rain Coats. The Sun Sets in the East.

A flash of lightning illuminated the Ward, followed by a low rolling boom reverberating in my chest. The storm had reached the city. Drops of rain smacked against the screen of my phone. In the hero biz, this served as an omen. Something wicked was about to unfold.

My back straightened as I reread the message. The Centurions had an elaborate system of codes should we find ourselves compromised. Was it Lix sending a distress call? Had she broadcasted it to the rest of the team? Team... Even if we were no longer sanctioned by the government, once a Centurion, always a Centurion.

"I'm coming."

Southland didn't have as many heroes as the rest of the city. One day, out of nowhere, Hyperion emerged as its advocate and defender. Thanks to his efforts, the crime rate declined for the first time in a decade. He might not be one of the famous heroes, but he rested in my good-people column. As I flew across Southland, I thought I might need to spend some time with him and see what I could do to help.

The abandoned factory was one of many in the city. Flying through the derelict property, I reached the back wall. What appeared like the rest of the corrugated steel sat a single out-of-place square. Placing my hand on it, I waited for it to awaken. The plate glowed a soft blue before a red line scanned my palm.

"Really? Nothing?" That was rude, Gideon.

Checking over my shoulder like a child about to pilfer the cookie jar, I pushed the lightning from my fingertips. The panel lit up before turning black.

"Gideon, I always disliked you."

The steel separated a few inches, revealing a concealed door. I pulled it open. If it were like the other safe rooms across the city, it'd hold medical supplies along with food and water. If the technicians at headquarters paid attention, they'd see the distress beacon. We didn't have long until the new team arrived. I almost wanted to wait and see who they enlisted.

I let the electricity ride the outside of my skin, casting a light in the empty room. There were racks of supplies, and at the end, a mobile command center supplied by the Machinist. Based on the amount of dust, it hadn't been occupied in years.

Was this a trap? I nearly rolled my eyes. Why would somebody lure me here when they could just—

The metal pushed against the back of my head.

"Take another step, and I'll blow a hole in the back of

your head." I recognized the voice. I was accustomed to her barking orders. Her threatening to kill me was a recent development in our professional relationship.

"Director?"

"Bernard?"

If it were any other crook, I'd risk a bullet to the head. It'd hurt in the morning, but it wouldn't kill me. But she'd know that. Director LaToya had a contingency plan in place for any Centurions should we go rogue. On her supervisor evaluation, I always included the word 'ruthless.' It'd be a mistake to not take her seriously.

"What's going on?"

"The Centurions are not to be trusted."

She had a deliberate word choice, as if she had watched one too many spy movies. If she didn't have a background in espionage and overthrowing governments, I'd say it was an act. But as I turned around and saw the barrel of the gun pointed between my eyes, I realized she meant business.

"There are no more Centurions."

"He's put together a new team."

"He? You mean Damien?"

"I know everything about the operation. He didn't fire me. He got *rid* of me. I believe it's all connected."

"Director—"

"Carmen. I'm not your director anymore."

"Carmen," I started. She released the hammer on the pistol. In all the years I worked with her, I had never seen her shaken up. Even more than the heroes, she maintained a stoic facade. When we first started, she used her connections to help direct the Centurions. She had never been wrong. I let this play out. "I'm listening."

"Your identity is revealed. The board disbands the Centurions. Damien Vex takes over and assembles his own team. None of these events could happen on their own."

"Coincidence."

"In my former life, we spit on the word. Everything is connected."

Griffin and Sebastian painted a bleak portrait of Damien Vex. They claimed his goal was to undermine the integrity of heroes. His magazine reflected his opinions on superheroes. But did a magazine mogul have it in him to put the entire planet in jeopardy? That seemed far-fetched, even for a world filled with supervillains.

"Damien set this in motion."

"Are you certain?"

She gave a slight nod. "I'd stake my life on it."

"Have you talked to the others?"

Her gaze dropped. Something in my chest tightened. Together, we served as the world's most formidable protectors. But individually, we were vulnerable. Was that the goal? Split up the team and pick us off one by one?

"Carmen."

She shook her head. "You're the only one who came."

"That means nothing. Lix is probably in Vermont with her family already."

"Or..."

The unsaid. We knew the stakes when we joined. Hell, we signed waivers about death in combat. But in all my years, we had never had to talk about our own in the past tense. I had attended plenty of funerals for my colleagues, but it never hit this close to home.

"They're fine." My voice lacked conviction.

A boom shook the walls of the safe room. Valiant might be the fastest flier on the team, but his landings ended in sonic booms. I let out a sigh. At least somebody else answered the call. Even if we weren't the Centurions, we still had each other's backs.

"At least Valiant—"

Carmen cocked the gun.

"That's not Valiant."

9

LaToya was fearless.

She eased out of the safe room, leading with the barrel of her pistol. It didn't matter that we could hurl cars across the street or wield the powers of nature. She didn't care. I expected another standoff with Valiant. If she were lucky, he wouldn't toss her across the factory.

I summoned the lightning—just in case. Tiny bolts jumped between my fingers, lighting the dark end of the factory. I waited for the loud boasting, the only thing louder than Valiant's landings. There were no quips, no one-liners, and no man in a red and gold suit. Something felt off.

The lightning intensified, burning away my t-shirt.

"Glad you're in the game."

For an unpowered person, she had brass.

"Sentinel."

Whoever spoke, their voice resembled thunder. It lacked the excitement of Valiant. The sound came from nowhere, produced by shadows. There was enough equipment littering the sides of the factory that it'd take forever to find them if they wanted to play hide and seek.

"Who are you?" It wasn't Bernard speaking anymore. My voice dropped an octave as I hurled lightning across the factory. LaToya used the opportunity to spin about, searching for the speaker.

"I forget, heroes like labels."

His voice might ricochet off the walls of the factory, but the condescending tone served as a jab. Villains came in a variety of categories. Some liked to grandstand while they put their genius on display. Others thrived in chaos. But they all had a way of speaking that reminded me of Griffin's comic books.

"Come out and discuss this like a man."

"Sexist," LaToya said.

"Call Human Resources."

My sneakers left the floor as I started hovering. Southlands had a host of supervillains. Was this a wayward criminal who saw a moment of opportunity? Or did it have something to do with LaToya and her conspiracy? If she was right, then we had a mastermind on our hands.

"You're all alone," said the voice.

"I'm standing right here," LaToya added.

With a volley of lightning flashing through the middle of the factory, I could see the outline of a man hovering in the air. His cape caught the wind from the storm. A single villain, this hardly warranted—

"Bernard," he whispered in my ear. I spun around, lightning pouring from my chest, tearing apart the wall of the factory. LaToya's worries left me jumpy. A pillar of control, I acted like a rookie.

"Who are you." Not a question, a statement, one that demanded an answer.

"I am darkness personified." Great, one of those cryptic villains. At least he wasn't speaking in riddles. "You can call me..." They always had a long pause, as if a cameraman zoomed in on their faces for the big reveal. "Havoc."

"No idea," LaToya whispered. If she didn't know the name, it meant they were new to the scene. Did this somehow play into her conspiracy?

"You need to find the others," I said.

"Who gives the orders here?"

"Why would I listen to your unemployed ass?"

While she oversaw Centurion operations, *I* led the team in the field. We had clashed heads more than once. But she always deferred to my expertise. But if she was right, and that was a big if, I needed her to find the others.

She holstered the gun. It was the closest I'd get to an agreement. "I'll take care of our—"

A hand wrapped around my throat before I could finish

the statement. The force of the grip hurled me against the machine on the far side of the factory. The force left a dent in the side of an oil drum. An acidic scent of fuel filled my nostrils.

I pushed myself free, dropping to my feet. I hadn't gotten a look at the man before he threw me like a rag doll. If taking punches meant LaToya could get away, I'd gladly divert his attention.

She had nearly reached the spot where my lightning had torn through the factory wall. Havoc hovered above her, stalking the director like prey. I needed her to get away and find the others. If what she said was true, I'd need the Centurions.

Hurling bolts of lightning, he probably thought I had horrific aim. Controlling a force of nature had required practice, but I didn't want him dead. I needed him caged and alive. Then I'd beat the answers out of him.

He vanished, but it didn't matter. LaToya had gotten away.

Havoc stepped out of the shadows as if blinking into existence. Teleportation? His entire suit was as black as, no, not a suit. Unless it was the tightest latex I'd ever seen, he wore darkness like fabric. He was more menacing than the average villain because the shadows made it impossible to see his face.

The dots connected, and the coincidences vanished. Supervillains with shadowy powers had terrorized the city.

One of them had released my identity to the media. LaToya's conspiracy didn't seem so wild anymore.

"I've been looking forward to meeting you."

His knowing my identity put me at a tactical disadvantage. But it's not as if I hadn't done these types of threat assessments in the field. Teleportation. Shadows. Speed. Flier. Strength. Nothing I hadn't dealt with before.

"Another nobody trying to make a name for himself," I hissed.

I shoved my hands against his chest, pouring electricity into my palms. Odd, they normally passed out. The darkness around the man appeared to swallow the light, siphoning the electricity as if it were nothing more than a flashlight.

"I'll find her when I'm done with you."

Arrogance. I clenched my fist, hammering my knuckles against his face. By the third blow, he laughed. If beating him would not net results, I'd rely on a classic move.

"What do you want?"

"The Centurions have been defeated. Not by a villain. No, a corporate boardroom defeated them. How's it feel to be designated an antique?"

I hovered backward until my back pressed against the oil drum. As he talked, it appeared as if his mouth didn't move. If he wore darkness, that might be a clue about how to defeat him. Unfortunately, he wasn't giving me much wiggle room to test the theory.

"I bested the great Sentinel."

"I wouldn't go that far," I said.

He pressed forward, closing the distance until there was only a foot between us. I could smell the oil, most likely coated in it from the throw. I'd be showering for days before the smell went away.

"Cowering? I thought the mighty Sentinel would fight until his dying breath."

He still had said nothing useful. "You're in charge of the shadow villains, aren't you?"

"Guilty." Confirmation. It meant LaToya had been right. The confession wasn't much, but it was a start.

"What do you want with the Centurions?"

"Ha." He leaned close. "I defeated the Centurions."

I grabbed him by the shoulders and spun him around. He did nothing to stop me. Did Havoc really think himself superior like every other villain? There was a prison full of my victories. This would just be one more to add to the list.

"I'm not sure you understand who you're dealing with."

He got uncomfortably close. I tried to pull my hands away, but the shadows clung to my hands, drawing me into him. His skin wasn't a common cold. It bordered on bone-chilling, like the vacuum of space.

"I know everything I need, Bernard." He continued dropping my name as if it were a curse.

"That's Sentinel." Quip successful.

Summoning lightning didn't require that it come *from*

me. The ceiling of the factory blew apart as a bolt of lightning slammed into us. The oil tank ignited, and the explosion sent us hurtling across the factory. Tumbling along the cement floor, I jumped to my knees and, in a skid, fist drawn back, ready to fight.

The fire clung to his form, but it didn't cast enough light to push away the shadows. His arms... unlike the rest of him, I could see the paleness of his skin. It wasn't much, but it meant he wasn't as powerful as he thought. It only took blowing up part of a factory to damage the villain.

Another drum of oil exploded, raining fire across the building. I covered my head as melted shards pelted my bare hide. I'd need to invest in getting a suit made if I was going to protect the city. They considered it a faux pas to fly around buck-naked.

Havoc vanished with a trace.

"Pity." I coughed. "I wanted my cryptic conversation."

I wouldn't call it a victory, perhaps a stalemate. But whoever they were, they knew my identity. I could only hope that LaToya had gotten away. Now I waited until she found the rest of the team.

"No," I shook my head, standing on my feet. I wanted her to find them, so I knew they were safe. But the Centurions had run its course. If I could stop Havoc and untangle this mess, they wouldn't have to worry. LaToya had nearly died trying to bring us back together.

This was *my* responsibility. I'd do this alone. I made it

out of this fight unscathed, naked, but unscathed. It was time to go to the source and see how far LaToya's conspiracy reached. There was no more sitting back and playing defense.

Skivvies first. Save the world second.

10

A: WE HAVE A SURPRISE FOR YOU.

X: Stop taunting. Bernard, hurry the hell up.

G: Alejandro broke the rules.

A: Tattletale.

It had been a long night of tossing and turning. By the time I fell asleep, I swear the sun had come up. I had questions about the villain last night, and how it all played into the Centurions. I felt like I was missing an obvious piece of the puzzle. But without somebody to toss around ideas, I was left stewing in my thoughts.

I flexed my fingers, still fighting the lingering cold left by Havoc's suit. The ache in my bones had me debating if I should show up to breakfast. I checked over my shoulder, convinced the reign of misfortune followed me. Every time I showed my face, I risked their lives. And if another super-hero battle erupted in the HideOut, Chad would have a meltdown.

B: Maybe tomorrow.
    A: We see your location.

Dammit. There was no point in shrinking into the shadows. We needed to discuss boundaries. How the hell did they know where I was? I bet it was WoofR. I needed to uninstall that when I got home. The last thing I needed was a bearish supervillain wrestling me to the... okay, maybe I wouldn't get rid of it just yet.

I rounded the corner and held my breath. What could they possibly have for a surprise? I hoped it was doughnuts.

Walking into the HideOut, I froze. My usual chair was occupied. I didn't need to see his face to recognize the curves of his shoulders and the thick biceps. I'd recognize Jason a mile away. How had they found him? I blamed Alejandro. He was the only one who knew about Jason. Yes, definitely his fault.

"Surprise." Xander held up a cup of coffee in a salute.

Alejandro could see the confusion. "It's not my fault, sort of."

Jason patted a chair next to him. Somebody had violated the rules. To curve the influx of Alejandro's one-night stands, we had a standing agreement that others, significant or not, couldn't join. Griffin had fought to change the rule when he and Sebastian got serious, but we vetoed him. Partners were an evening event. For breakfast, it had always been us four.

Now, five.

"Morning," Jason said with a smile. It wasn't any smile. Not a pleasant, great to see you after great sex smile. No, the slight crookedness had been a signature. He knew he was going to be in trouble, but he didn't care. But damn, it was a sexy grin.

As I took my seat, Chad appeared with a mug full of coffee. The way he avoided eye contact, there was no doubt he was to blame. "Sorry. He came in for coffee and we started talking. I mean, have you seen him? Damn. But he asked about you, and one thing led to another. Sorry, not sorry." Dammit, even my barista conspired against me. I sensed a theme as nefarious as any supervillain league.

Even Griffin had a shit-eating grin. "Jason was just telling us—"

"Nothing. Absolutely nothing." I prayed a villain came barging in the door and blew up the HideOut.

"I was just telling them how we met."

"Parks, big guy?" Xander gave me an elbow. "You were old back then, too."

"I hate you all."

"He was reading this fantasy book. I remember he was sitting in the middle of the park bench. It was obvious he didn't want to be disturbed. So, I did just that."

"Liking him so much," Alejandro added.

"He didn't even know I was hitting on him. When I asked for his cell number, he said he didn't have one. I thought he was shooting me down. I got up to leave and could tell he was confused. Then he pulled out his bookmark, scribbled his phone number on it, tore it off, and handed it to me. Took days to catch him when he was home. Who only has a landline?"

"Papi." Alejandro batted his eyes at me. I wanted to slap the smirk off his face. But I remember that day. A cute guy struck up a conversation with me about fantasy books. He didn't like them. In fact, he hadn't read one since *Lord of the Rings* in high school. But he held his own. Being dense, I almost let him get away.

"I kept the other half," I admitted.

Griffin's jaw dropped. "Who are you? Clone? Mirror dimension? There's no way this softie is *our* Bernard."

Jason laughed. "Are you pretending to be a tough guy?"

"Not tough," Xander said. "More like quietly stoic."

"I guess that's better than listening to him sob at the end of a Hallmark movie."

They all froze.

"First person to open their mouth gets electrocuted."

Each of them sipped their coffee. Threatening friends might be bad form, but they left me no choice. I preferred listening to Alejandro's escapades in the bedroom or Griffin talking about superheroes. Hell, I'd settle for Xander diving into inappropriate levels of gore in the ambulance. But all eyes turned on me? I'd rather arm-wrestle a giant lizard monster.

I should have known it'd be Griffin to call my bluff. "So, what brings you to town?"

Okay, he'd live... for now. But it brought up a good question. I had been bowled over seeing Jason at Bottoms Up. The shock hadn't quite worn off when he enchanted me with his exposed backside. Would he confess to seeking me out? Or that he catfished me on WoofR?

"Emotional resilience conference for elementary school teachers."

I held back my surprise. I don't know why I thought my picture on the television would have been enough to have him show up at the bar. I'd never admit it, but I hoped it was a lie to save me embarrassment.

"You're a teacher?" Alejandro asked. "You're doing God's work. The thought of dealing with anybody under twenty-one gives me hives."

"Trust me. I have my moments. You know how many

hand-traced turkeys I've had to admire? How many ways can you praise their artistic genius?"

"You mean my teacher's lied?" Griffin gasped.

Xander reached across the table and patted Griffin on the head. "It's okay. I'm sure you were the exception."

"Not all heroes wear capes," I said.

Xander pointed at me. "That. That, right there. That's what he does now. He sits quietly and doles out epic one-liners. How did we not know he was a superhero?"

"I knew," Griffin said.

"Me too," Alejandro added.

Xander gave them both a slow, extended middle finger.

"They grow on you," I said. "I couldn't get rid of them if I tried."

"You love us," Alejandro said, curling his bottom lip into a pout.

"I *love* coffee."

The banter continued as I hid behind a mug colored like the rainbow flag. As the warm nectar of the gods revived my soul, something tapped my foot. With a quick glance down, I found Jason's foot rhythmically tapping the toe of my shoe. Like a teenager, I moved my foot. But before he could retract his, I returned the tapping motion.

Yes, Bernard Castle had a doctorate in footsies. Sue me.

"It's been fun, boys." Xander got up. "But one of us needs to go save lives."

"And one of us needs to go to bed," Alejandro added.

I eyed Griffin. He pointed at himself. "Me? I'm sleeping with the boss. I can stroll into work whenever."

Xander picked up Griffin's coffee and finished it. "Come on, lover boy. We've got jobs to do like responsible adults."

Seconds later, the table emptied, leaving me alone with Jason. I'd give them credit. It was more tactful an exit than I expected. But as Alejandro returned, kissing me on top of the forehead, I realized I had spoken too soon.

"Papi, be careful. I know you're out of practice. Call me if you need pointers."

Almost tactful.

"Papi?"

I gave Jason a shrug. "I've learned to pick my fights with that one. Most of them I lose."

"Your friends seem—"

"Intense? Difficult? Pains in my butt? Should I go on?"

Jason fidgeted with his coffee mug. "I was going to say loyal." Despite my insistence on a fresh pot in the house every day, I never converted him. He tried to make me a tea drinker, but I threatened to call the authorities if he insisted I replace my caffeine.

"When I got to Vanguard, I didn't know anybody. I met Xander at the bar and..." Did I confess to a few dates and a night of awkward sex?

"I would have banged him too."

"It was another in a string of bad decisions. We started the Breakfast club to slow down. I had just joined the

Centurions, and everything felt larger than life. Coffee with them kept me from losing touch."

Jason squeezed my thigh. "I'm glad they were taking care of you."

I was about to protest and say that was my job. But as I eyed the empty white chairs, I couldn't imagine what would have become of me without their antics. We drove each other mad, and we argued like family. The moment the word crossed my mind, I smiled. Jason was right. While I thought I was the parental figure, they were the ones keeping an eye on me.

"I guess they have been. But notice that none of them left money for breakfast."

"How else are they supposed to say they need you without making a scene?"

"I hate when you're right."

"It's a curse." He squeezed my thigh again. I never wanted him to move that hand again. It rested in the danger zone. The area where it could be seen as a friendly gesture, or intimate enough, that it served as a possibility of something more. I jerked off twice before calling it a night, and already I could feel my jeans tighten.

"Are you in a rush this morning?"

He shook his head. "I'm free until this afternoon." He raised an eyebrow. "What did you have in mind?"

"Consider it a surprise."

"The park?"

"You sound disappointed."

For years, I stopped here before heading to work. Vanguard took care to protect its green spaces. Winding paths were filled with joggers and women pushing strollers. Villains weren't morning people, which meant the park became a safe bastion away from my life as Sentinel.

"I thought this surprise involved you naked."

"Police officers frown on nudity in the park."

"Sounds like experience talking," he laughed.

We strolled past a woman, tearing pieces of a croissant apart before tossing them to the pigeons. Dozens of feathered rats fought over the bits of bread before one emerged victorious, flapping its wings to celebrate. But it wasn't the blood-thirsty birds I wanted to show him.

I checked my watch, and we only had a few minutes before the surprise revealed itself. Spinning about to do a quick check if somebody followed, I pulled the hood further over my head. When I was certain we wouldn't be disturbed, I gestured to an empty park bench.

The path widened until it surrounded a large water fountain. Right now, it wasn't anything impressive. The three tiers of angels holding trumpets had dried out overnight. He took a seat next to me, turning to stare.

"You couldn't look more suspicious if you tried."

"Tell that to the paparazzi staked outside my building."

"Is any of it a relief? Your identity being out there, I mean."

I shook my head. "We wear masks for a long list of reasons. It allows us normalcy."

"You hurl lightning. The normal ship sailed a while ago."

"There are heroes who live their persona all the time. They lose touch with reality. I couldn't do it. But the masks keep other people safe, too."

He cocked his head to the side. His eyes widened as he read between the lines. "You're hiding... for me?"

In the movies, this is where the main character said something moving, an admission that'd win them points with the viewers. I recounted the hundred movies and the formula they followed. When I watched, I admired the moment the hero put everything on the line, risking their happiness. Then there'd be a moment of debate as their words sank in. It'd end in a kiss, and suddenly, their pasts were forgiven.

My heart wanted to speak, to weave a string of words together in a way that'd leave Jason breathless. But to what end? To put his life in jeopardy? I'd continue swallowing my feelings, locking them away where they wouldn't get him killed. Instead of tapping into my inner romantic, I let the silence speak for me.

"You're not my protector, Bernard."

"I can't protect you. But Sentinel can."

"You're going to make a therapist very rich."

If I couldn't speak my heart, I could at least appeal to his logic. "Here's a hypothetical. You're Sentinel and a villain attacks. My life is in jeopardy. What do you do?"

He leaned back, narrowing his eyes with skepticism. "I save you."

"Easy, right?"

"But..."

"But if you save me, you can't save your classroom. What do you decide?"

He laced his fingers together and twiddled his thumbs. For years, I watched him spin his thumbs around one another as he thought through conundrums. At the time, I hadn't noticed, but seeing the nervous habit now offered familiarity. I ran my hands along my thighs to resist the urge to force my hand into his.

"It's a lose/lose situation."

I shook my head. "There's a right answer. That's the problem."

"The kids?"

Silence. I didn't have the strength to confess it aloud. How did you admit to somebody that they wouldn't survive a hypothetical? But that wasn't the *real* problem. Should I be presented with the situation, I wouldn't have a fast answer. Could I be Sentinel if I wasn't willing to save help-less children? But how could I live with myself if I allowed something to... no, I couldn't let myself dwell on the thought.

"You make these decisions?"

"This is why I keep my distance."

His hand slid across his lap, fingers walking along my thigh until he reached mine. He hesitated before squeezing my fingers. For a man who wielded lightning, I shouldn't notice the jolt of electricity along my arm and the way it jump-started something in my chest.

Dammit, Jason.

"It sounds lonely."

Before my photograph appeared on television, I hadn't had time to think about it. If the bed felt empty, I'd focus on the thousands of people I saved. If I got lost in the what if's, there were planets thankful for the Centurions. I had a monogamous relationship with duty, and while she was a cold bitch, she gave me purpose.

I pointed at the fountain.

The water sputtered from the trumpets. As the pumps drew water from the basin, the streams turned steady. The top tier filled, and seconds later, it spilled into the second. Once they reached their peak, the sound of trickling water filled the park. I closed my eyes as I let the babbling water ease the tension between my shoulder blades. While that was magical on its own, it was the least impressive aspect.

The sun had barely broken over the buildings. Rays of light hit the brass angel, making it appear heavenly. Over time, the rays would work their way down the fountain until they reached the bottom, highlighting the greenish patina.

"Life is complicated. We make a million decisions every day. Some good, some bad. We bury ourselves in the regrets of yesterday and, at the same time, we race toward tomorrow. But for just a split second, it's literally drowned out."

"Yesterday is gone. Tomorrow has not yet come. We have only today."

"Let us begin." Mother Teresa, a quote I needed to embrace more often. Jason had hung the quote in needle-point above the monitor in his office.

"It reminds me of..." He stared at the water fountain for a minute. Among his many admirable traits, his ability to recall the past teetered on dangerous. "The fountain in Chicago?"

Our first vacation as a couple. He had visited the Windy City a dozen times as a kid. When I said I had never gone, he not only demanded we change that, he surprised me with an impromptu trip. Of the many sights, the one that always stuck out was Buckingham Fountain. Before we could inspect it, the wind had picked up, spraying us with water. Drenched and shivering in Chicago, I remember kissing the man.

I wanted to kiss him now.

My phone buzzed. I took my larger-than-life feelings

and shoved them into the box. Locked and sealed, I tucked it away on a shelf that I'd stare at but never open. When I saw the number came from Centurion headquarters, I glanced at Jason.

"Don't stop on my account."

"I'm so sorry." I answered the call, pressing the phone against my ear. "Hello, Bernard speaking."

"Mr. Castle, I'm calling on behalf of Damien Vex. Mr. Vex would like to arrange a meeting with you."

"About?" Why on Earth did the man who took over *my* team want to meet? Was it a job offer, or did he want the Wi-Fi password?

"He didn't say."

"He wants me to drop everything at his beck and call?"

"We could do Thursday at—"

"I'll be there in fifteen."

"But—"

"Tell him to prepare."

I hung up. If I was going to meet the notorious Damien Vex, it'd be on my terms. As I put the phone down, I realized my hot-headedness brought our morning to an end.

Jason squeezed my fingers again. "Go be Sentinel. I need to get ready for meetings this afternoon."

"Sorry." It seemed I constantly needed to apologize to the man.

"You're forgiven if..." The smile spread across his face.

I'd never tire of that devious smirk. "Only if you show me you can fly."

As I stood from the bench, it was as if I had stepped on invisible asphalt inches above the path. Hovering, I turned around and gave him a low bow. If he wanted to see my powers in action, it was the least I could do. They were good for something other than electric nipple-play. But not nearly as fun.

"Go save the city." He waved me off.

Off I went, rocketing toward the sky.

11

THE ELEVATOR DOORS OPENED ONTO THE 99TH FLOOR. I
stepped into a spacious lobby. Damien had already
removed all of LaToya's paintings in place for stark gray
walls with geometric art. It screamed effort, as if he were
trying to show off overt modernism. Griffin would have a
field day if I asked him to critique the room. Sterile and
lacking personality, I expected nothing less from
Damien Vex.

A woman with a headset strapped to her ear sat behind
a large desk to the left of double glass doors. I stormed
through the office. My grimace and clenched fists didn't
stop her from jumping to her feet and blocking the doorway. Had Damien fired Rachel and replaced her with his
own secretary? My opinion of the jerk continued to
plummet.

"Sir, you can't go in there."

"Damien wanted a meeting. He got his meeting."

I gave her credit. She knew exactly who I was and the power I wielded. But she refused to budge. She'd hold the line even if it meant a standoff. If she threw up a force field or shot lasers from her eyes, I'd understand. But the petite administrative assistant held her fountain pen as if it were a sword.

"Mr. Vex is occupied."

"Unoccupy him."

"You'll have to wait."

"That's not happening."

"You'll have to wait."

I hovered upward a few inches, emphasizing the powers. As she tapped her headset, her eyes remained locked with mine. Despite putting my powers on display, she held her ground. No matter how much Damien paid her, she deserved more. I pressed forward and her hand shot up, demanding I stop.

"Mr. Vex, Sentinel is here to see you." She nodded. "He's being rather persistent." More nodding. "Okay, thank you."

Her back straightened, and she stepped to the side. She gestured to the glass doors. "Mr. Vex will see you now."

And just like that, she granted me permission to barge into Damien's office. Him aware I was coming stole my thunder, but at least I didn't wait for a meeting next week.

"No matter how much he's paying you..." I landed, pulling the glass door open. "It's not enough."

"If that ain't the truth," she said with a smile. At least he didn't surround himself with arrogant pricks. Apparently, he needed to be the biggest dick in the room. Well, I was prepared to whip it out and measure.

On either side of the hallway were large meeting rooms where the board would meet to decide on the operations budget or discuss public opinion. Being a superhero sounded easy. Save the planet, stop the bad guys, and then kiss a few babies. But after fighting a skirmish, the property damage needed to be dealt with. The lost lives, heck, even the lawsuits from the villains, all of it required damage control. That's when Bernard Castle worked his magic.

At the end of the hallway, an opaque glass door led into LaToya's office. Shockingly, after years of being on the team, I had only set foot inside once. The office had been incredibly bare, and even her desk required every item at a forty-five-degree angle. I imagined Damien had a giant portrait of himself with eyes that would follow you as you walked into the room.

I didn't slow as I reached the door. Instead of reaching for the handle, I walked through the glass. Shards fell to the floor as I stepped through. Petty, I know. But I wanted to make a statement. If what LaToya said was true, it meant Damien was at the heart of the conspiracy. A little broken glass would serve as a reminder of who he dealt with.

"Vex."

The man wore a black suit and a neon pink dress shirt. He skipped the tie, preferring an informal open top button. Not only did he want to put his wealth on display, but he also wanted to maintain his sex appeal.

"Gretchen could have opened the door for you."

Assessment. He remained seated, resting his elbows on an oversized desk. There was no portrait of him on the wall, but he had blown-up covers of his magazine and littered the wall with them. Each issue took jabs at the superhero community. I was surprised the issue describing me as an egomaniac didn't sit with the others. Sprinkled between them were photographs of him with prominent politicians. Damien wanted every person who entered to know that he was important, *very* important.

"This isn't a social call, Vex."

He leaned back in his chair, letting the black leather outline his upper body. If he had a cat in his lap, he'd be a picture-perfect supervillain. I expected my entrance to raise an eyebrow, but the dark beard made it impossible to tell if he clenched his jaw. Even his perfectly manicured eyebrows held their place. Damien Vex was either unimpressed or capable of locking away his emotions.

"I was hoping we could talk, like gentlemen."

There was nothing about him that said gentleman. He attempted to manipulate the situation. I'm sure a man like that didn't require superpowers to be a villain. As the owner of Revelations, he had been a thorn in the superhero community's side. Now that he had powered minions at his beck and call, he'd leveled-up. Damien Vex had become dangerous.

"Unfortunately, there's only one gentleman here." Petty, I admitted it. But I didn't want him believing I thought of him as anything other than a thug in a tailored suit.

"It's unfortunate what happened to you and the rest of the Centurions. Your presence is sorely missed."

"Didn't your magazine label us the world's greatest terror?"

"The people deserve to hear about the other side of your career choices. You spent your days covering up your messes. I simply exposed them."

I hadn't thought about it in that manner. Revelations served as the antithesis to everything I did for the Centurions. At least Damien acknowledged it. I didn't miss the subtle jab that we hid away our messes. Since I took over, we owned our shortcomings, no matter how brutal. Each decision weighed on me, and I refused to let the Centurions stand as gods.

"If you're going to be coy, I'll see myself out." As much as I wanted to throw LaToya's allegations at him, I doubted he'd crack. I had dealt with people like him for years. Their iron-clad demeanor meant sussing out information was futile. Instead, I could be home relaxing, staring at my phone, and waiting for a text from Jason.

I turned to leave.

"You've undoubtedly heard I'm ready to launch a new team."

I froze. He folded as I called his bluff. I faced the man, stepping closer to his desk. While we spoke, I wanted to look down at him. "I have."

"The world needs the Centurions. We both know that. But the public opinion polls have been less than stellar."

I cracked a smile. "You want my expertise. That's downright laughable."

"No. I don't need to waste more money on a public relations department. I have no use for Bernard Castle. I need Sentinel."

"Are you offering me a job?"

It was his turn to laugh. I overplayed my hand, and once again, he held all the cards. "No. You're yesterday's news. But our team could use your endorsement. A handing of the baton from the leader of the Centurions to the next generation."

"An endorsement?"

He gave a slight nod. At first, I thought he might be joking. But with the level of arrogance about him, he expected me to agree. Griffin had talked about the man's bold behavior. This wasn't bold. It was more like outlandish.

"Are you that much of a narcissist to think I'd say yes?"

"Perhaps." He stood, taking a moment to straighten his

jacket. Everything about him screamed—vain. I wanted to know who willingly allied themselves with a man who believed himself a god.

"Heroes have no checks, no balances. You wield a power that makes you dangerous. Should you go rogue, could the police stop a misguided rampage? What about the military?"

He led the conversation toward a trap. Damien Vex thought himself a brilliant man protecting the masses. From what? Me? Heroes? Arrogant.

"Get on with your point, Vex."

"You operate without supervision. Revelations ensures these larger-than-life heroes remember we're watching. We police heroes with social opinion."

I laughed. "You think your magazine stops me from being a bad guy? Vex, you think highly of yourself. You might need to step off that pedestal. Careful, it's a long drop."

"The magazine? Oh no, Bernard. That was only the first step."

I raised an eyebrow. He made my skin crawl. The hair on the back of my neck stood on end, and I half expected him to start in with maniacal laughter. Knowing LaToya believed him to be the center of the conspiracy, it took a moment before I caught up with his logic.

"You're going to use the Centurions to police heroes?"

A smile spread across his face.

"The heroes will rally against you, Vex."

"Whether or not you stand behind us, heroes rallying against the world's greatest team... it wouldn't be good for their public image."

The man had a point. If anybody stood against the Centurions, they'd look like rogue heroes. Damien Vex had created a public relations nightmare. His new team, even if they were fresh faces, carried a name that could create havoc for anybody who spoke out against them. The man had literally bought himself superhero bodyguards.

"I don't know what your endgame is..."

"Endgame? There's no endgame. I am making sure the people of Earth are protected. I'm also making sure heroes aren't causing more mayhem than good."

He couldn't resist the smug smirk. Perhaps he believed himself the judge and jury of superheroes. But he also wanted it known that there were more secrets to uncover. Griffin's description of the man didn't include a sadistic streak. Damien Vex was up to no good, and he only told half the story. I suspected the other half involved LaToya's theories.

"Let me be clear, Vex. I don't trust you. I don't believe the events in the last couple of weeks are a coincidence. Some might say you've been careless, leaving clues. But I think you're just that arrogant."

"Sentinel, are you threatening me?"

"I've known plenty of men like you."

"You've never met somebody like me."

I laughed. "I've filled a prison with men with more talent, more brains, and..." I gave him the once-over. "Better looking. I'm watching you, Vex."

I hadn't realized my fingers curled into fists. Despite thinking him a plague on mankind, I resisted the urge to drive my knuckles into his jaw. Nothing would have brought me more pleasure, but it'd have proven him right. No, heroes had a code, and I'd maintain my morals while I beat him at his own game.

I turned around, ready to walk through the shattered door. I wanted to fly out his window, shattering more glass, but decided I had already made my point.

"Leaving so soon? Does this mean your answer is no?"

It shouldn't surprise me. He believed I'd help him. Griffin had seriously undersold the man's self-righteous ego. "I have nothing more to say to you."

"I suppose I'd want to get home to my man, too. How did Jason's interview go?"

I froze. Interview? I tucked away that question for later. But the underlying threat toward Jason had been the exact reason I had kept my distance. Just like any villain, Damien didn't care about the collateral damage. If he saw a way to manipulate Sentinel, he'd certainly take it.

There was no point in hurling insults or making idle threats. He had shielded himself, and any attack on him would only reinforce his argument that the new Centurions were needed to protect the world from so-called heroes.

I spun around and stormed past Damien. Lightning jumped from my chest, crashing against the floor-to-ceiling windows. As they melted away, I leapt from my former headquarters. I wouldn't repeat the same mistakes as before. I'd protect Jason or die trying.

12

"Guild of Ash."

Anywhere else in the city, the storefront would be out of place. Sandwiched between two brick buildings with large display windows, the Guild had an old-world feeling. The wooden trim and carved sign with the store's name made it look as if it belonged in England a century ago.

When it came to tailoring, nobody surpassed Asher. They had a knack for tailoring a shirt in a way that hid every flaw and still made biceps bulge. When I wanted to look my best, Asher was the only person I trusted.

I checked my phone again. The exchange with Jason had been brief, but it gave me butterflies.

· · ·

J: That's done and over with. I'm famished.

B: Code for dinner?

J: Do you want a formal invitation?

B: Yup. Written. Calligraphy. Singing telegram.

J: Sir Bernard Castle, would you accompany me to dinner?

B: Sir Bernard Castle? I like the sound of that.

J: Play your cards right and I'll say it in person.

J: Dinner?

B: It's a date.

Damien Vex threatened all of Vanguard. That was bad enough, but when he spoke Jason's name, he made it personal. It had only been a few days and already being in proximity to me put him in jeopardy. I should run and distance myself. Every instinct screamed to remove him from the splash zone around Sentinel.

But Bernard didn't want distance. He wanted...

"Now I'm referring to myself in the third person. I've become *that* guy."

Easing the door open, a small ornate bell above the frame jingled. Of all the senses, the Guild of Ash had a smell to it. The ornate shelves, slick with lacquer, caused my nose to tingle. But the smell of cloth, rich, warm, and fuzzy, elicited a smile. The small shop was like a warm hug while wearing your favorite sweater. I could spend all day running my fingers over the clothes, appreciating the many textures covering the tables.

Asher was nowhere to be found, which meant they were most likely in the back of the shop helping size a customer. I wasn't in any rush, but leaving me to wander the store always left my credit card smoking. If I asked myself if I needed another sweater to prepare for the cold, the answer was always a resounding yes.

Walking along the wall, I stood in front of the suit jackets. Damien might have spent thousands on his suit, but it'd never look as good as anything Asher created. They had a knack for fine detail, and it easily put Damien to shame. It might be vain, but the next time I ran into the egomaniac, I might have to be wearing one of Asher's suits. Let's see how Vex enjoyed being the least dapper man in the room.

"Bernard, my favorite burly bear."

"Oh, stop it."

"Is it time to get you out of these pants and into a kilt?"

Asher walked from behind the counter and struck a pose. They wore an ornate jacket that reminded me of a modern-day pirate. The crimson chest and sleeves hugged their upper body tightly, but the bottom of the jacket served as a skirt. Asher made the finest tailored garments in Vanguard, but they also loved to take risks in fashion. It wasn't something I'd wear, but it screamed

Asher. It also gave away subtle hints as to why I was really here.

"The world isn't ready to see these calves bare."

"Honey, we're ready to see all of you bare."

For somebody who created exquisite clothes, I think Asher appreciated the naked form even more. Maybe someday I'd be ready for a kilt, but for now, I had a very specific request for the tailor.

"I need to see your special collection."

"Bernard Castle, I thought you'd never ask." Asher clapped their hands with a little jump of excitement. "I've wanted to dress you for ages."

Asher took a bow, gesturing for me to head to the backroom. We walked past the counter through a doorway covered with fabric. They covered tables in rolls of cloth and half-cut patterns. The mannequins were dressed with what would be a bit more radical designs than what made it to the front of the shop. If the front of the shop contained the commercial clothes, back here, Asher reveled in the avant-garde.

"How special are we talking?"

"Super special."

"Finally!"

Asher raced to a wall, drowning in sketches and cloth swatches. Pressing their hand against a bare spot, the hidden panel glowed. Once the red light finished reading his palm, the wall pivoted, revealing a hidden room with a spiral staircase. While Sentinel saved the planet from diabolical villains, people like Xander and Asher supported their efforts. Xander bandaged the superhero's wounds, and Asher equipped them with the tools necessary to fight crime.

I worked my way down the stairs. Unlike the old-world vibe from the storefront, nothing in the basement said 'old.' Soft blue lights flooded the room. Along the far wall, mannequins wore all manner of suits. But these weren't for a night on the town. Capes, cowls, and masks in an assortment of colors were ready to be worn while protecting Vanguard. Asher might be well known as a great tailor, but in the super community, Asher was *the* designer.

"I'm gonna dress Sentinel." Asher sang the words, clapping their hands as they followed down the stairs. "It's gonna be a super day todaaaaay." I couldn't help but smile at their enthusiasm.

I eyed the sketches littering a giant table in the middle of the room. Some heroes I recognized. "Redesigning Zipper's suit?"

"Frictionless technology. It'll increase his speed by ten percent."

It was like superhero eye candy. I'd like to think I wasn't vain, but every hero knew a costume made the first impression. Seeing our signature colors and chest emblems were as effective as yelling, "Stop!" But many of them included technology protecting the wearer. Not everybody was bulletproof or capable of flying. Where our powers fell short, that's when Asher stepped up to the plate.

"So what exactly are we looking for, my burly protector?"

"You've seen the news. Centurions are no more."

"It's all anybody is talking about these days. And Damien Vex in charge? He's hot enough to shag, but that's a one-night stand full of regrets."

I had been so angry I hadn't stopped to think of him as anything other than a jerk. But I guess he was handsome enough. His ego drowned any sexiness. Damien Vex knew he was handsome and flaunted it. That instantly dropped him down a few pegs.

"Sentinel needs a new suit." Even before the news broke, Asher knew of my alter ego. They knew the identity of every super in Vanguard. How they hadn't been kidnapped and beaten for information was beyond me. But perhaps if they could keep the secret without repercussions, Jason could do the same?

"Are we thinking dark and brooding? Sexy? A show stopper? What about a thirty-foot cape?"

I hadn't given it any consideration. My old suit did its job, but I wouldn't call it a fashion statement. I eyed an all-black suit. Monochrome, that seemed striking?

"No," Asher said.

I pointed at a dark maroon suit with black panels on the chest.

"No, again."

"The gauntlets?"

"Nope."

I threw my hands in the air. "I have no idea."

"Do you trust me?"

I raised an eyebrow. "You're not going to give me a choice, are you?"

"Sentinel needs a makeover. New team, new suit."

"There's no new team." I paused, studying Asher. Despite biting their bottom lip, it was obvious there was a secret dying to get out. "What do you know, Asher?"

"Hellcat!" Asher covered their mouth. "Hellcat is going to kill me."

I shook my head. "Hellcat can try all she wants. Sentinel is going solo."

"I won't tell you how to do your job. But Sentinel doesn't strike me as a solo hero. He's a leader."

"*Was* a leader."

Asher rolled their eyes. "Somebody is trying too hard to run away from their past."

If only they knew everything going on with Sentinel... and Jason. Their statement hit home. The past had a way of dogging at my heels. Maybe it was time to stop running?

"I trust you." Would I regret those three words?

Asher pulled a tape measure off the work table. They stalked around me in a wide circle, eyes narrowed as if they might pounce. I had to remind myself that it'd be worth it in the long run. This was the hidden life of heroes, being accosted by costume designers so we could uphold this heroic facade. If only the world knew what we went through to keep the streets safe.

Asher snapped the tape measure at me. "Strip, big boy."

13

I CHECKED MY WATCH. FIFTEEN MINUTES EARLY, WHICH translated to 'exactly on time.' When I mentioned needing to head home to get ready for a date, Asher wouldn't let me leave the Guild without a new outfit. Despite his attempts to get me in a kilt, I talked him down to a snug pair of jeans and a dark green sweater. He promised it gave my eyes a little extra shimmer. Who could say no to shimmering eyes?

Vanguard had a beautiful way about it that blended the immensity of a city with quaint areas that left it feeling homey. The Ward personified the small-town feel despite the skyscrapers in the distance. The Night Market was an event that made it even more special. Even though the sun had set an hour ago, Christmas lights hanging from poles illuminated the intersecting alleys. Flowery, perfumed wax from the candle tent filled the air.

A young couple held hands as they walked by. There was something romantic about the space. It reminded me of walking through a portal into another world. As he placed his hand on the small of her back, sneakily pulling her closer, I smiled. While my intentions weren't to lure Jason into this ethereal place and run my hands along his back, I didn't *not* want that to happen.

"Of course, you're still early." I didn't need to turn around to know it was Jason. I played it cool, despite wanting to give him a kiss. The memory of his lips from the other night hadn't faded.

"If you're not fifteen minutes early—"

"You're late. That's going into the annoying column."

He could act irked, but I could hear the smile. As he stood close to me, he bumped into my shoulder and I returned the gesture. "Fancy meeting you here." Awkward, I know. But it was either light body contact or a high-five, and that seemed wrong after railing him.

"It's beautiful," he said. He wore a t-shirt that hugged his body. I loved a big guy willing to show off his girth. It didn't hurt that the shirt was just short enough that if he raised his arms, I'd catch a glimpse of his belly.

"Yes. Yes, it is."

The dim lights didn't hide the red as it crept into his

cheeks. He took my hand and pulled me along as we went into the market. We had barely passed the man selling pretzels when he paused. His eyes went wide as he followed the strings of lights. I remembered having the same reaction the first time I had discovered it. But there was something magical about getting to experience it through a fresh set of eyes.

The Night Market wasn't much wider than an alley, but they filled both sides with small businesses. It was the only place in the city where somebody could buy vegetables, artisanal cutting boards, and quilts. There were hundreds of people milling about, treating it as their date night.

Was this a date?

"This city continues to amaze me. I can't believe I never visited growing up."

"Finally warming up to city life?" Jason had grown up in the country and preferred his wide-open green spaces to the concrete jungle. I loved the rolling hills and lush woodlands, but there was something to be said about having a mall nearby.

"Maybe I just needed a reason to visit?"

It was my turn to blush. "Still a fan of pretzels?"

"Only if they have yellow mustard."

I glared. "Brown mustard or nothing." Yes, we were the couple that argued over condiments. Despite my refusal to eat the vile pedestrian mustard, I always made sure it fell into my basket at the grocery store.

I ordered a pretzel, and yes, I even added yellow

mustard to the top. I broke off a piece and handed him the rest. He made a show of tearing off a piece with his teeth, loudly making delightful noises as he chewed. They weren't so different from the noises he made in the bedroom. I never thought the bright yellow condiment would have me stiff in my pants. Jason knew exactly what he was doing. Not even a supervillain would be that evil.

We continued our stroll, journeying into the heart of the market. In the darkness, nobody gave me a second glance. If they recognized my identity, they didn't let on. With heroes being a dime a dozen, I appreciated they let me go about my business undisturbed. It made me think that maybe there was a life after being revealed. If the people here treated me like an average Joe, then perhaps the rest of the world would as well.

"Hey!" shouted a man. I stopped walking, back straightening and shoulders going wide. I didn't clench my fist, but the lightning was ready should I need it. "A handsome, bearded couple like yourselves should check this out."

A couple? The man's words didn't deter Jason as he walked up to the vendor. I grinned at the name of his company. The Burly Bear Balm. The man behind the table had a beard only a few inches above his belt and a mustache that curled like he was born in the Victorian era.

"I'm not saying a good-smelling beard will get you laid, but—"

"Oh, it definitely will," Jason said. "I can assure you of that."

They laughed. Just like that, the two of them started talking about Vanguard, the Night Market, and ultimately the importance of a man who smelled like leather. I almost forgot about Jason's superpower. He treated every person like a friend he hadn't met. If I let him go long enough, we'd be invited to dinner.

"Smell this." He passed a small bottle under my nose. It reminded me of fresh leather with a hint of sandalwood. I'd be lying if I said I didn't spend copious amounts of time hydrating my facial hair, but I typically avoided scents. But before I could argue, Jason bought a bottle. "You'll thank me later."

"Somebody's getting lucky tonight," the man said, twirling his mustache.

"Only if he begs," Jason said. Between the scent of leather and the thought of Jason naked... I adjusted my pants.

We continued walking. "Do you still make stuffed manicotti?"

"Yeah, I..." I tried to think of the last time I made the dish. It was a recipe Jason's mother had given me. She swore it was the fastest way to cheer up her son. "Wow, I guess not. The last time was for your birthday. Why do you ask?"

He pointed to a young woman selling jars of homemade tomato sauce. "Sometimes when I'm sitting at home, I'll hear something on television or catch the whiff of the neighbors cooking and…" He shrugged. I caught the tinge of sadness as it crossed his face. "It reminds me of you, that's all."

I caught him by the belt loop. I pulled harder than I expected, causing us to collide. There's a moment to decide, to come up with something sentimental. With his admission, he offered me an opening to bare my heart. I decided it was better to keep Jason close than to push him away. I worried about villains using him for leverage, but keeping people safe was my job. But just because I made the decision didn't mean I knew how to get the ball rolling. What could I say that summarized my feelings?

I cupped Jason's cheeks before planting a kiss on his forehead. Words wouldn't do the trick. Poets spent a lifetime trying to illustrate the emotion bubbling in the pit of my stomach. But where words fell short, actions would speak volumes.

I stepped around Jason and picked up two jars of sauce. I exchanged pleasantries with the woman before paying. When I turned around, Jason hadn't moved. When I returned, he eyed the jars. I could see the confusion as he weighed a ruined moment against my Night Market purchase.

"I'll need sauce if I'm going to make you stuffed manicotti."

"I guess I went overboard."

I eyed the three bags resting next to us on the bench. "You never could resist coffee cups with pithy sayings."

We had reached the end of the market. The alley opened into a small courtyard with an old fountain in the middle. It seemed no matter where we went, a fountain served as a sign. We had taken a seat on the small bench, forced close enough that I couldn't ignore the heat radiating from his torso. It bordered on painful to not reach out and wrap my arm around his shoulders.

"Hero in the streets, villain in the sheets?" I gave him a dirty look.

"I mean…" He patted me on the cheek. "It seems a pretty accurate description. Or was that another hero pinning me to the wall in the bathroom?"

Playing coy seemed foolish. It wasn't like I hadn't replayed every touch of his body a hundred times since. There was a familiarity to his skin, comfortable, like putting on your favorite hoodie. But unlike before, where I thought I had the two of us figured out, this came with uncertainty. It wasn't only Bernard I had to think about. Sentinel had his own issues to work through. And how did Jason—

"You're thinking really hard."

"Am not." Childish, I'll admit it.

"You bite your lip when you're having an inner monologue."

"I do?"

He put a hand on my thigh, giving it a squeeze. I never wanted that hand to move. "You've always had it."

"And you're just now bringing it up?"

He leaned in close... for a kiss? I could feel the heat of his breath against my cheek. "We each have our little secrets, don't we?"

"Touche."

To emphasize his point, I held my hand above his. With just a bit of effort, sparks jumped from my hand to his. Not strong enough to sting, just enough to leave the hair across his knuckles standing on end. Sure, I could throw a man through a wall or race around the globe. That was Sentinel's job. But this was the first time I shared an average man with extraordinary powers with somebody.

"Does it hurt?"

I shook my head. "When I summon lightning bolts, it tingles a little. That's it."

He laughed. "That's it. No big deal. Just thousands of volts running through your body."

He turned his hand over, and little jolts arced between our skin. His middle finger caressed the center of my palm. The softest of touches made my stomach turn as if a truck had struck me. Even I was aware of biting my lip as I suppressed a gasp.

"Can you feel that?"

I nodded.

"You can withstand a punch, but that..."

One finger at a time, I squeezed his hand. Between the cool night air and the twinkle of the lights in the Night Market, I stopped resisting. I pushed the inner monologue aside and spoke with action. It was like our first date all over again, and I thought the butterflies in my stomach might rip from my chest.

"I feel it." When I brought his hands to my lips, I kissed his knuckles, barely touching the skin. "Every bit of it."

Jason didn't hide the gasp.

"What are we doing?" His words came out as a whisper. Even I heard the willingness to ignore the big question and let himself live in the moment. But blocking our way forward stood a massive hurdle. It just so happened it was shaped like my alter ego.

"I..." I couldn't act my way out of this. Jason needed... no, he deserved words. An explanation, a plan, an apology. There were so many things he deserved and, as I shoved my fears aside, I offered them. "I made the biggest mistake of my life that night."

I hid behind protecting him. They had been at my heels for years, and I let my sense of duty hold the emotions at bay. I left him to protect him. I said it so many times I believed it. I left because I feared losing him. At least this way, I thought he could move on and lead his life. But it seemed neither of us could let go of the past.

"I've done amazing things. I've seen worlds unlike anything you could imagine. I've saved the world."

"Starting to sound like bragging."

"But every night I crawl into bed... my side of the bed. I tried to move on. I tried to forget you. But..." I pressed his hand to my cheek. "You're unforgettable."

"I'm not going to wake up to an empty bed again, am I?"

"I can't promise that." Letting the electricity flow through my body, I let my eyes shine. "The world needs Sentinel."

He nodded, and for a moment, I thought he might pull away. I braced myself for the reality. Jason never asked for the responsibility of the world, and if that was too much for him, I would never hold it against him.

"But you'll come back?" I wasn't the only one putting their heart in the line of fire. While I weighed the worry of villains hurting Jason and protecting him, I was the villain in this narrative. I had been the one to hurt him, and he cautiously opened the door to his heart.

"Not even the Cthulhu himself could stop me."

"You're kidding, right?"

"He's slimier than you'd think."

"I trust you. About the coming back, not the slime thing. Let's forget you mentioned that."

I leaned in for a kiss. There was no teasing, no hesitation. I wanted to taste the man. For too long, I relied on the memory of him. I had years to make up for, and I'd start tonight. And as he parted his lips, the flood of memories broke through the walls I had built. Every time he covered me in flour while baking, each time he threatened to turn the car around when I touched the radio dial, it pelted against my armor. The nights I spent nestled against his back, kissing his shoulders until we drifted asleep, left me defenseless. The possibilities hinged on a kiss, and I never wanted to let him go.

"Whoa," he backed away. "Does this mean an open relationship?"

Oh, I hadn't thought about it. It'd take time to—

"Cause I want to get fucked by Sentinel."

Oh. Oh! He laughed as my face went through the motions. Leave it to Jason to keep me on my toes.

"I can share with such a sexy superhero."

The laugh turned to eye-rolling. Okay, I needed to work on my sexy talk. "Good. Cause before the end of the night, I want him inside me."

His hand slid down my chest and, with a quick glance to make sure nobody was watching, he gave my package a squeeze. Had there not been a market full of people, I'd have bent him over the bench.

"You'll get his cock when he says."

Jason growled. "Yes, sir."

Hard. My jeans needed to be off now. I jumped to my

feet, holding out a hand. We stood belly-to-belly. If he wanted a night with Sentinel, it only seemed fitting we start it off correctly.

"Ready?"

"Here? But what about—"

"We're going up." I glanced at the sky.

His eyes went wide. "Oh! Are you serious?"

"How fast do you want my tongue in your ass?"

He glanced up and then back to my jeans. Any fear of heights vanished, dwarfed by the hardness in his pants.

"I want it, sir."

I scooped him up. As he clenched his arms around my neck, I grabbed his bags. If he called me sir one more time, I didn't care if people in the market watched. I'd be shoving my cock in him for all to see.

"I'll take it easy for your first time."

"Words Bernard Castle has never said before in his life."

It'd be the only thing I'd take easy tonight.

14

THE FLIGHT HAD BEEN SLOW AND STEADY. I TOOK THE LONG way to my apartment. Jason got a bird's-eye view of the city when he opened his eyes. There's an art to being airlifted by a superhero. Let the person capable of lifting a car do all the work and have faith they won't let go. If I had wanted to show off, we could have gone high enough to spot the other fliers protecting the city. Baby steps.

This time, when I opened the door to my apartment, I didn't think about the loneliness. Instead, Jason barged his way through the door, taking in the sight of my apartment.

"So, this is what it looks like when nobody decorates for Bernard Castle?"

Wounded. I had spent hours deciding on egg-white or off-white for the walls. The throw pillows on the couch were neon orange. "I decorated."

"It's like a model home. If somebody broke in, they wouldn't think anybody lived here." He gestured to a framed poster of Sentinel on the wall. "Really? No, really. A poster of yourself?"

I pushed out my lip, pouting. "That's the first ad campaign I worked on for the Centurions. I'm still proud of that. You have no idea how much they needed a facelift. The city needs to be reminded that we don't just blow up landmarks."

He pointed to the action figure of Sentinel on the coffee table. "And that?"

It was Jason who collected action figures. Our spare bedroom had shelves of them imported from around the world. They *were* pretty cool. He had rubbed off on me.

"Hush. He lights up and has three catchphrases."

"Do I get to see the suit?"

What was it with people and that damned suit? Did the world think that a mask and cape made the hero? I opened the hallway closet and pressed my hand against the false panel in the back. I pulled out the first suit I ever wore. Homemade, and not very good at that.

"You were never very domestic."

If only he knew how long it took me to thread the needle. "I'd put it on, but after a few years, I think it shrunk."

"Shrunk. Sure."

I put the suit away and walked up behind him. Wrapping my arms around his chest, I rested my head on his shoulder. It still had the groove that cradled my chin, as if we were two puzzle pieces that slid together. Having him in my house, my life, all the drama with work washed away. Perhaps I needed the Centurions to fall apart to remake my life, with room for him.

Swaying his hips back and forth, I moved with him. He turned, wrapping his arms around my neck. We moved as if we were at a high school dance. It blew my mind. Jason Jaynes, the one who got away, was here, in my apartment.

"You're staring."

"Admiring," I corrected. "I want to—"

He stopped me as he pulled my sweater over my head. Tossing the shirt on the kitchen table, he started running his fingers through the hair on my chest. Every time his fingertips connected with my skin, I felt a jolt, as if the lightning in my body had a mind of its own. When his fingers traced the outside of my nipples, I shuddered. But as his finger grazed the tip, I let out a long sigh. Where Jason liked it rough, my back arched at the soft teasing.

When he traded his finger for his tongue, I resisted the urge to tear the shirt off him. Before he could kiss down my chest, I picked him up in a bear hug. He laughed as I carried him to the bedroom.

"This is so not fair," he said. I tossed him on the bed. He bounced before breaking out in a laugh. "And I thought you could toss me around before."

"You have no idea." I had never shown off my abilities in the bedroom. I could either be Bernard or Sentinel. And as a Centurion, I never risked a scandal with my alter ego. But now, there was no need to hold back.

"Yes, sir." Jason bit his bottom lip, the insatiable hunger creeping into his eyes. In the streets, he might be a strong personality who took gruff from nobody, but in the bedroom, he preferred somebody else to take charge.

"Strip." It wasn't a suggestion. He didn't treat it as one, as he quickly undid his belt and kicked off his pants. All that remained was the jockstrap, already straining to contain his package. That's all it took for my cock to press against the zipper of my jeans. It surpassed anything my imagination could conjure.

Jason was the epitome of sexy.

"Roll over."

"Yes, sir." He accentuated the word, knowing full well that it'd get me worked up. I didn't budge as he rolled onto his stomach. He tilted his hips, raising his ass in the air to help motivate my actions. The way the straps framed his backside, it was like a target. And the arrow... Okay, maybe that was a bit too on the nose.

When I didn't move, he wiggled his ass. Our first time in the bedroom, I had taken things slowly, making sure he was comfortable. It wasn't until our second date he said, "Don't ask." He relinquished control, comfortable with me taking the lead. Jason wanted to be used, and it was a privilege that he let me. But when he uttered 'sir,' it tapped into a primal need. I wouldn't be satisfied until I drained my balls and he ached. We both had jobs to do, and I would not disappoint.

I kicked off my shoes and made enough noise with my zipper to get him excited. I reached inside my briefs, stroking my cock as I admired the beefy man in my bed. If he had misbehaved, I'd keep jerking my cock until I came. I'd let him watch me soak my briefs, and if he were lucky, I'd toss him my underwear. But for now, I needed to taste him.

Crawling between his legs, I dragged my fingers along his legs. The sparks were just enough to tickle, a reminder of who took ownership of his ass. I grabbed each cheek, hard enough to make him whimper. Bending down, I kissed the red outline left by my fingers. I could do this until he left a wet spot on the bed. Teasing got me worked up as well. Each sound he made, non-verbal cues begging for more, but never saying it. How long would he let me go before he asked?

When I bit the soft flesh, I didn't have to wait. "Fuck me, sir." I would. Eventually.

"Not yet."

"Yes, sir." It was a test of will to keep from straddling him and watching my cock slide into the valley in the middle of his ass. But I had an agenda, and I didn't want to be rushed. I wanted to savor years of missed kisses, missed touches, and missed affection. I'd make up for lost moments, one caress at a time.

He stifled a laugh as I ran my beard along the crack of his ass. As he tried to pull away, I held his hips in place. Breathing deep, I let the heat of my breath cover his skin before I flicked my tongue. When he moaned, I buried my face, dragging my tongue across his ass. Jason stopped trying to get away, instead pushing back until he was fucking himself.

I rested my hands on his ass, kneading the skin until I had to come up for air. With an inhale, I dove back in. His moans had me pushing my tongue further. He didn't need the spit, but the more I prepared him now, the rougher I could get later. If I had my way, I'd stay here while I stroked my cock and came.

"Fuck me." It was less a request and more of a desperate command. I couldn't wait any longer. Any longer, and I'd risk coming in my briefs. While that was hot, it wasn't nearly as amazing as feeling his ass grip my cock.

I slid off the bed and dropped my briefs. Grabbing him by the ankles, I dragged him to the edge of the bed. I pulled him back until he was on all fours. Now *that* was a sight to behold. I reached between his legs to find the front of his jock had turned damp. Knowing he enjoyed my tongue made it even hotter.

I rested a hand on his left cheek before drawing it back. Smack.

He muffled a groan into the blanket. The slap wasn't hard enough to bruise, but it'd leave a handprint for the next day or two. "Want another?" I couldn't make out the words, but the head nod was enough.

Smack.

I traced the red line of my hand with my fingertip, following the skin as it swelled. I waited until his body relaxed and added a third. Tomorrow morning, it'd serve as a reminder. I enjoyed knowing my handprint left him stiff. But that was enough teasing.

I pressed my cock against his ass. I wanted to tease, to make him beg, but my willpower dissolved ten minutes ago. Inch by inch, I watched as he greedily devoured my length. I didn't stop until my balls rested against his backside. I'd lie and say I paused, giving him time to adjust to my girth, but I needed a moment to stop myself from coming.

No, not like this. I pulled out and flipped him onto his back. His eyes were wide in disbelief. Perks of superhuman strength. I pushed his legs onto my shoulders as I slid back inside. His fingers pulled at the comforter as a moan escaped his lips.

I held those legs tight against my torso, enjoying the soft thickness of his thighs. Sawing back and forth, I skipped the quick strokes. I slammed into him hard enough that my balls slapped against his ass. Leaning forward, I could see the lust in the way he bit his lip. Or maybe it reflected my own?

Letting go of his legs, I reached down, holding the back of his neck. I risked sliding out of him to steal a kiss.

"Come, sir," he said with a growl, begging as much as it commanded. Another night, I might make him beg, but I would write tonight off as a lust-filled escapade.

I reached between our bellies, wrapping my hand around his cock. Every time I shoved in, he swelled in my hand. I picked up the pace, racing toward the tingling starting just behind my balls.

"I'm coming."

He tightened as he covered the space between our stomachs in cum. The tingling transformed into flashes of lightning in a summer storm. I fought the urge to let it flow from my body even as my skin glowed.

I didn't need to announce reaching the finish line. My cock pulsed, thickening to where Jason didn't hold back the moans. He continued squeezing, milking the load from me. It was my turn to join in the chorus.

I collapsed on him, my cock slipping out as the last few pulses wracked my body. I'd need to wash the floors in the morning. His legs clung to my hips as my chest heaved against his.

"That wasn't bad." I glanced up to see the smirk on his face.

"Leave your comment card on the way out," I managed.

"Five out of five. Would recommend. Worth the tip."

"You got more than just the tip."

We laughed. In our post-orgasmic glow, we couldn't help but laugh at each other. *This* was perfection.

"I forgot."

"Forgot what?"

"That your arms feel like home."

Jason Jaynes simply fit. His back pressed against my chest, while my cock rested snuggly down the crack of his ass. One hand reached over, slowly rubbing his belly while the other snaked under him, palm pressed against his chest. Our legs tangled together as if we'd attempt to trip the other to prevent them from leaving the bed. With Jason in here, there was no need for a blanket. He *was* my comforter.

I could hear my phone vibrate. I tried to ignore it, to pretend that nothing outside this room could be more important than breathing in the scent of him. But when the vibrating turned into a muffled siren, I realized it was more than a wayward text message.

Vanguard needed Sentinel.

"Can you ignore it?" He wiggled his butt against my cock. Temptress.

"That's an all-city alert. Something big is happening."

He rolled over, burying his face in my chest. "Is this how it's going to be?"

"It's the downside of loving a superhero."

"Can't crime wait until breakfast?"

I couldn't tell if he was joking or not. He kissed me on the nose before giving me a pat on the cheek. "I guess if you're okay with me shagging Sentinel, I can live with sharing him."

"I'm saving them, not plowing them."

He groaned. "You should go before I find a way to keep you here." His hand wrapped around my cock, giving it a tight squeeze. Jason had all the makings of a villain. It was almost worth letting Vanguard burn, to let him keep stroking.

"You're evil," I whispered, kissing him on the forehead.

"Go." He threw himself back on the bed. "I'll just be here all alone." The dramatic tone and slight flailing made me laugh. "Go be a hero."

As I slid out of bed, I realized I didn't have time for a shower. The electricity sizzled around my skin, burning away the remnants of last night.

"That's one way to get cum out of your chest hair."

"Comes in handy." I slid on my briefs, careful to tuck away my erect cock. Yeah, the entirety of Vanguard better be thankful. As much as I loved being a hero, sliding inside Jason and falling asleep sounded like the better way to spend the rest of the night.

"I have to be out before breakfast."

"Oh?" I hunted for a t-shirt in my bureau. It wasn't a superhero outfit, but it'd suffice. "You can come join us for breakfast."

"First rule of Breakfast club..."

I laughed. "I see Griffin informed you. But I'd break the rules for you."

"You live on the edge."

Black t-shirt and jeans. Not quite a super suit, but it'd do in a pinch.

"I have another day of conferencing. I assure you, it's riveting."

Damien had asked about Jason's interview. He didn't strike me as a man who told the truth, but it raised some questions.

"Learning anything useful?"

"Methodology. Pedagogy. So many o-g's."

The phone started with another wave of sirens. I didn't have time to ask questions. Even if Jason wasn't giving me the whole truth, he'd have a reason. When he was ready, he'd come around. I had faith in him. Hopefully, he trusted me to do the same.

I kissed him on the forehead. "I'm off to save the world."

"Suddenly, my job doesn't seem as important."

"Hey, if it wasn't for the education system, I wouldn't have villains to fight."

He shot me a dirty look before rolling onto his belly. He

buried his face in the pillow, and I had a moment to admire this beautiful naked man in my bed. Hours later and his left cheek still had an outline of my hand. Good, I wanted him to have something to think about today.

The world owed me.

15

FLYING ABOVE THE CITY, I COULD SEE SOMETHING HAD RILED up the villains. The heroes were out in force, saving innocent bystanders while trying to suppress the bad guys. I stayed close to the tops of buildings, looking for any group of heroes in need of support.

None of this was by chance.

Without the Centurions, heroes had stepped up for planet-wide threats. It meant the streets weren't safe. Vigilantes had been called to help support those with powers. Whatever their endgame, it seemed like it was working. But behind it all, somebody had to be pulling their strings. There was a mastermind behind this chaos.

Something struck me in the back, driving me toward the street. Spinning about, I glimpsed the shadow vanishing in a puff of smoke. LaToya claimed there were no such things as coincidences. And as I rolled along the ground, jumping to my feet, I stood in front of the Centurion's skyscraper.

Even if I didn't agree with her, there were too many coincidences at once.

"About time you showed up."

The shadowy figure from the warehouse stepped out of an equally dark portal. It had been a long time since I faced somebody capable of clobbering me. I had never backed down before, and I wouldn't start now. I clenched my fists. It just meant I'd need to hit harder.

"Let's get this over with," I shouted. "I have things to do today."

I'd gladly call down lightning and eradicate him in a swift blow, but I needed him to go into a monologue. There was no point in vaporizing him if I didn't know the purpose of all the attacks. They always wanted something. Power? Money? Perhaps his parents skipped out on his piano recital?

"Were you waiting for a reveal? A plan, perhaps?"

Self-aware villains were the most annoying.

He held his hands out to his sides. Two portals opened, and out stepped a woman clad in black smoke and a man in an all-white suit. The woman I didn't recognize, but the man, I owed him a beating. Eclipse was the villain who revealed my identity. I thought EO and Stonewall had put him away, but it seemed like our prison system needed an overhaul.

"Sorry for outing you, Sentinel." Even Eclipse's voice grated on my nerves. But the man in the middle had already made an error. Revealing Eclipse meant that my identity being shared with the world was part of a bigger plan. Eclipse hadn't been working alone. Now I knew the mastermind behind this operation.

Now I could hit. Hard.

The sky lit up, a bolt of lightning cutting through the night. I didn't flinch as the searing white light struck the leader. I would take out all three, but I wanted to make sure Eclipse got what had been coming his way. Clouds gathered overhead, and as I tensed my muscles, several more flashes struck the ground. Summoning lightning wasn't a science, and the forces of nature would do as they pleased, but when the last one sent Eclipse sailing into the lobby of Centurion headquarters, I resisted a victory dance.

Eclipse might have suffered my wrath, but his leader stepped out of a portal, unfazed. Similarly, smoke gathered from the ground until it formed into his lady companion. It was foolish to think I'd cripple them with a single strike. As much as I wanted to trade blows with evil wannabes, there was a man in my bed I'd rather be blowing.

The tug on my boot brought my attention to my feet. The black smoke swirled around my legs. If it wasn't for super strength, the pressure would have crushed bones. I tried to kick, but the smoke held, refusing to let go. Okay, we had a trio of darkness-related goons. At least they thought through the motif of their superpowered league of evil.

The light about my body intensified until quick jolts of lightning tore through my clothes. Great, at this rate, I'd be fighting naked. I understood why everybody harped on getting a suit. Nobody wanted to see a burly bear fighting naked. Well, *almost* nobody.

The shadows pushed back enough for me to jump into the air. Tendrils chased, trying to wrap around my ankles. A few well-placed blasts of electricity and they retreated. Focused on my feet, I didn't see Havoc's fist racing toward my face.

He packed a punch. It must have been three blocks before I started slowing. Pushing off a dump truck, I flew back, fist drawn, ready to return the favor. But I didn't make it as the smoky woman intercepted. Her momentum sent the two of us crashing into a firehouse and burying me in the water tank in the back of the truck. Before I could close my fingers around her neck, she dissolved in the water.

Tearing at the metal, I hopped out of the truck. A crew of firemen gathered to see what happened. Jumping onto the ground, I gave them a wave. "Sorry about that."

A man stepped through his crew and gave me a head nod. "Give 'em hell, Sentinel."

"I owe you gentlemen some community service."

Before the captain could respond, I zipped out of the hole in their wall. Havoc stood in front of Centurion head-quarters, beneath a statue bearing my likeness. This time, I summoned the lightning strikes kicking up pavement around him as I flew closer.

Instead of slamming my fists into the man, I let the electricity pour out of my fists. Through the dust, I could see the jagged bolts slamming into his chest. Unlike before, I caught him off-guard, electrocuting him before he could step into a portal.

Or... so I thought.

Havoc stepped from the cloud, hand held out, stopping my lightning as if it was a jet of water from a squirt gun. By himself, I might have had a chance, but tendrils of smoke broke through the street, clutching at my arms and legs.

Havoc laughed. "It's great to have a team, isn't it?"

I was about to hurl an insult when Eclipse appeared overhead, his white cape flapping in the wind. I listened to Alejandro talk about his experience with the villain. Mental manipulation. Fear driven. He couldn't throw a punch like Havoc. I'd clobber him, and then I'd move on to the real...

I was standing in my apartment. No... *our* apartment. I had relived this moment a thousand times. Eclipse might pull at my fear, but it was nothing compared to what I did to myself. The soft snoring captured Jason's just as I remembered it. He had shimmied backward in my absence, seeking warmth. But I had left, leaving a void in the bed where I should have been.

This was the moment where I decided to leave. I could either be a hero and protect the world, or I could be mundane and wrap myself in happy ignorance. Six years ago, I made the wrong choice. But standing here, I could fix it. I could crawl into bed and press myself against his back and bury my face in his neck.

But as I tried to pull back the blanket, it refused to budge. There was no point in being gentle. The floorboards groaned under the weight, but even calling on the extent of my strength, it held fast. I refused to be defeated by a blanket.

It lifted.

In a puff of smoke, the scene changed, and I found Jason squaring off against a giant monster composed of shadows. Havoc. The word crossed my mind, a fragment of reality shaking... Eclipse. He used his powers to trap me in my worst fear.

"Havoc!" my voice bellowed in the empty space, shaking as if it might shatter imaginary walls. Eclipse pulled at my worst fear, Jason between me and danger. The villain wouldn't succeed. I had made up my mind. If this was going to work, I needed to be more than Vanguard's protector. My duty couldn't only be to the masses. There was a single man who deserved his own hero.

As the shadow lunged at Jason, lightning burst from my

chest. The brilliant, blinding light punctured the shadow. As the beast recoiled, lightning thrust downward, smashing against the empty landscape. I opened my eyes to see Vanguard and Havoc's henchmen by his side.

Eclipse failed, and I was mad. Very mad.

"Welcome back."

I barely glanced at Hellcat. I appreciated the vigilante keeping the streets of Vanguard safe, but this wasn't her fight. EO stepped out of a portal joined by Hyperion and Lionheart. The vigilante had been busy collecting super-heroes. Despite the impressive powers at their disposal, they would have to be spectators as I wrapped up with Havoc.

"What's the plan?"

"You stay here. I break their jaws."

She cursed under her breath. "He's going rogue, guys."

I shot forward. I let the lightning surge along my skin, burning away my shirt. The smoke covering the ground shot upward in jagged spikes. Whatever *her* powers were, I was prepared. A line of lightning poured from my chest, skipping along the street. Each place it struck, her powers retreated, clearing a direct path between me and Havoc.

A third black figure joined them. Havoc's monochrome companions were flying toward me. As Eclipse grew close, I darted to the right, grabbing him by the cape. Slinging him about, I whipped him into the newcomer. When the woman appeared out of a burst of smoke, I propelled toward her, fists out.

A bolt of lightning struck me in the back, charging my battery. This would be the spot where I normally wielded the axe, more of a showman's tactic than an actual weapon. Without the weapon between my shoulders, I let the lightning rush down my arms, firing it at her. Just like I expected, she evaporated.

There was nobody left between me and my target.

Fist drawn back, I picked up speed. I should have felt his face against my knuckles. The force of the shattering windows should have made me wince. I should have done a lot of things, but all I could do was gag as he clutched my throat and flew upward with me in tow.

"The infamous Sentinel, a has-been. You've reached your end."

I clawed at his hand, but there was no breaking his grip. I tried to summon the lightning, but he dodged every strike. Then he rushed through the clouds above the storm I created. His fingers closed tighter around my throat. As he brought my face level, he slammed his other fist across my jaw.

"One by one, the Centurions have fallen. You're all that remains of a crumbling dynasty. Good riddance. All that remains is havoc."

"Bad form." I coughed. Villains using their names in speeches always sounded tacky. It had been so long since I lost a battle, I didn't recognize the fatigue. As he tossed me upward, he slammed both fists against my chest. It sounded like a bomb went off and...

Falling? The cold air caught the remnants of my t-shirt. The world had grown dark. I tried to slow my descent, but there was no juice left in the tank. I lost? Twice Havoc bested me. My limbs struggled to follow orders, and before I knew it, I struck something. Dirt? Gravel? Pavement? I couldn't tell. I'd conserve my energy. In a minute, I'd be fine. I'd chase the villain. I'd win. I couldn't lose a third time.

It was almost as dark as when Eclipse used his powers. I could still feel my body, but, as if I were standing outside of it. Everything drifted in and out. I caught a glimpse of a man in a red suit, stubble covering his chin. Seconds later, I could feel lips against mine. It reminded me of Jason.

Jason. I had a reason to win, to be victorious. Havoc wouldn't make me a liar. I'd get up. I'd beat the bad guy. Then I'd go home to the best thing to ever walk into my life. I'd smile. We'd laugh. We'd grow old together. I just needed to get up. But right now, I needed a few seconds to rest my eyes.

"Don't quit on me, big guy."

Just... a... few...

16

I CAME TO AS A WOMAN HELD BACK MY EYELID, FLASHING A bright light from one eye to the next. The jolt of electricity to her hand had her cursing as she cradled her hand.

"That's it," she yelled. "I quit. I'm going back to private practice. Nobody there shoots lightning at me. Nobody sets fire to the hospital room. Superheroes, you're on your own."

She stormed off. It took me a second to realize I was in a medical bay in a superhero hospital. Unlike a normal hospital, they reinforced the walls with steel, and the doors were like bank vaults. I had never been in a public super-hero-based medical facility. Between Lix and the medical staff at headquarters, we treated our bruises in-house. Even thinking it, I sounded entitled.

They'd glued half a dozen little square pads to my

chest. The heart monitor screen had turned a bright green while wafts of smoke drifted from the back. The nurse wasn't the only one to get a shock. I'm sure I'd see a bill for the equipment before they let me check out.

"You leave an impression wherever you go. That nurse is currently cursing your descendants."

"Xander?"

He wore his paramedic uniform. I'd seen him in it plenty while we sipped coffee, but I never suspected I'd need his services. Alright, maybe I *had* grown entitled and cocky.

"Got the call that a sexy daddy bear got his ass handed to him."

My expression soured. He was one of my closest friends, but it'd take time before I incorporated Sentinel into my everyday life. Having him know I just got pummeled somehow felt humiliating.

"Did you save me?"

"Hellcat is my witness. I performed CPR. It was *definitely* not a make-out session."

"You wish." Chuckling hurt. Not as bad as my ego, but Havoc had left bruises. I didn't know I *could* bruise. Today was filled with new experiences.

"I saw the tail end of the fight. It was painful to watch."

"I could have handled him."

Xander laughed as he approached. He poked a finger

into my side, forcing a groan. "Yup. The nurse was right. You're a pain in the ass. Careful, or I'll send her back in."

Xander had spent the last few years patching up heroes. I never expected him to save my life. How do you respond? Man, I really was out of practice with showing appreciation. Was I like this all the time? I was about to ask if I was a dick when Xander sat on the edge of the bed.

"So you got your ass handed to you—"

"Are you going to keep reminding me?"

"Shut up," he scolded. "I'm trying to make a point."

He glared. His brow furrowed until I finally nodded. Of the guys, Xander was the first one to call me out. I guess I was long overdue for some tough love.

"Everybody has an off day. Don't let it define you."

I waited for the rest. When he didn't add anything, I raised an eyebrow. "*That* is your pep talk?"

He patted me on the leg. "I remember Sentinel was one of the heroes that charged into battle when he was depowered." True. There were hundreds of us assisting Lionheart that day. He proved himself to be a hero. We all did. It was a proud moment for Vanguard.

"You don't need a pep talk. You need to be told to get your head out of your ass." There it was, the Xander we all loved. "When you're getting tossed around like a sack of rocks, let the Deviants help you."

"Deviants?"

He shrugged. "Don't change the subject."

"Fine."

"Fine, you're going to listen to me? Or fine, I want Xander to shut up and I'll ignore his advice?"

I flopped back on the bed, my head sinking into the oversized pillow. Griffin and Alejandro would have let the conversation stand. They'd have moved on to another topic. But Xander, he knew me well, and somehow it always came down to which of us was more stubborn. Hint, it wasn't me.

"I'll consider it."

It was embarrassing as one of the world's greatest superheroes to let the bad guy get away, let alone be knocked unconscious. Now we added being rescued by non-powered people. My ego continued to bruise. The worst of it was realizing that Sentinel wasn't enough, that he couldn't solve the world's problems on his own. But had he ever?

When I came to Vanguard, I had barely started heroing before we formed the Centurions. Each of us had a skill set, and together we... I pushed the thought out of my head.

"Are you here to rub salt in the wound?"

A candy striper walked in with a tray. She paused, giving me the once-over. "You certainly don't look like the devil incarnate. Maybe Jackie meant the man with horns in 2B?" Just to be safe, she slowly reached out, placing the tray on a nearby table.

Before she left, Xander was already pilfering the tray,

saying a prayer as he peeled back the foil on the Jell-O. He skipped the plastic spoon and squeezed the contents into his mouth. It bordered on sinful how he smiled, his eyes rolling back in his head as he swallowed it in one gulp.

"Do you and my Jell-O need some privacy?"

He let out a content sigh before grinning ear to ear. "Nah, I enjoy having an audience."

The way he deep-throated Jell-O was less unsettling than the smile. Since meeting Aiden, something had changed. He had become more confident, but not in a cocky way. The quick-to-anger version of him hadn't vanished, but it *had* been tempered. Now he was more like a giant marshmallow.

"What?" He wiped his face, looking for tiny green remnants. "Did I miss some?"

"Admiring the smile."

He hopped to his feet. "Bernard, it's understandable that you have a crush on me. But I'm a taken man." Good grief, I think I liked him better when he was throwing punches through walls. "What we had was special, but our love is forbidden."

"Uncomfortable being happy, huh?"

He flashed two middle fingers. He wasn't the only one capable of detecting bullshit. "It's a good look on you."

"Thanks. It's—" He shoved his hands in his pockets and kicked the ground like a school child. "I'm not going to say it's because of Aiden, 'cause that's only part of it. But he challenges me to—"

"See the good in the world?"

He nodded. "Sounds like somebody knows exactly what I'm talking about."

I sighed. "It's just so... complicated."

He cleared his throat and dropped his voice an octave. "When life gets complicated, uncomplicate it."

"You do a horrible impression."

"Maybe. But it's true. A wise man once said it to me."

He patted me on the leg one last time before heading to the door. Damn, he knew how to drop a bomb and make an exit. But he wasn't wrong. A wise man had once said that. Perhaps it was time I took my own advice.

But first, I needed to go apologize to a cursing nurse.

17

"Are you sure they allow my kind in here?"

"You make it sound like you're an alien."

"I mean—"

"They allow aliens too."

Midnight Alley, the premiere hotspot for superhero nightlife. I hadn't come since Alejandro took over as the general manager. But if I was going to introduce Jason to the world of superheroes, I might as well throw him into the deep end.

From the outside, it was just another ominous door leading into a windowless warehouse. But with three gentle taps on the door, the bouncer pulled back a spot in the door where he could inspect the newest arrivals. I didn't remember them being this stringent about security. What was the point when the club contained enough firepower to hurtle a planet into the sun?

The door opened quickly. "Sentinel! Sorry about that. We've been getting a lot of reporters lately."

"I know the feeling." Yes, the vultures continued circling my apartment. Thankfully, the helicopters over my building had stopped.

"Come right in, gentlemen." He gave a slight bow as I led the way inside.

"Wow." I glanced over my shoulder to see Jason's face lit up. "I thought you meant like a club. You know, caged dancers and guys in thongs serving shots." I'd need to ask him what clubs he had been frequenting.

"Less go-go dancers, more speakeasy."

It wasn't a huge crowd tonight, but there were enough capes present to do the trick. I wasn't expecting the curious stares, followed by whispers. Nobody in the room had ever seen Sentinel without a mask. I'd have preferred Jason's first experience didn't remind him of tween girls at the lunch table.

"Do I have something on my shirt?"

"They're staring at me. Being unmasked is a big deal for heroes."

Scarlet stood on stage, her lips steadily turning down into a frown. Funny enough, she was one of the few people who would understand my situation. Giving up the mask, she founded the club before stepping down and letting

Alejandro take the reins. She might not be the owner anymore, but she'd be damned if a room full of patrons weren't focused on her.

She sang before the music started. Her voice held a sultry sensuality to it, and not because she used her powers to gain the attention of the room. Unable to resist her siren's call, Jason fixated on her, mesmerized, just as she intended.

As the song continued, she released her hold on the patrons and Jason turned slowly. "It was like..."

"You couldn't resist? Scarlet does that. Even heroes like their moment in the limelight. She also throws a mean right hook."

"You mean she's a hero?"

"Retired. She gave it up when she opened Midnight Alley. Now she just pops in for a song or two."

"So heroes *do* retire." He shot me a look. I couldn't tell if he was giving me grief or if he wanted to put the option on the table. For a split second, I considered it when Eclipse revealed my identity, but the world needed Sentinel. Retirement was nowhere in sight for this hero.

"Let's grab a drink." I rested my hand on Jason's lower back as I guided him toward the bar. More than one hero gave a slight nod of the head, acknowledging me as we went. Nobody displayed pity, but they wanted to make sure I knew they understood. Like me, almost all of them separated their identities. We all had our reasons.

"Is that the Arachniman?"

I never understood why the man with only two arms called himself the Arachniman. It only got weirder when one of his abilities was to levitate. He referred to it as the 'Arachnileap.' He found a theme and stuck with it. At least he didn't have arachnid-shaped boomerangs.

"Just don't ask for their signatures. Half would roll their eyes, and the others would grandstand while they regaled you with their latest triumphs."

We reached the bar. Alejandro showed a bartender how to execute his infamous cocktail, the Hero Chaser. I'd describe him as quick to laugh, and sometimes hard to take seriously. But as he flipped a bottle from behind his back, I realized he had a bit of dramatic flare as well. When he spun the bottle in one hand while snatching another, pouring them both into the tumbler, he looked up and winked at me.

"Now shake like you hate it." His trainee picked it up and gave it a good shake. "I said hate it, not like you're making sweet love." Alejandro took the tumbler and threw his hips into the shake. I'm pretty sure what I witnessed bordered on vulgar. I recognized a hate fuck when I saw one.

"Now give these two fine gentlemen a pour."

A second later, Jason and I clanked our glasses together and started sipping. It was sweet, almost too much, but then the alcohol hit the tongue. I almost coughed at the strength.

"Damn," Jason whistled. "Now that's a cocktail."

Alejandro directed his trainee to see to a pair of heroes in matching purple suits. "What brings you two here?"

Before I could answer, Jason leaned across the bar. "He brought me here to freak me out with his side hustle."

Alejandro raised an eyebrow. Jason wasn't wrong, but I would have put it a bit more gracefully. Alejandro patted him on the cheek. "Is it working?"

"I've seen worse at leather night at the gay bar."

Alejandro belted out, laughing. "Bernard, if you're not careful, I'll steal him."

"He can't fly, multiply himself, burst into flame, or lift a car over his head. Not exactly your type."

Alejandro gave Jason a wink. "I bet he has *other* powers."

Both of them stared at me. The heat rushed to my cheeks as the blush settled in. I could control it when it was just Alejandro baiting me. But Jason? I didn't like this team up. Not one bit.

"He does this thing with his tongue—"

"Alright, enough of that!" If my face got any hotter, I'd burst into flames. I'd need a lot more alcohol if I were going to survive these two ganging up on me.

"It's cute when he blushes." Jason's devilish grin gave

away his plan. He wouldn't have finished the sentence... I think. He just wanted a reaction.

"Papi, I approve. I *really* approve."

"Gentlemen, excuse me for a few. I need to hit the head," said Jason.

Alejandro pointed to the doors off the side of the bar. "Ignore the graffiti. Though *you* can still call me for a good time."

Alejandro waited for Jason to leave before he threw himself on the bar, grabbing my wrists as if his life depended on it. "Papi, this is your chance. The one that got away. He's back."

I couldn't believe it. It wasn't long ago I confessed to Alejandro that Jason existed, that he had a long-term lease in my head. I continued to struggle with—

"No, Papi. No! I can see you rationalizing."

"It's complicated."

"No. It. Is. Not." His eyes narrowed.

Never did I think I'd be taking relationship advice from Alejandro. He might be dynamite in the bedroom, but... something had changed. As his face softened, I could swear he attempted to communicate telepathically.

"Relationships are difficult. But, amar? Love is never complicated."

Alejandro cut through my defenses. He leaped over my walls and reached into my chest. The only man capable of calling me daddy without getting spanked spoke to my heart.

I leaned forward, kissing him on the cheek. I needed to get out of my own way. If I let my heart do the thinking, I imagined nights curled up on the couch. We'd fight for the blanket as I used his belly as a pillow. I'd fall asleep holding him. We'd argue about the best way to cook bacon.

If my heart did the thinking, I saw a future filled with love.

"There it is." Alejandro released his death grip. Sliding behind the bar, he straightened his tie, dusting himself off as if he had just moved a mountain. "Now get out of here. He doesn't need to see Sentinel's world. He needs to see this new Bernard."

"Al..." Thank you, didn't seem to cover the tab.

"It's what friends are for."

18

AT THIS HEIGHT, THE WIND WHIPPED VIOLENTLY. JASON scooted closer, his body pressing tightly against my arm until I finally draped it over his shoulder. He hadn't wanted the night to end. When I offered to take him to my favorite spot, he thought I meant the bench in the park. I should have clarified. *Sentinel's* favorite spot.

From atop the bridge tower, we could see half of Vanguard. At this hour, there weren't many cars, not that we'd be able to hear them over the howling winds. After a long night, something about this spot made the city appear peaceful. There were nearly a million people going about their lives, but here, the city held its breath. From afar, it was impossible to see it as anything but beautiful.

"This is going to take getting used to."

I peered over the ledge. Jason clutched a belt loop on

my jeans, as if it might be the only thing stopping me from falling. I lost count of how many evenings I spent here as I decompressed. But with Jason, it was like I was seeing the headlights passing underneath us for the first time. This was only one of the many things I wanted to show him.

"Wait until we leave Earth."

"I can't tell. Are you kidding?"

He let go of the loop as I sat back. His head rested on my shoulder. There were so many things I wanted to experience with him. Every mundane aspect of life would be new for us.

I kissed the top of his head. "I can reach out to the Plitachs. They're a peaceful people, mostly scientists. But they do enjoy their late-night drinking sessions."

"Now you're just making up alien races."

"Their planet has two suns. It's amazing to see the suns set."

"I'm going to veto this one. I'm barely functional on Earth."

"I question your sense of adventure."

"Maybe we should try something local first? I've never been to Boston?"

I forgot how little Jason traveled. Even Vanguard was a leap for him. He'd left his comfort zone coming to the big city. My heart swelled as I realized how many firsts he experienced, and why? For me? I squeezed him tighter.

"Let's compromise," I said. "We'll stay on Earth. What about Scotland?"

"I do like men in kilts. Wait, are you going to carry me across the ocean?"

It started as a grin. But as I imagined him clutching my neck while lugging suitcases, I broke down laughing. I might make the trip myself, but subjecting Jason to that never crossed my mind.

"I was thinking of a plane. You know, like normal people. Maybe splurge for economy plus?"

"How mundane," he said.

"I know. I'm just this boring guy. Sexy as all hell, but oh, so boring."

"The perfect teddy bear."

Everything about the conversation came naturally. It was as if we picked up right where we left off. It had been six years since *us*, but we fell into a rhythm like a day hadn't passed. But there was a glaring difference, one I needed to make sure he understood before we could move forward.

"Are you ready to date a superhero?"

His face scrunched up as he thought about the question. His lips tightened and moved to one side of his face. It served as his thinking expression. He had jested up to this point, but I was glad he paused to flesh out what it meant.

"Are you ready to date an elementary school teacher?"

"I'm sure they're dangerous, but can they blow up your house?"

"Do yours ask where babies come from?"

"Touche."

"If you're asking if I'm worried about a villain showing up on my doorstep? Yeah. I guess I am."

I appreciated he was being honest. If this was going to work out, we needed to communicate. This wasn't as simple as deciding which sci-fi-inspired artwork to hang on the wall. It could be life or death.

"I'm more concerned about dating two men."

The statement caught me off-guard. Alejandro had been dating EO for months now. I hadn't thought to ask how he handled EO's average, everyday alter ego. I never gave it much thought. Dating a superhero was like a weird threesome with two people.

"How do you mean?"

"I know Bernard. I'm excited to see him again. But Sentinel? He's new. I don't know him. And here I am wondering what it'd be like to be in a relationship with both?"

"Sentinel isn't a bad guy. He's stubborn. But he leads with his heart. I have it on good authority he's gotten in trouble for doing the right thing versus the logical thing. He sees the world is broken, and if he can make it better, he'd..."

"Lay down his life?"

The ultimate sacrifice. It hung over the head of every superhero. We wanted to believe that we'd be willing to go the distance. Each of us hoped it never came to that. But would Sentinel? Jason nodded his head as he interpreted the debate happening on my face. I worried it'd be too big a sacrifice for Jason. Hell, even *I* lost sleep thinking about it.

"I guess it's no different from a police officer." He gave me the once-over. "That shoots laser beams."

"Lightning bolts."

He glared.

I stood up. He quickly gripped a massive rivet to his side, holding onto it for dear life. I started pacing back and forth, no different than if we were standing in the living room. He needed to see the differences. I wanted him to think about this beyond a romantic reconnection.

"You're going to give me a heart attack."

Then I stepped off the tower. Jason yelped. I stood on air, continuing my pacing. "We can't pick up where we left off," I admitted. "But we can start something new."

If he squeezed any tighter, he'd crush the rivet. "I get your point," he said. He gestured to the tower, a furious demand for me to stop showing off my ability to fly.

"I left all those years ago because I feared something happening to you. I'd have never forgiven myself. But..." I smiled as I stepped onto the tower, kneeling before him. "I can protect you."

His death grip relaxed. Resting my hands on his thighs, he had grown chilly. It'd take me a while before I recalibrated to what it was like to be an average human again.

"I don't want your protection."

The words were slow, carefully selected, and deliberate. I didn't know how to respond. If I was going to make this work, to put Jason's life in danger simply by loving him, I'd need to protect him. There was no way around this, whether or not he wanted it.

"You can't shelter me from the world. If it's not a villain, it could be a drunk driver. One of my students could poison my coffee." Damn, the fourth grade had gotten ruthless. "This is my choice. *My* choice."

Was I truly bad at reading a situation? I couldn't formulate words. What was it he wanted?

"Bernard, I have loved you since the park. I have loved you every day since. When you left, I hated you." The truth stung. "I hated you because I couldn't stop loving you."

"I love you," I replied. The words were natural and comfortable. But inside, I felt the walls around my heart tremble. I never thought they'd crumble. But with five words, Jason shattered the prison I had built for myself.

"I don't need a superhero, just a regular one. I need *you.*"

I hung my head. If Jason asked me to give up the mask, to put away my alter ego, could I? Even if I could, the real question was, *would* I? I had been so consumed with what I'd need from Jason that I forgot to ask what he'd want from this relationship.

"Go be Sentinel for them." He cupped my face, lifting

my chin. I wanted to be lost in those eyes. They crinkled around the edges when he smiled. Even when they narrowed, threatening to push me off the couch, the playfulness never vanished. But right now, they were hopeful. I wasn't the only one watching the fortress around their heart obliterate.

"Are you—"

"Be Sentinel for them. Give me time. Maybe I'll learn to love him. But he damn well better make sure Bernard comes home."

I lunged forward, wrapping my arms around Jason's chest. It was too soon for him to see tears. I pinned him to the platform while he flailed, shouting as I dampened the collar of his shirt.

"You're going to kill us!" For an average human, I was surprised by just how tightly his arms squeezed my neck. As much as I didn't want to move from that spot, his pulse raced fast enough I could feel the vein in his neck ready to burst.

"I love you." I meant every word, and I'd repeat myself until my voice turned raspy.

"I'll love you when I'm kissing grass."

Pulling back, I stood, holding out my hand for him. "Then I guess we're going for a stroll." He moved slowly until I picked him up. His arms remained locked around my head. He clenched his eyes shut as I stepped off the tower. Instead of flying to the nearest park to make good on his promise, I opted for gently lowering us to the sidewalk along the side of the bridge.

He dared to open an eye. I moved slow enough that he had to check that we were descending. "Okay, maybe I don't *hate* Sentinel." His grip said otherwise. But it was a start.

19

"... BUT WHAT IF THE OWNER OF THE PENIS IS IN ANOTHER galaxy?"

Griffin threw his hands into the air. "Alejandro! How the hell did we get here? I only asked if you knew the daily specials?"

"You should know better," Xander said. "Daily. Special. Every one of those words are sex-related to Al."

"¡Dios mío! It's like you don't even know me."

While they launched into a heated debate over sausage links or patties, I sat silently with my coffee. They provided entertainment day after day, and usually, I listened for the perfect moment to place a Bernard-defying zinger. But all I could think about was standing on a stranger's front lawn, kicking my shoes off to feel the grass beneath my feet.

Jason had laughed. But it didn't take prompting for him

to take off a single shoe and sock. I waited in anticipation as he described the chill of dew under his foot. The way he closed his eyes and savored the moment was almost sinful. He dragged it out until I pressed against him, holding his hands.

"Bernard Castle..." More pausing. More savoring. More watching me squirm. "I have, and always will, love you."

The air grew crisp and lights along the street brightened. His words healed a self-inflicted wound I had been triaging for years. It was easy to get swept up in the endless possibilities of the future. But I didn't want to think about the future, not yet. I wanted to live in this moment, with this beautiful one-shoed man.

"Bernard!"

I remembered the taste of his lips, his warm, soft lips. Overcome with emotion, my feet had left the grass, threatening to pull away from Jason. Figuratively and literally, he grounded me. I lived in that moment. The walls had come down as Jason jump-started my heart. He hid his face as I spun about, shouting, "I love this man."

Slap.

Breakfast. Xander and Griffin stared at me as Alejandro wound up for another smack. This time I caught him by the wrist. He threw his arms around my neck as if I had come back from the dead.

"Did Shinasta possess your body?" Asked Xander.

"She only possesses women," Griffin corrected.

"Lord Hypnotic?"

"Only within eyesight."

"The Blue—"

"Not even the right species. Xander, do you know anything about superheroes?"

"Papi, are you all right?"

Alejandro pulled away, taking his seat. All three waited for my response. "Did I zone out?"

Griffin shook his head. "Silence is kind of your thing. We're more concerned with what happened to your face."

"My face?"

Xander poked at the edge of my lip. "You were smiling."

I rolled my eyes. How hard would it be to make new friends? Could I trade in these heathens? Was there a return policy?

"Shut up." Mature, I know. But they had caught me off-guard while daydreaming. And true to form, they weren't going to relent.

"I didn't know he could smile," Griffin said.

"It makes your face look weird, Papi."

Did I confess I lost myself in a memory of Jason admitting he loved me? Or did I play coy and hope they returned to the conversation of sausage links being superior because of their phallic shape?

"Does this have anything to do with a sexy man you left Midnight Alley with?" Alejandro knew exactly what was going through my head. His superpower might detect fresh sex, but it was a close cousin to sniffing out romance. I'd be safe as long as—

"That's the smile of a man who just said, 'I love you,'" Chad said over my shoulder.

—as long as Chad didn't come into the conversation. The barista considered himself an expert in all things relationship. I needed to find a new group of friends. Maybe I'd take out an ad in the local paper.

"Papi?" Alejandro's eyes grew wide. "Really?"

"Guilty."

"Guilty?" Xander chimed in. "Two seconds ago, we thought you were being telepathically controlled by MindMeld—"

"Not how his power works," Griffin said.

"Shut up, Griffin. And we find out you're in love? Tell us everything," he finished.

Behind Xander was a large glass window looking onto the street. I imagined the glass exploding as a team of supervillains threatened to kill us all if I didn't go with them. I'd rather be a hostage for nefarious plans to conquer the world than recount this story.

I wanted to tell them everything, but not yet. I feared they'd lose their intensity if I shared my emotions. Foolish, I know. But I wanted to live in this *thing* that belonged to only Jason and me. Eventually, they'd hear the tale as Jason and I forced them to attend an ugly-sweater party. Someday, but not now.

Alejandro cupped my hand, squeezing it. "Savor it, Papi. But we need to know, are you happy?"

I hid the smile behind another sip of coffee. Happy. We all strived for that sense of satisfaction. Happy was so far in my rear-view mirror I almost chuckled. I experienced happiness when I remembered where I'd put the television remote. This was as if happy drank rocket fuel.

"I am."

The four of them cheered as if I'd saved a puppy from a burning building. They held coffee cups high as Alejandro declared, "Sausage penises for the table!"

Chad patted me on the shoulder before heading back to the counter. I thought they were ready to move on when Alejandro snatched my phone from the table. I'd need to change my password when he wasn't around. With a few clicks, he looked up, far more serious than I was used to seeing.

"It's time to take the next step in your relationship, Papi."

"Wait. You don't mean..." Xander's eyes went wide.

"Is he ready for that?" Asked Griffin.

"There's no going back." Xander added a hiss for emphasis.

Next step? Was he about to text Jason and ask him to go steady? Did people still do that? Maybe he meant making the relationship exclusive. Giving him a key to my apartment? The anxiety built until I caved.

"What next step?"

With a poke of the screen. He set it on the table, spun it around and slid it in front of me. WoofR, relationship status? He had changed it from 'single' to 'taken.'

"You made it sound like it was a big deal."

With a tap on the screen, he clicked on Jason's profile. There, clear as day, he had updated his status to 'taken.' I wanted to laugh it off as being ridiculous. But I couldn't fight off the smile as I realized he had already shouted to the world that he was off the market.

"Think it's a big deal now?" Asked Griffin.

"Aww," Xander said. "Looks like Jason is taken. Sorry to hear that, buddy. Maybe he's shagging that Sentinel fellow."

"Good point." Alejandro snatched my phone again.

"Hey!" I didn't know which of them made me madder. Changing a relationship status on an app shouldn't be a big deal. But if I got excited seeing Jason's availability, then hopefully, it'd do the same.

Alejandro returned the phone. The new relationship status was set to 'It's Complicated.' I shot him a dirty look.

"What? There's not a setting for my alter ego is taken, but my superhero persona is ready to mingle."

I facepalmed. They were insufferable. "Okay, maybe it *is* complicated."

Chad returned with an order of sausages. Before they hit the table, Xander grabbed a couple, jumping to his feet.

"I have to head to work. Apparently, there are superheroes that just don't know how to take a punch."

He shot me a look. I appreciated his discretion. I didn't need Griffin and Alejandro worrying about my superhero escapades. The way Griffin stayed glued to the HeroApp™, I'm sure he knew about the fight. But hopefully, it didn't detail Xander showing up and taking me to the hospital.

Xander kissed my cheek before shoving sausages in his mouth. Okay, Alejandro had been right. Watching him slurp them down like a cock-starved man made links superior to patties.

"Everybody take care of themselves." He patted me on the shoulder. "You too, Sentinel. Don't do anything stupid, big guy."

Big guy?

Xander dashed out the door. I shifted in my seat to see him leaving with his duffle bag in tow. My brain wrestled with the disbelief. Had he bent the truth to justify where he was during the fight with Havoc? He had been the first person to arrive at the hospital. There were too many coincidences. Xander? A superhero? It'd be rude to ask, but did I ignore it?

What about Griffin or Alejandro? "Are either of you superheroes or have superpowers?"

"I wish," Griffin said. "I'd be a comic book legend."

"Does what happens in my bedroom count?"

Well, that answered my question.

20

"I<small>T'S LIKE</small> I <small>DON'T EVEN KNOW YOU.</small>"

I ignored Griffin's statement as I followed him into the comic book store. Out of the Breakfast club, Griffin held the title of Senior Director of Geek. He had proven to be a walking dictionary of all things comic books. By extension, it meant he was the most knowledgeable person I knew about superheroes. Even Gideon, an artificial intelligence, would struggle to keep up.

"How long have we known each other? Never once have you come with me to the comic shop. He's changing you, Bernard." He looked over his shoulder and gave me a ridiculously exaggerated wink. "And I don't hate it."

"Griffin!"

The woman behind the counter jumped up and down, waving her arms. Was Griffin popular? In the world of geekdom, had he reached the level of godhood? I hated to admit it, but I had entered his world. I would have to keep my mouth shut and learn his people's customs.

"What do we have here? Griffin, are you bringing me dessert before dinner?"

She wore a neon pink t-shirt with the phrase, 'Hero in the streets, villain in the sheets,' across the bust. She flipped hair over her shoulder as she licked her lips, leaning on the counter like a cat ready to pounce. How did such a small woman have so much energy coursing through her body? I wielded lightning, and even after downing four cups of coffee, I couldn't compete.

"Gay."

"Griffin. Buddy. Pal. Brother from another mother. How many times have we talked about this? You need to branch out to hot, straight men."

"Aren't you married?"

"I didn't say I wanted to touch him."

As he approached the counter, I trailed behind. He and Lydia were working together on a comic book. Griffin created the artwork while she wrote the stories. Hearing him talk about their project with such passion and vigor always made me smile. I might have Jason to blame for my mood, but Sebastian did the same for him. Who would have thought an abundance of love pushed us to take risks?

The shop had an entire wall plastered with comic books. Hundreds. Beneath the display were boxes filled with more comics. There must have been thousands. The opposite wall was covered in action figures. It surprised me to see a poster of the Centurions, a promotional piece created for the documentary they released. It was surreal to see our lives mixed with fictional heroes. Did it matter to the person reading? I hoped they found both to be inspirational.

"Wait, aren't you that Sentinel guy?"

I spun about to see Lydia studying me with her head cocked to one side. She held up her hand, blocking the top of my face. It was only then she let out a low whistle.

Griffin chuckled. "Lydia, meet Bernard Castle. You might know him better as Sentinel."

"Know him? I have his life-sized pillow boyfriend on my bed. The hubby isn't thrilled, but it's our happy threesome."

Pillow boyfriends. I had overseen the public relations side of the Centurions, and it created a constant battle with our branding director. If he found a way to squeeze pennies from the Centurion brand, he jumped on it. Comics and action figures, it made sense. The body pillow boyfriend? We're going to put that in the epic-failure column.

"Nice to meet you." As fast as I could hold my hand to greet the shop owner, she shoved a box in my direction.

"Will you sign my Sentinel action figure?"

Taking the box, I couldn't help but laugh. It'd have been surreal to see my tiny likeness, but I had one of my own.

Griffin often chastised me for taking it out of the box. I'd never confess that I had already lost one of its bolts of lightning.

"I think I can handle that."

I scribbled Sentinel across the front of the box. I added my signature underneath. It'd take getting used to not having an alter ego.

"Are you still heroing? Retiring?"

"I'm a solo act as of late."

Lydia gave me a once-over. "I'm not saying I'm mad with this…" She gestured up and down my body. "You should rebrand. It might be time for a new identity."

Heroes were known for changing their names and costumes regularly. What was one more alter ego? It made keeping track of heroes a pain in the butt. But as they upped their game or went through major life changes, sometimes they needed a new identity. Was she right? Should I shelf Sentinel and come up with a new name? I wonder if Thor: God of Thunder was taken?

"Right now, I'm focused on being Bernard."

"He's smitten with a new guy," Griffin said. "He's giving pseudo-normal a trial run."

Lydia took the box out of my hand, inspecting the signature. "That's a shame. Sentinel kicked ass with the Centurions. So starting a new team is out of the question? Then maybe Revelations wouldn't be trashing you so hard."

If Hellcat had her way, I'd already be running with the Deviants. I didn't have a good reason not to start a new team or join an existing one. Every time I sat down and thought about my future as Sentinel, I stumbled through a fog until I hit a wall. I attributed it to the amount of change happening around me. A creature of habit, I think I reached my limit with new.

"What is Damien Vex saying now?" I asked.

"I really hate that guy," Griffin said.

"The usual. Sounds like you destroyed half the city yesterday. Did you really get angry and blow up a fire station?"

"No. Well, not exactly."

"You seem to have gotten under that man's skin. Ex-lover?"

Griffin gagged. "I'd disown you."

"It's just his normal anti-hero rhetoric. Only now, he's in control of the new Centurions. It's most likely a publicity maneuver." I'd need to pay Damien another visit. He was sending a message, and if he wanted my attention, he'd get it.

Her face scrunched up as if my answer offended her. "I'm not going to tell you how to hero."

"She's going to tell you how to hero," Griffin interjected.

"You led the world's most awesome group of super-heroes. Teach a new generation of heroes. Once a leader, always a leader. It's going to happen, eventually." She rested a hand on my face. Okay, this had gotten weirdly uncomfortable. "Why are you fighting it?"

"Told you," Griffin said. "It's best just to give in."

I stared at the signature on the box. Sentinel. Bernard Castle. Maybe Lydia had the answers? If I resisted the inevitable, was I just dragging out the misery of uncertainty? I followed Griffin here, thinking I might buy something to satiate Jason's love of science fiction. Instead, I was being schooled by Griffin's vivacious and spunky counterpart.

"But what do I know? It's not like I'm an expert in all things superhero. They're just my life."

Things were going so well with Jason. But maybe I needed to see what picture these scattered puzzle pieces created. Could I have the guy *and* serve the city? Jason said he needed to warm up to Sentinel. I hadn't considered putting Sentinel away and creating a new identity, one that Jason was always part of.

"I'm going to need that." I snatched the box out of her hands.

"Hey!"

"I'll sign all of them for you."

Her eyes widened. "In that case..."

Griffin gave me a swift pat on the butt. "You should only play with your little Sentinel in private." Try as I might to glare at him, he batted his eyelashes with a smile that nearly went from ear to ear. "Do you want me to show you how it's done?"

When did *I* become the target of their teasing? The world had gone mad, and I stood at the epicenter of the storm. But it was Lydia who gave me an eyebrow waggle that left me feeling like my zipper was down.

"Only if I can watch."

I needed a shower. But first, I needed to have words with Vex.

Centurion headquarters. Staring at the skyscraper, it no longer stood as a beacon of pride. Seldom a day went by where I wasn't meeting with directors or collaborating with other heroes within those walls. But in just a few days, Damien robbed it of warm memories. Now, it represented a thorn in my side, and it was going to end.

At this hour, most people were already at their desks. When I walked inside, I was surprised to see how few people were coming and going through the lobby. It served as an industrial marvel, an expansive room with a giant water fountain. In the middle, a glass elevator moved upward, giving its occupants a bird's-eye view of the building's interior. Along one wall, technicians replaced a series of shattered windows. But there weren't the usual people using the space for impromptu meetings or working away from their offices.

"Bet it has something to do with Damien."

Revelations labeled me a menace. I wanted to fly through Damien's office window and make an entrance. He should be lucky I considered myself a level-headed guy or I might strangle him. If Xander had his way, I'd be trading fists with the bully. For now, I'd attempt to have a man-to-man conversation. If that didn't work, who knows, maybe I'd have to lawyer up and take him to court for libel.

I stood at the mouth of the lion's den, and checked my phone again, hoping LaToya had sent word. Nothing, not from her or the rest of the Centurions. If she was right, the magazine's hate toward me might be the least of my worries. But until I had confirmation from Carmen, or proof of my own, I needed to deal with the immediate problem. I couldn't deal with a conspiracy if all eyes were watching me for my next destructive act.

"Sentinel, to what do we owe this pleasure?"

I spun about to see a woman in a vibrant blue leather suit. The strokes of neon pink wrapped over her shoulders, between her cleavage and along her legs. The cape matched the pink streaks and the angular mask covering her eyes. I couldn't place the heroine. But the way she commanded the space, it was clear she belonged to the new iteration of Centurions.

"I'm here to speak with Damien Vex."

She descended but held her position several feet above the floor. I recognized the power play. Either I flew to meet her, which could be seen as an act of aggression, or I remained on the floor, surrendering the high ground. I already didn't like her.

"Do you have an appointment? He doesn't have time for riffraff coming off the street."

"I want to have a chat about him dragging my name through the mud."

"Seems like you're doing a fine job of that all on your own. I had to help put out a fire this morning. Apparently, the local fire department couldn't answer the call. They have you to thank for that?"

She spun the details masterfully, pulling just enough from reality that it came across as plausible. Use the facts, but withhold enough that the listener paints their own narrative. I had used my skills as the public relations director to raise awareness and create trust between the public and my team. But this woman, she was like my antithesis. I *really* disliked her.

"What's your name?"

"Hoax."

I didn't recognize the name. But with the number of heroes in the world, it'd be impossible to memorize them all. For all I knew, she created this persona as part of her contract with the Centurions. But as much as I'd love to trade industry secrets, I had to see a man about a magazine.

"Hoax, tell your boss I need to speak with him."

She laughed. Forced. Fake. Condescending. "You had your chance. He offered you a collaboration." She dropped to the floor, getting close, but staying just out of arm's reach. "You're a has-been, Bernard. Hang up the cape. The world doesn't need you anymore."

It didn't come as a surprise that Damien recruited heroes with the personality of dirt. The public thought all heroes were this noble respected breed. But there were as many jerks. They ranged from stoic to arrogant, hero to anti-hero. If this was one of his recruits, I couldn't fathom wrangling the egos for a mission.

"I'm not here to spar with a whelp."

I turned to walk toward the elevator. She moved quickly, blocking my path. Her arms folded over her chest like she had already won the fight. Unlike her, I knew the danger of two heroes slugging it out. She might be willing to tarnish her reputation, but I wouldn't sink to that level.

"You're not welcome, old man."

I'd earned every gray hair in my beard. Most of them, probably before she was born. "I'm asking politely."

The air thickened, as if a storm had moved in. She bordered on sinister as her eyes filled with black. If she thought I was going to flinch from a little flex of power, she'd have to try harder. After fighting demons, her parlor tricks were quaint at best.

"Hoax, stand down." Stepping out of the elevator, it

surprised me that Damien would be caught mingling with commoners. But with a single command, Hoax's eyes returned to normal. The snarl on her lip said she didn't like her master's command, but she followed orders.

"We need to talk, Damien." I tried stepping around Hoax, but she stayed between me and her boss. With a hand on my chest, she made it clear she still wanted a fight.

"Have you reconsidered my offer?"

I couldn't hide the disgust on my face. He published a magazine labeling me a menace to Vanguard, and yet he thought I came begging for a job? The man's audacity had no limits. If I was any other hero, I'd have lost my cool, and lightning would have smashed more than a few windows.

"Get my name out of your mouth," I barked. "Find another target."

"Stop making yourself a target."

Gaslighting? Really? He wanted to spin this as being my fault? I wanted to wipe the arrogance from his face. But as he sauntered forward, his hands held behind his back, he held no fear. I could wield a primal force of nature. And yet, he didn't hesitate as he approached.

"Saving the world, you meet some interesting people," I said, shouldering my way past Hoax. "Celebrities. Politicians. Lawyers. I'm sure a few of them would gladly support the man who saved their lives. Do I need to reach out and see which of them would see a menace in handcuffs?"

The thinly veiled threat caused the man's eyebrow to rise. Damien let very little slip, the definition of control. The perfectly plucked brow remained high. It was enough.

"Sentinel, did you just threaten me?"

"Threat is such a violent word," I corrected. "Let me use words that make more sense. Libel. Litigation. Courtroom. Public opinion. Corruption. Sentinel has nothing to do with this. Bernard Castle is the name that should worry you. I will make this a public relations nightmare. Then let's see how you operate with the world breathing down your neck."

I expected when backed into a corner, a man like Damien would puff out his chest and grandstand. But when he started with a slow clap and a chuckle, I didn't know how to respond.

"Well played, Bernard. I'm glad to see you haven't lost your bite. It's cute, really, it is. But if you think a single person can win against a media giant, perhaps I gave you too much credit."

Heroes had sought to shut down Revelations for years. Despite the best lawyers, somehow Damien Vex stayed just within the confines of the law. If anybody in this lobby proved themselves a menace, it was him.

"I'm putting you on alert, Damien."

Bernard wanted to drag his knuckles across the man's chiseled jaw. Bullies preyed on a good guy's morals. But as Sentinel, I had to stay above petty squabbles. A superhero beating an average citizen, even a nefarious asshole like Damien, it'd create unease with the public. He knew my ethics protected him. I curled my fists. I didn't want to be the bigger man.

"Your final warning, Damien. Unless you want me to unravel the mystery behind how a magazine mogul climbed his way to overseeing the greatest heroes on Earth."

Cheap blow, I know. But if he would not listen to logic, then I hoped his need for self-preservation would calm his attacks. Damien shook his head, adding a tsk-tsk sound to make it even more pretentious.

"I don't have the faintest clue what you're alluding to, Bernard. Go protect Jason. At the rate you're making enemies, he's going to need a bodyguard more than a boyfriend."

My fists tightened and electricity jumped along my skin. Hoax's fingers dug into my shoulder as a warning. I batted her arm away. I could have hurled her across the room, but with the number of security cameras hidden in the lobby and the building's A.I. watching me, I didn't dare make a scene.

Damien spoke to my greatest fear. If Jason hadn't come to Vanguard, he'd be out of reach and safe. It was the exact reason I walked away that night. I had to resist the urge to pull the same disappearing act. I wouldn't be that man again. But Damien had a point. If he stayed in my radius,

I'd need to be ready to throw fists any time a villain decided hurting me wasn't enough.

"This isn't over." It wasn't a threat. It served as a reminder to me. I had faced men like Damien before. He'd push until I was ready to break or until I pushed back.

I turned and walked away, a literal storm as lightning flickered from my fingertips to the lobby floor. I needed to speak with LaToya and see proof Damien was a tyrant. Then I'd push back with everything I had. But first, I needed to make sure Jason was safe.

21

Who knew bad singing could be this painful? Right now, my ears hurt.

"Thank you for that, ahem, creative rendition," said the DJ. "Who knew you could yodel during a rap?"

I eyed Jason, trying to telepathically ferret out why he insisted we go to Bottoms Up on karaoke night. While I questioned my life choices, he clapped as if the train wreck were a masterpiece. I caved and gave the woman a clap as she took a bow on the small stage.

"If we wanted singing, we could have gone to Midnight Alley."

"Nope." He shot that idea down quickly. "Tonight you're Bernard—average grumpy bear. No powers."

"Average?"

Jason reached under the table and gave my package a

squeeze. "Yup, average." He gave me a wink before kissing my cheek.

Unlike jocks and socks, Bottoms Up had a mixed crowd tonight. Mick had figured out how to make everybody in the Ward feel welcome at his bar. There wasn't as much eye candy with their asses exposed, but the night was young. Who knew what would happen when a singer got frisky on stage?

"Want me to put your name in? Maybe we can do a duet?"

I tensed at the suggestion. The thought of getting on the stage and singing made the hair on the back of my neck stand on end. I'd rather face the Rat Overlord than stand up there. Just the thought made my palms sweat.

"Your face right now. You're debating on flying away, aren't you?"

The sound of his laughter put my body at ease. He knew how to push my buttons. While I should have shot him a dirty look, the familiarity with one another forced a smile. Even the mention of me flying away instead of running. The fractured life I led was coming together.

"Be glad I love you."

"Someday..." He tussled my hair. "It's going to happen."

The server put two pint glasses on the table, and I slid one in front of Jason. I had almost forgotten what it meant to go on a date. This wasn't a random hookup or an awkward 'get to know you.' This was a good ol' fashioned date.

As he took a sip of his beer, swishing it around in his mouth to savor the taste, I couldn't help but admire the man. Since the other night, his stubble started to show on his cheek. Knowing him, he forgot to pack his razor. But the way the tiny hairs grew along his cheek only emphasized his jaw. I looked forward to them brushing against my face.

"What?"

I looked forward to the days ahead. He'd have to learn to accept my constant staring. There were years to make up for, and I wanted to relearn every inch of his body. As the smile spread across my face, his cheeks turned red.

"Is this going to be a thing?"

"Yup. There will be plenty of admiring."

"I can't handle it."

"You don't have much choice."

"Can you wait till I'm asleep?"

I laughed. "Like I don't already watch you sleep."

Jason gave his signature pout—bottom lip curled as he crossed his arms. He held the pose for a second before leaning over, resting his head on my shoulder. The singer on the stage belted out an 80s classic, and something about the situation... felt right? Wrapping an arm around him, I gave him a squeeze.

"I was going to wait to ask, but this conference..."

I didn't want to push him, not this soon into our rekindling. But things were going well, and I didn't want Damien's voice in my head driving a wedge between us.

"I lied." Just like that, he confessed. Did he come to Vanguard for me?

"And…"

He held his position until the song ended. He sat upright as we clapped. Jason seldom hid the truth, and even when he did, he usually had a good reason. If he didn't want to talk about something, he'd let me know.

"I came to Vanguard for a job interview. I had eleven lined up."

"Job interview? What about your students?"

"Not so funny story…" The smile vanished. "I got fired."

I rested a hand on his leg, giving it a squeeze. He snaked his fingers through mine, gripping them. I'm not one for public displays of affection, but considering we were only twenty feet from the bathroom where I fucked him, hand-holding no longer counted.

"Long story or short?"

"Whatever you want to share."

"Did you know that schools now have Superhero Protocols?"

I nodded. "I've gone to a few schools in the city for assemblies. They never tell you that saving the day from a villain could put bystanders in harm's way."

"You know me. There isn't a volunteer opportunity I refuse. I offered to be on the committee at the elementary school. Maybe six of us? We had to come up with a plan and present it. It's pretty standard. Lock doors, pull down the shades, common sense stuff. It shouldn't have been that difficult."

"But..."

"Enter our jerk of a principal. He got the job because he knew somebody at city hall. He was unqualified, and I'm pretty sure he didn't like kids. Can you guess who got put in charge?"

I rolled my eyes. I had been thankful that LaToya had her finger on the pulse of Vanguard. We might not always agree, but I never felt she had been adversarial. Even now, she was somewhere out there putting her life on the line for the Centurions. Perhaps I should have been doing the same?

"We're in the meeting, going through everything. We're laying out the rules he's going to take credit for. Then the secretary comes in and says we need to turn on the news. What do you know, my ex-boyfriend is a superhero?"

I already didn't like where this was going.

"The principal goes on a tirade. He's anti hero. Claims they're all menaces. He's been a jerk this whole meeting, and I lost it. So I chimed in."

"You didn't..."

He gave a slow nod. "I can't even remember what he said. But I slammed my hands on the table. Not my greatest moment. I was flustered from seeing my ex-boyfriend turned superhero on the television. Maybe I lost my cool."

I should have left it alone. But nosey me needed the rest of the story. "What did you say?"

"If you have a problem with heroes, fine. But Sentinel, Bernard Castle is a good man."

"That's sweet."

"Then he asked how I knew."

"Oh, no." I knew where this disaster was headed. "You didn't."

"Yup. Apparently, confessing to dating a superhero was not the right move. I went back to teaching, but by the end of the day, he sent an email firing me. The coward couldn't even say it in person."

"I'm so sorry."

"It's not your fault. Funny thing is, when I went back to class, the kids were having quiet reading time and I had already found positions. Plenty of openings in Vanguard."

"We go through teachers kind of fast. Something about kids coming to school with superpowers freaks them out."

He chuckled. "By the time I got home, I had a request for an interview. I packed my bag to do a whirlwind tour of as many as I could. Who knew I'd see you in person. I was bored in my hotel room when this new profile popped up. What do you know..."

"Wow. Never tell Alejandro. He'll want all the credit."

"He can have it. I owe him."

He leaned over, resting his head on my shoulder again. I kissed the side of his head, giving his leg a pat. Before I even saw him, I had come barging into his life. I might be able to protect him from sentient robots, but prejudice like that? There were some villains that couldn't be conquered with a punch.

"I've had ten interviews. No callbacks. I'm getting worried I'll have to wait for the next school year."

"You know what they say about lucky eleven."

"Optimism appreciated, but it's not your best trait."

True. If he was worried about finances, I'd gladly help him out. He'd hate it, but I wouldn't let him go into debt. But I doubt it had anything to do with money. Jason loved having a sense of purpose. If being a teacher had become that purpose, he'd feel incomplete until he stood in front of the classroom.

I couldn't let him wallow in his misery. Sentinel couldn't fix this problem, but Bernard could. I slid off my bar stool.

"Where are you going?"

I didn't answer as I walked toward the DJ. He played an old tune between brave souls taking the stage. I gave him a nod.

"Do you have "Hero" by Scarlet Drozdov?"

"Hey, I was next."

"Sorry." I gave a bow to the young woman. "That man back there is having a rough day. We just... he's my boyfriend."

Glancing over her shoulder, she nodded. "I wish *my* boyfriend would sing to me."

The music started, and when I stepped onto the stage, I could see Jason's jaw hanging open. Never in a million years would he think me brave enough to sing in a room full of people. But never in a million years did I think I'd have a reason. Life is funny like that.

I had listened to Scarlet's song a thousand times. Every time it came on the radio, it made me think of him. Taking the microphone in my hand, I gave him a wink. I didn't need to watch the little bouncing ball move across the teleprompter. I had performed this in the shower until I knew it by heart.

Time to be brave.

"This is the story of a hero..." The heat rushed into my cheeks as my voice cracked. I thought I'd die of embarrassment. Jason placed a hand over his heart. The woman in the front row cheered, and the crowd followed.

"If I could get a second chance to set you free." By the chorus, my voice deepened, filling Bottoms Up with a tale of rediscovering love. I pulled the mic from the stand, stepping off the stage. A woman eagerly shoved a dollar bill into the waistband of my jeans.

I paced myself, waiting for the chorus. "Regret swallows my days. Then I see those eyes, vibrant and filled with surprise. It starts with a hello, a long time no see. The story picks up as we turn the page. And before we know it, we find ourselves lost in a second-chance romance."

He wiped the tears from the corners of his eyes. When I stood next to him, he leapt from his stool, throwing his arms around my neck. Kissing Jason was more important than finishing the song. The crowd cheered as I wrapped an arm around Jas... my boyfriend.

As Scarlet said, this was the start of our second-chance romance.

22

"I'M GOING TO EXPECT MORE SINGING," JASON SAID AS HIS hand slid around my arm.

"I wouldn't hold your breath. One-time show. I'm going into retirement before the groupies get out of hand."

We found a rhythm to our walking, letting Jason hang onto my arm as if his life might depend on it. Out of habit, I had led us toward my apartment. I realized I never asked him if he wanted to spend the night. Did we skip that step? I should probably ask.

"Do you want to come over to my place?"

"No. Yes, I mean, yes. But I should go to the hotel."

I'd be lying if I said the statement didn't feel like a kick in the gut. But it was best to take things slow.

"I want to. Trust me. I *really* want to. But I have one more interview tomorrow."

"Oh." That took away the sting.

"And if I go to your place. I'll be exhausted in the morning." He pulled away, the edge of his lip turning up. "And a little sore."

"Hey! I can keep my hands to myself." Even to me, it sounded like a lie. If I had my way, I'd be tearing him out of his clothes before the door shut. I'd be spending the night curled up behind him, and most likely *in* him.

"Maybe you could—" A steady whistle filled the air. Jason spun about, looking for the source. This is where experience in the field came in handy. I grabbed Jason from behind, spinning about and covering his body with mine.

BOOM. I braced for the concussion from the missile. The fire wrapped around us. Holding Jason tight to my chest, I feared I didn't cover enough of his body. It only lasted a second, then I flew forward with him in tow, putting distance between us and the crater. Before landing and giving Jason the once-over to make sure he was uninjured.

"What was that?" he yelled. A blast that size would leave his ears ringing for a few minutes. Hopefully, by then, I'd have the culprit in cuffs and ready for local law enforcement.

"Remember me?" Great, another supervillain seeking revenge. All I wanted was to kiss Jason good night. But no, some idiot with delusions of self-grandeur needed to interrupt date night. I didn't need to summon the lightning. The anger did that for me.

Gauntlet. Advanced cybernetics integrated into a suit stolen from the Machinist. The Centurions provided backup last time he held the city's machines hostage. Apparently, he held a grudge.

"I'm giving you a chance to walk away." I didn't want a fight tonight. It killed the mood.

"I think we both know that isn't going to happen."

He wasn't *my* arch nemesis, but attacking me and Jason on an otherwise quiet stroll, I'd make an exception.

"Jason, stay back."

Lightning poured from my fists and raced toward him. A cannon on his shoulder sent out a wave of decoys. The light crashed into the small canisters, nowhere near close to annihilating Gauntlet. Okay, maybe this wasn't going to be a fast punch and cuff.

"Who's your little friend?" A villain even acknowledging Jason made my blood boil. I rose off the ground, ready to square off against the hacker-has-been. The lightning arced from my fists to my chest, and I said farewell to another t-shirt. I really needed to make the suit from Ash a priority.

"I owe you some payback."

"Oh, just shut up."

He listened. Two missiles flew from his forearms, intertwining as they sped toward me. One I blasted into a harmless explosion. The other, I caught out of the air and threw into the sky before it burst into a flurry of orange and red sparks.

I barely had time to see Gauntlet before he flew into me, his shoulder driving into my stomach. Smashing an elbow into his back, I was surprised to see he didn't relent. Somebody had made upgrades since I last saw them.

He stopped, changing direction to fly away. It had been a ruse as I spotted the black hexagon pressed against my chest. Wires flew out, wrapping around my body. The thin strands glowed a bright red, hot enough to burn against my skin. Flexing, I tried to tear them off, but they held tight, biting into my flesh.

"Somebody looks tied up at the moment." God, I hated when villains attempted to be witty. The man engineered a computer virus that rendered the entire city inert, and yet he couldn't come up with good quips. Griffin needed to teach a class.

I pushed the lightning to the surface. Instead of bolts of white light, the skin along my arms and chest glowed a brilliant yellow. With another shove, it turned white, burning through the cables. I wish I could see inside his helmet. The disbelief would be delightful.

"This is your last chance to surrender." He wouldn't take it. They never did. Instead, he'd make some grandiose statement about defeating me. For once, I'd like a villain to see he was outmatched and just give up.

"First, I'm going to drive you into the ground. Then, Vanguard will be mine." Not bad compared to his earlier statement. But he lacked flare.

I skipped the repartee and flew toward the man, fist drawn, ready to clobber him. Two drones detached from the back of his suit, firing tiny darts. A burst of lightning from my outstretched hand vaporized them. When my fist connected with his breast plate, I hoped to shatter it and end the fight. To my surprise, his suit not only held, but as thrusters fired from his hands and legs, he hardly moved.

"I've added some upgrades."

The thrusters changed direction, propelling him forward. The metallic fist under my jaw sent me reeling. Nobody had ever punched me before I got my powers, but I imagined this was what it felt like. Pain radiated along my face and neck. Before I recovered, something wet and slimy shot out of his chest.

The greenish fluid expanded, coating me from the neck down. With hands together like a club, he brought them down on my shoulder. The force sent me to the pavement, and as the green substance touched the street, it stuck. As I tried to muscle my way free, I realized it was non-lethal detainment technology from the Tower. The thief used Centurion tech against me.

"Poetic, isn't it? Defeated by your own creation. I'll have to thank them."

Gauntlet landed a few feet away. As he thrust a hand

down to his side, metal bits of his suit broke away, reforming into a small device in his hand. It produced a three-foot blade made of glowing blue light. A plasma sword? Great, more technology Gauntlet pilfered from hi-tech heroes. When I had him cuffed and safely behind bars, I'd need to talk to folks about keeping their gadgets under lock and key. But first, I needed to free myself from this nasty greenish goop.

"It seems our time together has come to an end."

"Just stop talking," I growled. "Your dialogue is horrible."

As he straddled my waist, he raised the sword overhead. Did I think he'd actually kill me? Perhaps he was a villain that didn't mind bloodying their hand. It wasn't enough to prove himself superior. He wanted a trophy. Thankfully, I wasn't out of tricks of my own.

The clouds over Vanguard swirled, turning dark. The static in the air grew ionized as it heeded my call. With the sword held high, it'd make for the perfect conductor. Another cocky villain, Gauntlet thought he had the upper hand. He couldn't fathom a hero laying a trap capable of incapacitating him. He was wrong.

I summoned the lightning.

"Get off him!"

"Jason, no!"

Jason struck Gauntlet on the back of his helmet with a metal patio chair. My eyes widened as a strip of searing white light left a jagged pattern in the sky, rocketing toward the three of us. Turning, a loud boom erupted from Gauntlet's palm. The sonic weapon hurled Jason backward just before the lightning slammed into us.

Gauntlet flailed as his suit went haywire. The electricity hammered away, vaporizing the green substance. I reached up, my fingers sank into the suit, pumping it with even more electricity. I tore at the power source, and the joints locked up, and he fell to the side. I didn't care about restraining Gauntlet. I needed to get to Jason.

I jumped to my feet, half-running, half-flying toward Jason's still form. The electricity from the lightning bolt had singed the fabric of his shirt, leaving tiny burn spots. "Jason, are you okay? Jason? Jason!"

I knelt by his side, checking his pulse. Good, he was alive.

"I'll never forgive myself if something—"

He coughed. His eyes fluttered open as he hissed. "Did I get him?"

I checked for broken bones as he tried to sit up. His eyes rolled back in his head, and he decided lying on the pavement was just fine. I lifted him onto my lap, cradling his head.

"Why the hell would you do that?"

He closed his eyes, but the grin let me know he'd be okay. "Boyfriend needed saving."

"He could have killed you." He reached up, patting me

on the cheek. "*I* could have killed you. What if my lightning—"

"I'm okay. Thanks for asking."

I'd never have forgiven myself. It would have been horrible if Gauntlet hurt him, but to think, my own lightning? I couldn't let Jason be collateral damage. But he was right. I needed to rein in the worry and be a good boyfriend.

"What hurts?"

"A little of everything?" He groaned, hamming it up. I didn't agree with the humor, but at least it meant he wasn't seriously hurt. "What was that thing?"

"Sonic boom, I'm guessing. At least he got you out of the way of the lightning. That could have—" I couldn't bring myself to say it.

"I'll be fine."

Sirens were somewhere nearby. I assumed somebody watching from their windows had called the police. They'd need me to go in and give a statement, but I wasn't leaving until I was sure Jason was okay. When the ambulance showed up, I'd be sure they checked him out. Then he'd get an escort to his door, hell, to his bed.

"I beat my first villain." His eyes opened, and he must have seen the panic on my face. "I'll be okay, I swear."

The seconds dragged on as I waited for the sirens to arrive. I cupped his head, letting my thumbs rub back and forth along his cheeks. It was as much for me as it was for him. If I could focus on the warmth of his skin, then I could focus on a different reality where Gauntlet showed up, and I hadn't been there to protect Jason. He had said it, his *first* villain. Dating me, it wouldn't be his last.

I thought I could protect him, but had that been a mistake? Was that a way to justify letting him into my life? There were a thousand questions, and as I stared at the rise and fall of his chest, I didn't like the dark places my mind went.

Two cop cars rounded the corner, with an ambulance in hot pursuit. I waved my arms, trying to get their attention. The cops were fast from their vehicles, ready with cuffs for Gauntlet. The ambulance stopped, and medics jumped out to check on Jason.

"He's going to be okay," one medic said.

"I told you," Jason said as he slipped from the back of the ambulance.

I eyed Jason and then the cops as they attempted to drag Gauntlet to the cop car. He patted me on the cheeks. "Do what you need to do. I'll be fine."

"Are you sure?"

"I just saved a superhero. I can handle myself."

He kissed my cheek and gave a slight groan. "Sore, but fine," he admitted.

I couldn't help but think to myself, he's going to be okay —*this time.*

23

"Disturbing the peace," I scoffed. "Try attempted murder. Two! Two attempted murders." As a Centurion, I had lobbied for years to have the crimes of villains be elevated. While the heroes busted their butts on the streets, the legal system struggled to keep pace. I'd have to call my senator and see where the Villain's Aggression Act stood.

"He'll be on the streets in a week."

Nobody thought about the difficulties superheroes faced. They saw us as caped crusaders whisking in and saving the day. But nobody thought about the amount of money heroes spent replacing their suits, or the time we sat in courtrooms giving testimony. Maybe Griffin's boyfriend could do an article for the magazine to help show all aspects of the job.

My brain fired on all cylinders. Even sitting atop the

bridge tower didn't bring the peace it usually did. The wind had stopped whipping about, making it possible to hear the car engines crossing into Vanguard. From up here, the troubles of the city shouldn't have been able to reach me. This worry had its own superpowers, and it clung to me for dear life.

When my phone vibrated, I fished it out. I expected another alert from the HeroApp™. I was delighted to see a text message from Jason. But when I saw a photo of him with the chair, clobbering Gauntlet, my chest tightened. The HeroApp™ watermark in the corner meant somebody had taken it and uploaded it to the app. Anybody in Vanguard could see my boyfriend putting his life on the line to help. It should have been sweet, but all I could think about was the villains with access to a phone.

More alarming was Jason's message. "Dynamic duo."

It had only taken days. Days! Already, the existence of Sentinel put Jason's life in jeopardy. I had feared him knowing my secret identity, but it paled compared to this.

"No, Jason," I muttered. Three emojis followed. Two caped men and a villain. I'm sure he saw it as an act of bravery, passion, even. He mustered the courage to help save the man he loved. While I should experience a heart full of love, I could only think about that plasma sword stabbing him.

His words about not wanting a protector echoed in the back of my head. They were great words. But as I shook the idea of him at the whims of Gauntlet, they weren't the reality. Even staying by his side put his life in jeopardy. I thought I'd be able to protect him from superpowered menaces, but it didn't change the fact proximity to me painted a target on his back.

"Maybe the wizards could make everybody forget?" They had messed with the fabric of reality before. But if I did that, then I'd be back to lying to Jason about my nightly excursions.

The image of a body on the ground with a white cloth draped over it flashed across my mind. I could control a force of nature, but I couldn't keep my mind from grasping at worst-case scenarios. Each of them ended with a body.

It was time to admit it. This wasn't a case of setting our baggage aside and rekindling a romance. It came down to life or death. I couldn't have it all. I couldn't be Sentinel and protect the city *and* be Bernard Castle. There was no putting the genie back in the bottle.

"I can't do this."

It hurt to admit. More than a punch to the face or lasers cutting through my suit, the truth cut deep. The people closest to me were in danger because I simply existed. It might not be my fault, but every action since my reveal, that was on me. Returning to my lone wolf ways was the only responsible decision. I didn't have to like it. What I wanted and what I needed rarely aligned.

I wanted to open a debate. I wanted to go kicking and

screaming against logic. The fortress I built about myself had crumbled, and for a moment, I had a glimpse of the life I could have had. Its obliterated walls had been glorious. It was feeling the stones fit back into place as I erected the new walls that hurt. I wanted to scream.

Bernard Castle, a pillar of calm and a provider of logic, wrapped around me like Sentinel's suit. The skies overhead swirled, a storm spreading along the borders of Vanguard. Thunder rumbled, a low, deep growl that shook the girders of the bridge. Specks of white filled the clouds, lighting building in between the roaring.

It started in the belly, a churning that clawed its way up my chest until it reached the back of my throat. Lightning struck the tower as the scream ripped from my mouth. The ferocity grew, the pain like sandpaper against my throat. The volume intensified, challenging nature itself. Brick by brick, I locked away my heart. Bernard Castle shrank, returning to the dark shadows cast by Sentinel.

"Literal screaming into the void."

If I had wanted privacy, I shouldn't have sat atop a Vanguard landmark. It didn't make Hyperion's approach any less intrusive. He dropped from the sky until he stood on the edge of the platform. No, not standing. He hovered, as if he might need to escape. I guess after manifesting a dark cloud overhead, I shouldn't be surprised.

"Everything... I dunno, okay?"

"If you're here to give another recruitment speech—"

"That's Hellcat's department. I was out patrolling. I thought Thundra might have escaped. Again. Man hasn't invented a cell that keeps that woman locked up."

When the rain started, I counted my blessings. It was one thing for him to see me as an emotional mess. But to see the tears streaming down my face? I didn't care about my image. I just didn't want to reveal how broken I might be.

"What do you want, Hyperion?"

He glided closer, his toes never touching the Tower. "Sitting in your Ivory Tower has made you bitter, Sentinel. On the streets, we look out for one another."

"Sorry." He might have been right. As much as I tried to return to being a solo act in the streets, the more I realized how removed I had become. I shouldn't be teaching the next generation of heroes. I should be taking notes.

"I saw what happened. Is Jason okay?"

My eyebrow raised. How did Hyperion know Jason's name? Sure, they could recognize him from the photo, but there hadn't been a name. I let out a deep sigh. LaToya's constant conspiracy theories were rubbing off. Everybody in the Ward respected Hyperion, and he had proved himself time and time again.

"Just a bump. He'll be okay."

"Same question. What about you?"

Physically, I barely had a scrape. Beneath the skin, that

was an epic-level train wreck. But I couldn't say that, not without having another emotional outburst.

"Dating a civie is rough."

That got my attention. "You?"

He nodded as his boots touched down. He took a spot on the giant rivet I considered my throne of self-pity. Hyperion was handsome, with a couple of days' worth of stubble covering the exposed jawline. It struck me just how many handsome bears saved the city on a nightly basis. It was as if Mick were spiking the drinks at Bottoms Up.

"For a little while. If we're speaking honestly..."

"Please do."

"He's the reason I wear a cape. I never wanted to be a hero. I resisted kicking and screaming. But he convinced me."

"Don't you worry about a villain finding out?"

"He's probably home right now, wearing my extra suit and watching superhero movies on Netflix."

I laughed. "Your boyfriend needs to meet a friend of mine. He's the biggest superhero geek I've ever met."

He laughed. "It hasn't been a walk in the park. But what relationship is?"

I leaned my head back, letting the droplets pelt my face. There was something calming about letting nature wash over me. It was almost the same as when I called the lightning. It was always there, waiting. When it ripped through my body, something about it felt right.

"I'm worried that—"

"He'll get hurt? Me too, Bernard, me too. But is it our right to dictate the risks they're willing to take?"

"I couldn't live with myself..."

"What if he got in a car crash? Or cancer?"

I saw his point, but this was different. There were forces in the world that we couldn't control. This, this I could control. I didn't want to increase the likelihood he'd bite the dust before it was his time.

"I don't want to be responsible."

He nodded his head. "Every day, we go out to save the world. But have you thought about how many people we don't help? Or how many people we put in jeopardy every time we face off against a gunman wearing clown makeup?"

There were casualties. Dwelling on those numbers crippled plenty of heroes. But if we didn't go put on the mask, the numbers would be higher. The damage would be greater, and who knew what would happen to civilization?

"It's different."

He shook his head. "It's only different because you know this one's name. It sounds like you're letting your fear ground you. Think about it."

"I should have taken a job selling furniture." I laughed. It was that or return to the hole of pity I dug for myself. "I could make a killing selling villain insurance."

"Bernard, you were born to be a hero."

"Sorry for being snappy earlier. I've been processing a lot."

He jumped to his feet, cape catching in the wind. "When you stop thinking you're alone in this, you'll be better off. We carry the burden of the world on our shoulders—"

"Is this a recruitment speech?"

He clasped his hands together as if he were begging. "Please. If Hellcat asks, tell her I gave it my all. I do *not* need her giving me attitude for a week."

I planted my face in my palm. I had to give it to the woman. She had a tenacity about her. I feared any villain who got in her way.

"Your secret is safe with me."

His feet lifted off the tower. "Speech aside, I'm serious, Bernard. You're not alone. You just have to ask."

He rocketed into the storm clouds above. I didn't expect to be sitting here wallowing only to be saved by a cape. I appreciated heroes did more than keep the city safe. The real question was, could I reconcile this internal battle? Punching bad guys was easy, but in the war of Bernard versus Sentinel, I wasn't sure either would walk away victorious.

24

AFTER A RESTLESS NIGHT, THE BIRDS CONSPIRED AGAINST ME. I must have stared at the alarm clock for hours before I nodded off. Were pigeons normally this loud? Even the sun shone brighter, determined to make me miserable. I should have stayed in bed and tried to catch a few hours, but Alejandro demanded I meet him. If I hadn't responded, he'd have sweet-talked my doorman and pounded at my door until I conceded.

If I wasn't warding off a sleep-deprived headache, the park would have been lovely at this hour. Joggers squeezed in a morning run before work. Chess players were already setting up their boards, preparing for a day of strategy. The only thing that mattered at this hour was the breakfast cart stationed near the playground.

I ordered two coffees and a breakfast sandwich. The

hair on Chad's neck probably stood on end as he sensed his most loyal customer drinking sludge. He'd say the chirping birds served me right. I'd have to order extra from him next time we were at the HideOut.

"You look like hell, Papi."

"You look like..." Despite working a late shift at Midnight Alley, not a hair was out of place. I couldn't fathom how he stayed out all night and functioned like a normal person. By this point, I'd expect stepping into the sunlight would cause his skin to burst into flames.

"Amazing? Handsome? Like you want to ravish me?"

"A solid seven."

He gasped. "We both know I'm a nine on a bad day."

I shoved the coffee into his hand. We both sipped, strolling along the winding path through the park. Chad might make the best coffee, but only a street vendor could make a breakfast sandwich this good. Before I knew it, I had devoured the entire thing. I almost considered turning around and going for another.

"Remember that night I showed up at your door a complete mess?"

I nodded. "You were having a rough night."

"Remember that time I invited me to the park for coffee and you were a complete mess?"

I raise my eyebrow. We had met here countless times, and never once would I describe myself as a mess. "I don't think—" I caught him giving me the once-over. "I'm not a hot mess."

"Subtle how you slid hot in there." We resumed our walking. I wish I could have argued with him. On the exterior, I wouldn't describe myself as a mess, but inside? Yeah, as of late, I always felt like a mess.

"I'm going to ask you a question, and I don't want you to read into it."

"Theo gave me a hall pass for you," he said.

"Wait. What?" I tried to fight the blush in my cheeks. I tried to hide it with the paper cup as I took a sip of coffee. Griffin and Xander worked to get a rise out of me, but with them, I could maintain the steely exterior. But not with Alejandro. My overtly sexual and charismatic Mexican knew how to push my buttons.

"If only you had asked before Jason showed up. EO could have watched."

Alejandro froze. His jaw dropped, as if he'd found out he'd won the lottery. "Good one." When I said nothing, I could see the swirl of possibilities in his eyes. If he wasn't imagining us naked, I'd be shocked. "All I had to do was ask?"

I shrugged. "I guess we'll never know."

After the failed date with Xander, I decided friends were more important than romance. But if I was going to break my rules, Alejandro would have given me a run for my money. Considering he kept my identity as Sentinel a secret, a heroic feat for him, the gamble had paid off.

"Stop distracting me with those nasty images of you naked in my bed. Oh, so nasty..." He snapped to. "What's going on, Papi? You had a question."

Oh, right. "When you started dating EO..."

"Was I worried I'd open my door and a villain would show up taking me hostage?"

Was I that transparent? Or could Alejandro read minds? His intuition bordered on a superpower. It was partly why I wanted to speak to him instead of Griffin or Xander.

"Yeah. That."

"Since I've been dating EO..." He trailed off as he started counting on his fingers. Everybody at breakfast knew Alejandro held the kidnapping record. But as he passed eleven, I realized we'd need to talk about him wandering around in the middle of the night.

"If you count the Girl Scout troop, thirteen times since we started dating."

"How many were because of him?"

"I see where this is going. Revenge kidnappings, if you include the Girl Scouts, seven. For a new hero, he's made a lot of villains pretty angry. I guess that's cause he's good at his job."

"And that doesn't bother you?"

"It bothers me when I'm late for work or they interrupt

dinner, but if you're asking if it bothers me that EO's job spills into my life, no. Not even a little."

"What if something happened to you?"

"Do you think Aiden worries about Xander in the ambulance?"

Xander had been part of the Superhero paramedic services for as long as I had known him. Aiden, on the other hand, was a mild-mannered reporter. Even if I ignored that Xander might have a caped alter ego, I had never given it a thought.

"Even if it wasn't superheroes. What if a family blamed Xander for not keeping somebody alive?"

"That's a lawsuit. This is life or death."

He shook his head. "You're not seeing my point, Papi. We don't get to pick the parts of a person we love."

"Love?" I raised an eyebrow. Alejandro, the bartender playboy, caught the feels? I feared we'd stepped through a portal into an alternate reality.

"Shut up." His face scrunched up as he gave me a gentle shove. "I haven't said it yet. The right moment hasn't happened."

I wrapped my arm around Alejandro. His head barely came to my chin as I gave him a kiss on the forehead. "Take it from an expert. The right moment will be when you say it."

"Thanks, Papi." As he pulled back, his smile stretching across his face, I felt happy for the man. "You're good at giving advice. Now if only you'd listen to yourself."

"I've been thinking about this—"

"That's your problem. Every time you dispense wisdom, that's not coming from up here." He poked me in the forehead. "It comes from here." He moved his hand to my chest. I ignored the slight rubbing. He earned a free pass. "What is your heart saying?"

I wished it was that simple. Between Hyperion and Alejandro, I was getting a better picture of what this happily-ever-after would be like. If only I could shut off that little voice trying to lace my feelings with a sense of fear.

"Gracias, osito," I said.

"What are friends for?"

That question had come to the surface in every facet of my life—from Hellcat's insistence on recruiting me to Cobalt setting me up with technology. I admired Alejandro as he gawked at a bearish man jogging toward us. When the man winked at Alejandro, I returned to my earlier thought about him having superpowers. No, not that he somehow managed to attract the sexiest of men, but in the way, he not only answered my question, but also reminded me I wasn't alone.

Perhaps he was right? I needed to get out of my own way.

Adjusting my tie, I gave my reflection in the dark glass a once-over. Under the cover of night, I could walk the street without many people giving me curious glances. I had to admit, I was feeling myself. With a little effort, I didn't look half bad. Hopefully, Jason agreed.

Date night. I forgot how much I loved going out with Jason. We'd have to continue the tradition of creating a bucket list of things to do in the city. It turned into a game to get us out of the house, and as soon as somebody declared a date night, the other picked from the bucket list. Already, I had a dozen places I wanted to experience with him by my side.

I opened the door to the restaurant, impressed with the romantic ambiance. Dim overhead lamps provided just enough light but also allowed the candles on the tables to create a sense of seduction. Staring at Jason across the table would be almost as gratifying as the food.

I stepped up to the maitre d', trying to ignore the sweat on my palms. "Bernard Castle."

He gave a slight bow. "Ah, yes. The other two members of your party are already seated."

Two? I tried to think if Jason mentioned knowing anybody in the city. If it had been breakfast, I could imagine one of the guys crashing. But a date? They wouldn't dare.

I followed the man through the restaurant. I had requested a secluded table, hopeful that nobody recognized a superhero slurping soup. Alejandro had said they were discreet about their clientele. I made the reservation and added the secret phrase, "What about the promenade?" The voice on the other line replied with a simple, "A lovely day for a stroll." I'd need to ask Alejandro for recommendations more often.

"Can I have the bar start a drink for you, Mr. Castle?"

"A whisky Old Fashioned. Thank you."

He stepped to the side, and I could see Jason sitting in the booth, but not the person sitting opposite of him.

"I look forward to this collaboration."

I froze. I didn't need to see the man in a black suit. The smooth voice was familiar. As Jason waved at me, getting up from the booth, Damien Vex did the same. Adjusting his jacket, buttoning it slowly, he gave me a show. Then he flashed that obnoxious smile. If he thought I'd hold my tongue with Jason nearby, he had another thing coming.

"Vex, what are you doing here?"

He chuckled, brushing off the growl in the question. "I don't want to interrupt date night. I'll let Mr. Jaynes explain it." He patted me on the shoulder as he walked by. "It's good to see you, Mr. Castle. I'm sure our paths will cross again."

No lightning. No lightning. No lightning. I kept repeating it, not wanting to blast the man as he exited.

When I turned around, Jason was already hugging me, giving me a kiss on the cheek.

"Today has been a whirlwind." The carefree tone meant Jason didn't understand the dangers of associating with Damien. The mogul had referenced Jason twice. Was this him reminding me how far his influence reached? I wanted nothing more than to chase him into the street and shake a confession from him.

A server stopped by the table. When it was clear that Damien wouldn't be returning, I joined Jason, sitting across from him in the booth, flexing my fingers. I didn't remember balling them into fists tight enough they ached. It wouldn't have come to blows, or at least I'd like to think that. But I'd be lying if I said I hadn't entertained the thought.

"What's wrong?" He truly didn't understand. Where did I begin? The facts were easy. He booted me from my position on the Centurions. He created a new group to replace us. Then there were the thinly veiled threats. But what I couldn't prove was what worried me most of all. If Damien had a hand in revealing my identity, it meant that this was all part of a plan that hadn't come to fruition. Yet.

"He's a dangerous man."

He raised an eyebrow. "You're going to need to give me more than that."

"He swooped in and took the reins of the Centurions. Mighty convenient if you ask me."

"That's why I met with him."

It was my turn to be confused. I could tell Jason was excited about something. Excitement with Damien didn't bode well.

"Did you know the Centurions have an education division?" Had we? I couldn't keep up with all the initiatives that headquarters created. "It's for school kids. Mostly elementary school. They get to come to Centurion Tower and learn about being superheroes. And that's the public-facing side. There is also a training program in the works for kids who show signs of powers."

"The sidekick initiative." It wasn't called that. But after a kid blew up their house, the Centurions came together to start the program. We always joked around that they were sidekicks in training. The first class had already graduated, and with their powers mastered, they weren't likely to hurt the people around them.

"Yes, he mentioned the heroes called it that."

"I'm not seeing a connection."

"The interview today..." His face lost its zeal. "It was obvious I wasn't the right candidate for the job. They wanted somebody rigid who followed the rules. I tried to work with them, but you know when you get that feeling you just don't belong? Yeah, that."

"It's their loss." I reached across the table, clutching his hand. "There will be more—"

"When I was leaving, I bumped into Damien. He was there to meet with the principal."

"Of course he was." Something about this seemed fishy. LaToya would claim that there was no such thing as coincidences. I was coming to understand why she saw conspiracies everywhere.

"He was hoping to recruit one of their teachers for the education division. I didn't even know who he was. But he had overheard my interview. We got to talking, and eventually, he mentioned running the Centurions."

"Did you say you knew me?"

Even to me, it sounded narcissistic. Was it? I know Jason had exciting news, but... When he pulled his hand away, sitting back in the booth, I realized I had stepped over a line.

"What's this about? You're acting kind of like a jerk."

I let out a long sigh. Bernard and Sentinel were about to clash again. "I think Damien is the one who outed me. The director of the... the former director of the Centurions is looking for evidence."

"So it's just a theory?" He didn't sound convinced. "Is this about Damien or your pride?"

My fist tightened again, and I fought the urge to slam it down on the table. Jason was thinking about a job, and it was sweet that this would give us an opportunity to live in the same city. But getting in bed with Damien meant putting his life on the line, I think. I believed the whole thing was orchestrated. It wouldn't surprise me if he was the reason Jason had landed none of the jobs.

"He's dangerous."

"So, this is about you trying to protect me? You want to shelter me from the world?"

"That's not what I meant."

"Do you know what this job would mean?" He leaned forward, folding his arms on the table. "With this job, I can move to Vanguard. And do you know why I'd want to do that?"

I didn't answer.

"So I can give you a second chance. The man who took it upon himself to make a decision without asking me. The man who is trying to decide for me again."

"This isn't about a job. Damien is as bad as the villains on the street. The only difference is he has a plaque on a door. He's dangerous, and I don't want to see you—"

"Get hurt?"

I hadn't prepared for this conversation. I'd expected expensive steak and congratulating Jason on a successful interview. There should be cocktails and laughing. But wherever Damien went, he sowed chaos. Had this been his plan all along?

"I could die tomorrow. We all could. Why are you fixated on the worst-case scenario?"

"You could have died yesterday." I blurted it out without thinking. It was on the table now. I spent my life being level-headed. But with Jason, the emotions were almost overwhelming.

"Gauntlet?"

"He came looking for me. Gauntlet wanted to take me out. It was *me* he was after. But you're the one who got hurt."

"Bernard, I'm going to say this once. I want to make sure you're hearing me." He paused, taking a deep breath. "Bernard Castle is not my protector. Sentinel is not my protector. If this is going to work, we're equals."

It made sense, or at least it should have. This wasn't a discussion about who paid what bills. I wished it was something that mundane. This was about him understanding that dating me could be dangerous.

"I don't want to be responsible for something bad happening to you."

"That's not your choice." He reached across the table, holding my hand. His eyes softened. "You can stay and make this work, Bernard. But we have to be partners. Or we call this off. That *is* your choice. This fight going on in your head needs to have a winner."

It wasn't an emotional statement. Jason could sort my baggage with a single statement. But his tone made it clear there wasn't room for negotiation. My brain fired on all cylinders, but the image of Gauntlet with his sword standing over a prone Jason continued popping up.

"I know you well enough, Bernard. This isn't a decision

you'll make lightly. I'm going to give you some space to process."

"Jason..." Tonight had taken a sharp turn. Despite trying to keep my insecurities under wraps, Jason put them on display. But as much as he treated it like a black-and-white choice, I still couldn't reach a conclusion.

"Regardless of your decision..." He sat back in the booth. "This time, tell me."

His words stung. I nodded. "I promise."

He got up from the table, slipping his jacket on. Coming over, he kissed me on the crown of my head. Wrapping my arms around his waist, I hugged him tightly. I didn't want him to go, not now, not ever.

"I'll check in on you."

When I let go, he walked away, heading to the door. I couldn't watch. The fear tightened in my chest as I worried I'd put a nail in the coffin of our relationship. I thought it would be different this time. With my secret out, we could start new. But as Jason rolled with the punches, I tore us apart.

"Congratulations on the job offer," I whispered.

I fought back the tears.

I lost the fight.

25

I PLOPPED ONTO THE PARK BENCH. IN THE MIDDLE OF THE night, this wasn't the safest part of town. It'd be a terrible night to pick a fight with me. I considered turning on the HeroApp™ and finding the biggest bruiser to throw down with, but with my mood, I didn't trust myself to pull punches. Maybe demons would invade? I never minded obliterating denizens of the underworld.

It had been hours since my botched dinner with Jason. When the light broke the horizon, I realized just how long I had been wandering about Vanguard. The air had grown chilly, dampness attempting to settle against my skin. With sparks of lightning, I glowed much like the tops of the skyscrapers in the distance.

Despite running through the situation, no matter what

angle I approached it, I didn't see a solution. Jason made it seem like an easy call. Was it? Did I just accept the dangers? More than that, was he right about me making decisions for him? I had lived in Sentinel's shadow for so long, being Bernard had gotten complicated.

It was complicated... for me.

I pulled my phone from my pocket. A couple of hours after Jason left, he texted me.

J: I know you're drowning in your head. Don't forget to breathe. Don't be afraid to ask for help.

Nobody knew me like him. For years he sat on the couch studying me as I lost myself to the perils of overthinking. When I started chewing my lip, he'd crawl across the couch and sit on my lap. When I drowned, he knew when to throw a lifeline.

I had composed at least a hundred messages. I'm sure he saw the three blinking dots. But just like when he knew when to rescue me, he also got my need to work through my issues. He navigated my baggage with such grace it made me appreciate him even more. Made me love him.

I had gone from leading the most successful team of heroes Earth had ever seen to... a pity party? Griffin would call me stubborn, but now I thought it wasn't as positive as

I believed. I had the rug pulled from under my feet, and instead of adapting, I hid. I claimed I wanted to be a solo act, but was that the truth? Or was I lying to myself to avoid looking like a fool as I built myself up? They would only consider these constant epiphanies growth if I stopped running.

Jason was right. I needed to ask for help.

I flicked the text away. After the disaster tonight, I needed somebody who wouldn't placate me. Of all the people stored in my contacts, there was only one person who'd call me out on my bullshit.

B: 911. Bridge tower.

I stared at the message, at the vulnerability in three words. Had I become one of those men who considered asking for help a weakness? I'd need to re-evaluate. I had received texts like this before. And each time I show up without hesitation. No, there was no weakness. I'd arrive, ready to be empathic and be the man they needed.

Yet again, Jason pushed me to be a better man. This would not be about me and my oversized ego. I didn't want to sink into the hole I had been digging. My path had overgrown with doubt and insecurities. I needed clarity.

It was time to make changes. Sentinel needed to step

aside for the night while Bernard figured out how to be a hero. There was only one man for this job.

I pushed send.

———

"When did you figure it out?"

Xander rose to the edge of the tower, his arms crossed as if he disapproved. I didn't out him, but the only way he'd be making it to the tower was to admit he was more than a run-of-the-mill paramedic.

"Who else would call Sentinel big guy?"

He snapped his fingers in defeat. "I knew it the moment I said it."

I couldn't help but laugh. He was the last to learn my identity, and I had to assume I was the first to discover his. I had a thousand questions, but I knew Lionheart's highlight reel. He had saved the entire superhero community. We owed him a debt of gratitude. More so, he stayed humble during coffee. If it had been Griffin, we'd never hear the end.

"What's going on, big guy?"

Before I could respond, my pocket shook. In unison, we grabbed for our phones. It was the HeroApp™. It appeared thinking of Thundra too often had summoned the beast. She and her cohort Lit had taken to terrorizing a... old folks' home?

"You've got to be kidding me," Xander said.

"Looks like the heroes are sleeping. Should we take this?"

"The old folks can probably take them," he said. "But if Sentinel wants to be my sidekick..." Without a word, his clothes transformed until I was looking at his black suit. When the mask formed around his face, I had to admit I was jealous. Heroes with the ability to summon their suits never had to powder their junk before getting dressed.

"Can you keep up with your sidekick?" Pushing off the tower, I sped past him. The fastest approach would have been staying above the buildings, but I wanted to see if Xander could keep up with an old man. As I zipped through the buildings, I glanced over my shoulder to see him quickly gaining.

The streets were mostly empty as I blew through a red light. With a tight right, I zigged and zagged through the financial district. Seconds later, the buildings shrank in size, skyscrapers replaced by green spaces. The retirement home sat in an otherwise peaceful community. The one-story building was big enough to have a few hundred residents, but it wasn't often they needed heroes for disagreements over bocce ball.

As I slowed my approach, Xander raced by. He had started a corkscrew, leaving a trail of spiraling fire in his wake.

"Dammit." When he landed in the parking lot, he

raised his hands over his head. Was that a victory dance? He gyrated his hips, and I wished I could avert my eyes.

I was about to ask if he was having a seizure when I spotted Thundra and Lit exiting the front doors of the building. Thundra had a pillowcase over her shoulder as if she were stealing presents from under the Christmas tree.

"Hey!" Xander yelled.

"Hey? Really? Have you learned nothing from Griffin? Watch a professional."

I walked forward, holding my hand up for Xander to keep his distance. "Sorry ladies, but it looks like your luck has—"

Bolts of lightning struck me. Another smashed against the parking lot, kicking asphalt up at my face. Lightning? Did she just hurl lightning at *me*?

Xander walked by, giving me a nudge with his elbow. "Look at me, not getting zapped by lightning."

Thundra dropped the sack. I shook my head as dozens of pill bottles rolled down the steps. Xander looked over his shoulder with a smile. Now that I knew his identity, I couldn't figure out how I hadn't spotted that handsome jawline.

"Talk while we work?"

I nodded as Thundra flew at me. "So this Jason thing."

"Dating a civie giving you issues?" Another bolt of lightning rocketed toward Xander. I flew overhead, shielding his body, letting it cascade along my back. Before I could touch down, Thundra grabbed me around the chest, knocking me to the pavement.

"Yeah." I skid to a stop. "I'm worried about some villain,"—I gestured to Thundra—"prime example, will come after him."

Xander ducked under a punch from Lit before crushing his forehead against her nose. Giving her a one-finger salute, he turned in my direction. "You have powers. He doesn't. Stop acting like that gives you the right to make decisions for him."

Ouch. "I know it doesn't give me the right. But I couldn't live with myself..."

I held up a finger, pausing the conversation as Thundra came down with both fists clenched together. Catching her wrist. I slammed her into the parking lot. "I don't want to be the reason he gets hurt."

"Sounds like you're doing a fine job hurting him plenty."

"Damn, Xan — Lionheart. Way to kick a man when he's down."

Lit lobbed balls of lightning at Xander. I was impressed with the accuracy of his fire, knocking her attacks off course. When that didn't work, she tried rushing him with an electrified fist posed to punch.

He turned his back on the woman. "You're being selfish

and making this all about you." Arms grew from the shoulder of his suit, smacking Lit across the face. He spun about, his arm coated in fire, clocking her in the jaw.

"Is wanting him to be safe selfish?"

"You're not giving him enough credit. He knew what he was doing when he messaged you."

"But—"

"Stop with the buts. Is he an adult?" The wind whipped around me, creating a cyclone as Xander talked. "Yes, he is. Can he make decisions for himself? I think he can. Is his decision to be with a brooding daddy? God help him, but all signs point to yes."

The cyclone grew fast enough to take me off my feet. Thundra cackled as she admired her handiwork. The force wasn't worrisome, but eventually, it'd siphon the oxygen, making it impossible to breathe. I had to give her credit. At least she figured out she couldn't slug it out and walk away victorious.

"Hold on," I shouted over deafening gusts.

Every time Lit threw lightning, the ionization tickled something in my chest. Pulling at the feeling, I hijacked one of her bolts, redirecting it at Thundra. The force knocked her into a minivan, and the cyclone vanished.

"Nifty trick," Xander said.

"It's new to me."

"As you were saying..." He turned, pressing his back against mine. I had to admit, having somebody at my side reminded me why I liked the Centurions. We might not talk this much during an onslaught, but we'd always talk about our encounters in the lounge. It might not be so bad having somebody I could talk to about heroing and life as a regular guy.

"Okay, I've been an idiot." Admitting I was wrong might as well have been a herculean task. But I could see his logic. It didn't solve the problem, but at least he confirmed the problem lied with me.

"Did Bernard Castle have a growth moment?"

"I should have called Griffin."

I could hear the impact of punches between him and Lit. They had traded using superpowers for good ol' fisticuffs. It appeared Thundra wanted to do the same. When it got to this stage of a fight, I wished they'd give up. We'd wait for law enforcement to arrive, then they'd be locked up. Give it a week, and they'd be free again. It was inevitable, but this method meant they'd walk away with bruises.

"How do I move forward?"

I ducked under her right hook but didn't move fast enough to dodge her knee. I staggered back until I bumped into Xander. "You two talk too much," Thundra said. She came in again, hoping to repeat the maneuver. This time when I ducked, I sidestepped her knee, grabbing her ankle.

"Nobody invited you to this conversation." I whipped

her about, slamming her into the ground. "Now, stay down while the grownups talk."

Thundra pushed off, but her muscles failed her. When I was convinced she wasn't getting up, I turned to help Xander. He wasn't even trying, as the extra arms did most of the fighting. At this point, he was toying with Lit.

"Have you just admitted you're scared?"

"I told him I was worried—"

"About him, yeah, I heard you. How about confessing why you're worried? That's not about him getting hurt. That's about *you* getting him hurt. Bernard, you can admit you're scared."

He spun about and, with a final punch, Lit fell backward. When she tried to get up, fire shot from his hands, slamming against her chest. With a last sigh, she groaned and surrendered.

"I know this is a novel concept, but talk to him. Ai—" he glanced over his shoulder to make sure Lit was unconscious. "Aiden and I had to set up some guidelines. Some of my suggestions, he said no. Some he agreed. Just like when we made things exclusive, we talked about what that meant to us."

"Example?"

"I get three days off a week from the ambulance. Aiden gets two of them. The other, sometimes I go out and save Vanguard, sometimes I sit at home and play video games."

"How mundane."

"You know me. As long as I'm punching something, I'm happy."

"But what if—"

"Stop it with the worst-case scenarios. You keep back pedaling. Do you want to live in the past, big guy? Or do you want to move forward with Jason?"

I wanted to see Jason's face before I went to sleep at night. Then I'd be eager to wake up, just so I could see the light making the hair on his arms glow. He probably had a list of science fiction movies to show me. I'd balk, but secretly, I'd enjoy every minute of arguing over the amount of butter on our popcorn.

"I want to move forward."

"How are you going to do that?"

"I was hoping you'd tell me."

He pulled Lit by the ankle, tossing her next to Thundra. "I just took out the bad guys for you, and now you want more?"

I frowned. If he thought I wouldn't slap him, he was about to be incredibly wrong.

"Fine, fine. Have you..." He paused, tapping his finger on his chin. "No, that won't work. What about..." He pursed his lips as if he was deep in thought. "Oh yes, that could work. Yeah, that's the solution."

"You're mocking me, aren't you?"

"It's borderline brilliant."

"Officer, he went crazy," I said. "He's in league with Thundra and Lit. I had to clobber him."

His eyes narrowed. "Talk to him, you goon."

"Your words of wisdom are a thing of legend."

He waved at the oncoming cop car. "I'm serious. Talk to him. Let him know what it means to be a hero. Once he knows the risks, then you can have an honest conversation. Together."

"How'd that go with Aiden?"

The cops slowed to a roll, getting out of the car. I could overhear them complaining about these two misfits getting out yet again. I was happy to hear I wasn't the only one who noticed the prison's inability to keep villains behind bars.

"It's a little different. I wasn't established when we met. We do a daily debrief over dinner. At least Jason isn't chasing danger. Since Aiden became a reporter, he's always in some sort of trouble."

"That doesn't freak you out?"

"Oh, it absolutely does. That's why I ask if he needs help. When he says yes, I come calling. When he says he's good, I trust him. He's a big boy. He can make decisions for himself."

Was I taking an everyday problem and blowing it up to epic proportions? Was the answer as simple as removing the "super" from the conversation? I had made this complicated, and all it took was coming together and acting like a normal couple. There'd be dangers, but I needed to respect

Jason's decisions just as he acknowledged my need to continue as Sentinel. Crap, I had been an idiot.

"I can see the gears turning."

"I've been a horrible boyfriend."

He patted me on the shoulder. "Yup. But now's your chance to be the man Jason deserves."

"When did you get so smart?"

"I don't want the other guys knowing I'm the wise one. I've got an image to protect."

I needed to stop being stubborn and refusing to accept the changes in my life. Once I did that, there was a list of things I needed to make right. Both Bernard and Sentinel needed to let go of the past and look toward the future. The weeds that had covered the path forward were of my own design.

"You do what you need to do. I'll handle the paperwork."

I gave Xander a hug, squeezing him tight enough to remind him of the strength at my disposal. "Thank you."

"Anytime." His voice cracked as he spoke. "You're never alone, big guy. Not with Jason, not with Sentinel. But in case you bump into Hellcat—"

"You tried your hardest to recruit me. Your pitch was so good I almost said yes."

"She'll never believe that."

"But you were *so* convincing."

"Okay, now you're mocking me."

"Yes, I am. I won't be at breakfast." I had a plan forming, a proverbial grand gesture. I needed a big change, something to remind me I was moving forward and to stop focusing on the past. A symbol...

"I need to see somebody about a suit."

"About damned time."

26

ASHER OPENED THE DOOR TO THE GUILD, LEANING AGAINST the frame as they gave me the once-over. Always showing off their talents, the tuxedo jacket cinched at the waist before cascading into a skirt. They blocked the entrance, holding up a hand.

"I've been watching you skulk about. You know we're not open for another..." With a dramatic turn of the wrist, I noticed there wasn't a watch, but that didn't stop them. Their eyes widened. "Morning, Bernard. It's still morning. I can't people at this ungodly hour."

"I'm not people."

Asher laughed. "Not even Bernard Castle—"

"I have coffee." I held up a paper cup, showing off the HideOut's logo.

"Bernard Castle, my favorite customer!"

They quickly swiped the coffee from my hand. It was amazing what a cup of coffee from the HideOut could achieve. Yet again, Chad kept the city moving. If only he knew how the citizens of Vanguard treated his concoctions like ambrosia.

"Come, come. Let me show you what we have for you."

I followed Asher through the store, taking in the smell of cedar. If Asher succeeded with this, I'd have to come back and have them tailor a suit for me. With one of their shirts stretched across my chest, Jason would be at the buttons. I followed to the back room and then into the basement.

I was surprised by the number of half-completed suits hanging from mannequins. It appeared as if Asher had been working overtime. I paused in front of the four suits. Each of them was unique, focusing on a different color scheme, but the belts around the waist displayed the same logo. It was a classic design for a team. From the gauntlets to the boots, the craftsmanship was downright phenomenal.

I jumped as a mannequin rocketed across Asher's studio. To my surprise, a young person shrunk as they hissed at the disaster. If Asher's work was legendary, it was only surpassed by their refusal to work with other designers.

"Sorry! So sorry. The force fields weren't calibrated

correctly." Their gloves continued glowing red. "Drats. I'm all thumbs."

"Bernard, this is Penelope. She's..." He gestured wildly. "I don't know what she's doing with those. She should be ironing."

Smoke drifted from metal gloves. I had seen them before, tech, no doubt, supplied by the Machinist. She took them off, hiding them behind her back.

Penelope's eyes went wide. "Bernard Castle? Sentinel? You're one of the Centurions." She tossed the gloves on the table and zipped across the room with her hand out. When we shook, she maintained a firm grip, shaking up and down longer than necessary.

"Former Centurion."

"When you stopped that giant dragon from stampeding the city..." She continued shaking. It had reached an awkward stage. "I've always been a fan."

"Enough of that, Penelope." Asher put their hands on her shoulders, guiding her to a table with capes and an iron. "No creases. The devil is in the details."

"You have an assistant?"

"Heroes destroy suits as fast as I can create them. I can barely keep up with Vanguard, and now I'm getting orders all the way to Starling City."

She picked up the iron and pressed the fabric. "Asher's going to write my recommendation for fashion school.

When they see a note from the Guild of Ash, there's no way they'll turn me down."

Her hand remained steady, the wrinkles in the cape vanishing. Asher had themselves a sidekick. I couldn't get over the shock. When she caught me watching, she gestured to the iron. It looked more high-tech than the one that hid in the back of my closet.

"We create the suits to withstand the elements. The only way to press them is with a thermal induction iron. If you're not careful, it'll burn through the cape, and the table... and the floor."

"Ask her how she knows," Asher chuckled.

"How many times do I have to say I'm sorry?"

"It's okay, dear. If I had a dollar for every time I set my first studio on fire..." Asher struck a pose, leaning against the table, arching their back as if a camera crew might be taking photographs. "It's no surprise I got evicted."

"Asher, any chance the suit is ready?"

"First, you won't let me design a kilt. Now you're asking if I rushed to finish your suit? What do you think this is? A fashionable sweatshop?" They walked toward me, poking a finger against my chest. "Genius takes time."

"Didn't we finish it yesterday?"

Asher rolled their eyes. "And my dramatic reveal is ruined."

Penelope raised an eyebrow, and I shrugged in response. Her straightforward approach might bring

Asher back to Earth. Maybe. She had her work cut out for her.

"It's done."

Asher walked over to a clothing rack. I got excited when I saw the black suit with yellow accents. It'd look amazing and highlight my chest while helping tuck my gut away. When Asher pushed it aside and lifted a box no bigger than my fist, I couldn't hide my confusion.

"For a man wielding lightning, we needed something capable of withstanding incredible heat. I don't need heroes thinking the Guild can't adapt to unique power sets. Despite my gifts in fashion, your suit needs to be functional."

"It uses liquid steel—"

Asher snapped their fingers, silencing Penelope. "Ruin this, and I'll have you designing outfits for cats." When she didn't continue, they walked toward me, holding the box out.

"My suit is in there?"

"You dare question—"

"No, no, no." They stopped, holding out the box. With a slow hand, they peeled back the lid of the box. Inside was a beautiful watch, nicer than I'd ever considered buying. Through the glass face, tiny gears moved, pushing the second hand along.

"Should I try it on to make sure it fits?"

Both Asher and Penelope laughed. They dismissed my

question, chuckling far longer than appropriate. When they stopped, Asher wiped invisible tears from their eye.

"It *always* fits."

"How does it—"

"Neural link. It'll know when you need it."

"Should I get the mirror?" Asked Penelope.

My phone vibrated. Reaching into my pocket, I expected a selfie of Xander at the police station with the officers. I couldn't imagine that by day he saved heroes from battle, and at night he was on the streets fighting crime. It explained why he no longer went to the gym. Keeping it a secret from Alejandro and Griffin would be the real challenge. They had known my identity. Maybe they already connected the dots?

It wasn't a selfie.

*: Ducks are in the desert. Games are played by children.

LaToya had information. I had to cycle through all the messages operations required us to learn. The first sentence served as the alert, but it was the second half I had to parse. It'd have been easier if she had given me a location. Was it the putt-putt golf course or the old penny arcade? No, wait, golf had something to do with fallen windmills. She must be hiding out in the arcade.

"I need to go."

"You are not leaving before we see this miraculous creation on—"

I swiped the box. "I owe you. Penelope, keep Asher's ego from getting out of control."

"Too late," she chimed.

"You owe me, Bernard Castle."

I gave them a quick handshake. "Next time I see you, we can talk about this kilt."

Asher's eyebrow raised, the silver hoop accentuating the surprise. The smile bordered on toothy, and I knew they were already picking out the tartan.

"The world deserves those calves," they said.

I was already dashing toward the stairs. "You're the only person I'd trust them with." By the time I reached the front of the Guild, my feet were hardly touching the floor.

"Penelope," Asher shouted from the basement, "fetch me the plaids!"

***

The arcade had long since closed. Dust had settled along the video games, undisturbed for years. It had once been filled with children swearing at screens. But now, as I passed a classic Pac-Man, it appeared like a scene from a dystopian movie. I found it hard to imagine the sound of teens running rampant as their parents snuck vodka into their slushies.

Unlike the secret room in the warehouse, the stairwell leading to the bunker below required buttons pressed on an out-of-order video game.

"They're *all* out of order," I grumbled.

"Don't worry," LaToya said, stepping out from behind a fighter jet game complete with cockpit. The unholstered firearm in her hand didn't escape me as she scanned the arcade. "It looks like hoodlums stole the door to our basement."

"Who knew the Centurions owned so much real estate?"

"I debated meeting at the mansion, but that felt gauche."

"Totally." I shook my head in disbelief. Nothing surprised me. "What's the emergency?"

"They're gone."

"Who?"

"The Centurions."

I didn't know how to respond. I feared asking questions, wanting to believe that by gone, she meant they were off the grid. The alternative made my stomach turn. A squeak from the floor had LaToya draw out her gun and drop to one knee.

A rat scurried from under a discarded pizza box.

"I've never seen you this jumpy."

"When the world's strongest superheroes go missing..." As she stood, she didn't bother holstering the gun. LaToya made it a point to demonstrate her nerves of steel. Being an unpowered person in charge of the Centurions meant she had to work harder than any of us. This was a side of her I wish I'd never experienced.

"Their families are missing as well. It's like they vanished in the middle of the night."

"No bodies, at least there's that," I said.

"I found the smoking gun."

"You need to be more specific, Miss Conspiracy Theory."

"Damien. He's been behind this all along."

"How do you know? I can't imagine—"

"He's an arrogant narcissist. The files were still on his computer at Revelations."

"You broke into the magazine?"

She laughed. "Does that sound like something I'd do?"

"Well..."

Her face didn't have an amused expression. "I found out his secretary is struggling to pay off her college debt. When I approached her, I was prepared to pay them off, to the penny."

"It sounds like a but is coming."

LaToya laughed. "Apparently, his personality rubs everybody the wrong way. She jumped at the chance to knock him down a peg. When I told her what I was looking for, she knew exactly where to find it."

"She just walked in and took the information?"

"She handed over his entire hard drive. I'll spare you the thousands of selfies of Damien at the gym flexing. The videos are damning enough."

With another quick inspection of the arcade, she holstered her gun and pulled out her phone. With a few clicks, I could hear Damien's voice shouting. Handing me the phone, I realized we were watching through a camera in his office. Had the secretary planted it?

"Who took the video?"

"Keep watching."

Damien sat at his desk, reclined and hands clasped as he twiddled his thumbs. But on the other side stood a young woman in a dress, hugging every curve. When she slammed her fists on his desk, I gasped. Black smoke spread from her hands while along the floor, tendrils of black rose like phantom limbs.

"I made you," Damien said. "There's no backing out now."

"You owe your success to me," she spat.

"I owe you nothing."

The black smoke enveloped the lower half of the woman as she rose off her feet. If I didn't know better, I'd believe she was about to beat Damien within an inch of his life. I had experienced her strength firsthand. The poor man wouldn't...

Damien inhaled sharply. The shadows in the room siphoned away. The man drank the darkness as if it were an aged bourbon. He hadn't been lying about making her. Seconds later, she dropped to her feet... powerless.

"He made the woman who attacked Hyperion?"

"It's not done."

Damien's skin turned black, as if he were wearing... When I looked up, LaToya was nodding. The arrogance of the man. He literally recorded and kept evidence of a secret that could destroy him.

Everything fell into place. I couldn't keep my jaw from hanging open. It wasn't enough that Damien hated heroes and used his magazine to slander them. I thought he'd sit on the sidelines and let people like this woman do his dirty work. I didn't think he'd get his hands dirty.

"Damien is Havoc," I muttered as the scene continued to unfold.

"Give them back, Damien. Or so help me..." the woman said.

"Rebekah, dear. I own you. You'll be free to go when I'm done with you. Do you understand?"

Her fists stayed clenched. Damien held all the cards. The black along his chest spread apart, revealing skin. In the middle sat a green gem, pulsing a soft light. The beam focused, enveloping Rebekah. A puff of smoke rose off her skin as she flexed her arms.

"Fine," she said. Turning, she prepared to storm off. I tapped the screen, freezing the frame. Zooming in, I recognized the woman. I couldn't quite place her, but the contextual clues were obvious now. She had been his bodyguard at Centurion headquarters.

"He's not recruiting heroes. The Centurions are villains."

LaToya snatched her phone. "What better way to destroy the reputation of heroes across the world? Seize control of the most recognized team and destroy heroes from within."

"He outed me so the board would disband the Centurions." I ran through everything that had happened. Eclipse had stolen the data. Before that, Smoke attempted to raise literal hell and by summoning a demon after robbing heroes of their powers. If it hadn't been for Xander, the world would be in chaos. And at the beginning, Wraith. Each of them attempted to tarnish the names of heroes.

"Does he classify as an evil genius?"

LaToya shook her head. "He's not a doctor. He goes in the mastermind category." She rested her hands on my shoulders. "You're the last Centurion."

I had gone toe-to-toe with the man and his squad of shadow-wielding psychos. At the time, Damien had the element of surprise. He could have killed me, but the fact he didn't...

"Jason." My worst fear had come true.

"Your boyfriend?"

"How do you know—"

"Have we met? I know things."

I ignored the fact LaToya spied on me. That'd be a discussion for another time. "You said the families were missing too? That explains why Damien offered Jason a job. He's using him to get to me. I need to stop him."

"You might take Damien, but with his soldiers? The man took out the rest of the Centurions."

I rose until my feet hovered above the arcade floor. "He had the element of surprise. Now it's my turn."

Reaching into my pocket, I pulled out my phone. Scrolling through my texts, I found Damien's number. With a click, it started ringing. I put it on speaker for LaToya to hear.

"Mr. Castle, I've been expecting your call."

"Vex. Or should I call you Havoc?"

LaToya sighed while shaking her head.

"Is this where you threaten me, Mr. Castle?"

"Vex, we're going to end this."

"Yes, I suppose we are."

I ended the call.

LaToya paced back and forth while throwing her arms

up in the arm. "You just alerted him you're coming. Why would you give up the element of surprise?"

"Surprising him isn't the advantage." She raised an eyebrow. "His arrogance, that's his weakness."

"I pray you're right, Bernard."

Me too. "Prepare for the worst, LaToya. If I don't stop him, you need to protect Jason. I can't lose him."

She nodded. "I promise."

I knew LaToya would put her life on the line to keep her word. Hopefully, it wouldn't come to that. First, I needed to stop Damien. Then I'd take Xander's advice and talk to Jason. If I could stop a megalomaniac and save the world, maybe I'd be able to save my love life.

27

F LYING THROUGH THE CITY, I HAD A RENEWED SENSE OF purpose. I could have flown through the lobby and taken the elevator like before, but it didn't quite make the right statement. I already pictured myself smashing through his office window and clobbering him before he defended himself.

This wouldn't be a long, drawn-out fight. A quick pummeling and handcuffs, and I'd be satisfied. Seeing Damien Vex behind bars would be a glorious victory.

From this perspective, the Centurion headquarters appeared no bigger than a finger. I cocked my head to the side, letting the bones crack.

"I'm coming for you, Vex," I growled.

Below, the city fast approached.

LaToya wanted in on the action to help stop Damien.

But her role wouldn't be trading blows with his lackeys. With the evidence at her disposal, we needed to expose Damien should I fail. She might not punch the man, but she'd deliver the final blow. When she reached the television studios, they'd have the fodder necessary to cripple Damien's empire.

The roar of the wind was deafening as I came down in a controlled fall. At the last minute, I'd use the momentum to barrel through the tower. Windows, walls, and furniture would be obliterated as I snatched Damien. The collateral damage would be...

"Shit."

My plan fell apart as I spotted Damien standing on the roof. Had he predicted my plan? Either way, it meant that this would turn into a slugfest. Tightening my fingers into a fist, I prepared to trade blows. With a quick glance, I couldn't see his minions. Would Damien confront me one-on-one? It seemed too noble for the arrogant prick.

"Damien!"

I dropped to one knee as I slammed into the roof terrace. Classic superhero entrance. The cracks ran along the concrete. Slow lift of the head. Rise with determination. I had considered focusing on street-level crimes, returning to my roots. It might be a cliche, but it also imbued me with a sense of dignity. No, there were bigger villains that needed my attention.

Sentinel had returned.

"What do I owe this pleasure?"

Arrogant or coy? I didn't care for either trait. "I know everything, Damien. Wraith, Smoke, and Eclipse, I know you're the puppet master."

"Of course you do."

Something in his tone. I couldn't quite place it. It wasn't condescending, but there was more to his words.

"Do you think I'd carelessly leave damning evidence lying around?"

"You wanted us to find out?"

"I didn't have faith you'd ever figure it out on your own. I thought you'd need a hand."

"Even your secretary?"

He laughed. "Oh no. She truly hates me. But I made sure she knew enough. People are so easy to manipulate."

That was enough talking. The lightning poured from my fist, crackling as it raced toward Damien. As it struck, his clothes tore away, leaving the black shadows of Havoc. Sliding backward, he drove his foot into the roof, holding his ground. Even as I raised the intensity, he leaned into it.

I gained ground as the black tore away from his body. The lightning stopped as I reached my limit. The moment it stopped hammering away, the black crawled back into place, covering the black stubble along his chest.

He brushed off his suit. He taunted me as he inspected it for imperfections. Damien Vex couldn't be more arrogant if he tried. It'd make defeating him even more glorious.

"Is that it? I expected more from the legendary Sentinel."

"I'm just warming up. You can't win, Damien."

"Perhaps." He shrugged. "But the past says I have the upper hand. Is the third time going to be any different?"

"I'll keep coming for you. You can't stop the inevitable."

"True, I can't stop Sentinel." There was a surprise behind the statement. Villains, especially masterminds, wanted to lead a hero into a confident place to sweep the rug out from under them. Damien thought he was unstoppable. That's what every other villain thought before I put them behind bars.

"But Bernard Castle," he said, "him I can hurt."

My body had already recharged. I let the lightning snap from my hands, smashing nearby planters. This time, I'd launch a volley to distract him before I advanced with an electrical uppercut. Even if he blocked the blow, it'd leave a bruise.

"I can't break your bones. But your spirit, your heart, that I can destroy."

It didn't take a genius to know he meant Jason. The muscle in my face ached as I clenched my jaw. The lightning grew more unwieldy, destroying furniture and the statues adorning the top of Centurion headquarters. If that wasn't enough voltage, the clouds overhead swirled, preparing to unleash a barrage of lethal strikes.

A cloud of black escaped his body, turning into a circle.

When the portal opened, I froze. Bound and gagged, Jason struggled against his restraints. When he looked up, our eyes connected, and he started shouting through the cloth tied about his face.

"Damien! He has nothing to do with this."

"Doesn't he though? It seems you made a tactical mistake. This is on you, Bernard."

The lightning overhead came storming down. Damien stepped into the portal, giving a slight wave as the black mist evaporated. The roof exploded as lightning struck where he had been standing. The entire building shook as a dozen more bolts hammered away. It was enough electricity to make the hair on my neck stand on end. But I had been too late.

"Damien!" I shouted into the emptiness. My worst fear had come true. A villain had decided the fastest way to hurt me was to strike at the man closest to me. I had led Jason into this fight, and now he'd suffer for my stupidity.

I dropped to my knees.

"No. No. No." The scream that escaped my chest was swallowed as lightning pounded against my shoulders. The storm responded to my distress. As quickly as it came, it vanished, leaving me staring at the spot where the portal had been.

"I'll save you, Jason." The determination in my voice faltered as fear laced my words. Shaking my head, I couldn't get the picture of him tied up out of my head. I could only hope that he was being used as bait and that Damien wouldn't stoop to hurting a bystander.

No. I couldn't dwell on what might happen. Right now, I needed to save Jason. I'd put Damien behind bars. Then Jason and I could have an honest conversation. And now that he saw the potential dangers, perhaps he'd understand my fears.

"Damien, I'm coming for you."

28

Since the sun came up, the HeroApp™ hadn't stopped vibrating. Approaching six in the morning, the innocent bystanders would soon fill the streets. Villains were out in force. While that would normally be a problem, they were the best chance I had of finding where Damien hid Jason.

I drew my fist back, ready to drive my knuckles into Miss Guidance's face. She held up her hands, begging for mercy.

"I swear, I know nothing. Nobody knows anything about Havoc."

My eighth villain of the night. Each had the same story. It appeared that Havoc kept to himself. I was growing impatient, and going by the blood dripping from Miss Guidance's nose, it showed in the force I used. At this rate,

I'd do something I'd regret and not be any closer to saving Jason.

"I don't even know how I got here."

I raised an eyebrow. Diamond, Cricket, Killer Bee — they all had identical bouts of amnesia. There was a growing trend, and I couldn't help but think Damien was behind it. It was time to admit I would not find Jason on my own.

I landed in front of the police station. A dozen police officers stood outside, wrangling villains dropped off by the heroes of Vanguard. The cells were going to be overflowing before the end of the night.

"Thanks, Sentinel." An officer slapped cuffs on the woman before dragging her into the station. I noticed the badges on several of the men and women were from neighboring cities. It appeared they had called in reinforcements, and as much as I hated to admit it. It was time I did the same.

B: Damien has Jason. I need help. 911.

X: HideOut. Ten minutes.

The HideOut? I took off, flying into the Ward. At this hour, Chad would have turned over the open sign. Of the thousand places in the city to meet, why pick our coffee shop? Did he worry I didn't know how to use GPS?

I landed a block away, careful to make sure pedestrians didn't spot my descent into the alley. As I walked, all I could think about was Jason. It wasn't the first time he'd been bound and tied, but usually, it was me with the rope. I doubt Damien would do anything in the meantime. He wanted me to suffer and... I refused to let my mind settle on the what-if?

I crossed the street, noting that the HideOut had its curtains drawn shut. Chad never closed them. Had Xander commandeered the coffee shop for this clandestine meeting? I opened the door, expecting to see Xander, suited and ready to fly into battle. But it looked like a party, with me, fashionably late.

"I told you he'd be confused," Griffin said.

"Leave him alone. Papi has had a rough night."

I narrowed my eyes, focusing on Xander. It was bad enough he invited Griffin and Alejandro. But everybody brought their boyfriend? Even Chad sat on the counter, waving while I tried to process what was unfolding.

"Xander, I... uhmm... This is a *special* situation."

Everybody laughed.

Xander patted my usual seat. Alejandro pushed it out with his foot. I didn't have time for witty jabs or discussing sex lives. I humored them, slowly sitting down.

When a burly man rested his hand on Alejandro's

shoulder, my eyes widened. I knew he had been dating EO, a teleporting hero. But I had never seen him out of his mask. "EO?"

"Theo," he winked.

"What's going on?" Even knowing EO's alter ego, I couldn't figure out the point of his gathering.

Xander patted me on the knee. "Bernard, we've been patient. We've waited."

"So long," Griffin added.

"So damned long," Xander continued. "You only ever needed to ask for help. We've always had your back."

Hearing that from Xander warmed my heart. He, Griffin, Alejandro, and Chad were my chosen family. They'd have done anything possible to help me. But I didn't see how it'd help stop a supervil—

"Griffin? You have powers?"

"I wish. I didn't win that lottery."

"It's okay." Sebastian gave him a peck on the cheek. "You're still cute."

"No." My brain caught up to the situation. Xander masqueraded as Lionheart, Theo as EO... we'd have to talk to him about being so obvious. And Sebastian?

"Hyperion." My jaw dropped. "Chad? You too?"

"Only if you count my wit and ability to remember customer orders."

"Deviants," I whispered.

"Papi," Alejandro laughed. "The name couldn't be any more obvious. I mean, look at us."

Two of us with powers. Two dating those with powers. It seemed none of us had been completely honest with one another. But to think each morning we talked about mundane news about Vanguard when each of us was part of the effort to keep the city safe.

"Still not fair. I don't have powers."

Alejandro patted Griffin on the head. "Maybe we can find a radioactive spider."

Griffin crossed his arms. "That's all I'm asking."

"We're here for you, buddy," Sebastian said. "Powers and not. We're ready to go to work."

Xander's eyes softened. "You've always been part of a team, big guy. This one just has more spandex. Ready to let us help?"

Before I could speak, the chimes above the door jingled. We all froze as Lydia walked in. She had dyed her hair a fiery red, letting it cascade onto her shoulders. Between that and the black collar, she looked as if she had just walked away from a punk concert.

Everybody held their tongues as she grabbed a chair, spun it around, and sat at the table. Nine men, one woman. Despite the odds against her, I didn't want to tussle with the woman. She controlled the space, ignoring the overwhelming amounts of testosterone. I shot Griffin a look, but he only shrugged in reply. Nobody dared to point out the obvious.

"Lydia." I feigned a smile. "It's nice to see you again. Is there something we can help you with?"

Her backpack dropped from her shoulder, landing on the floor with a thud. She rubbed the bridge of her nose as if we were trying her patience. I didn't want to be rude to Griffin's friend, but every second we danced around the awkward situation was another that Jason waited for a rescue.

"We were in the middle of—"

She smacked her forehead before reaching down to her bag. The zipper pulled back slowly as she fished through its contents. When she sat upright, her eyes rolled back in her head. Before they returned to their forward position, she held the mask in front of her face.

Everybody gasped.

"You're Hellcat?" I couldn't hide my surprise. The punkish and aggressively forward comic book store owner had an alter... Never mind, it made perfect sense. Reading about heroes all day long wasn't a hopeful aspiration. It served as inspiration for the moment she closed shop and took to the streets.

"Lionheart texted me you might need the Deviant's help."

"Havoc has Jason."

"Vex," she hissed. When my jaw dropped, she smiled.

She slid her phone across the desk. On the screen, every news article was about Damien's secret identity. Each of them cited an anonymous source, but it didn't take a rocket scientist to figure out who leaked the information. LaToya had made good on her promise.

"The empire of Vex has fallen," Aiden said as he scrolled through his cell phone. "Not even Revelations will survive this."

"Now for Havoc," Theo added.

I didn't know how to express my gratitude. It was one thing to provide a shoulder to cry on when times got hard. Offering advice might be sweet, but it didn't compare to risking one's life. Eyeing each of them, I knew they'd cover my back just as I would theirs.

"From the bottom of my heart, thank you." Alejandro reached out, taking my hand. Out of instinct, I reached for Lydia's hand.

She pulled it away quickly. "We're work friends at best. Now, are we going to get our asses in gear, or should we share our feelings some more?"

Lydia and Hellcat were two entirely distinct personalities. The socially awkward comic geek vanished, replaced by the militant vigilante leader. Her laser focus was something to admire.

Griffin threw his arms up in the air. "This is not fair. Next, I'll find out Alejandro has superpowers."

"Speak for yourself." Alejandro slapped Theo on the ass. "I save my powers for the bedroom."

A collective groan.

Hellcat stood, tossing the backpack over her shoulder. "I hope you resolved the suit situation, B. You're going to need it."

"So, Hellcat, what's the plan?" Xander put his arm around Aiden, holding his boyfriend close. He tried to maintain the gruff demeanor, but as Aiden leaned against him, I could only see happiness.

Hellcat turned to give me the once-over. "I'm not the leader of this sausage-fest. I was only standing in until we found a suitable replacement." She took a step back, giving me the floor.

When my identity splashed across the television, I never thought it'd begin this cascade of events. From the Centurions falling apart to Jason waltzing into my life, Damien thought he had defeated me. As I moved from one set of eyes to the next, each focused on me. I almost chuckled. Damien didn't understand a novel concept like friendship. He thought he had destroyed me when all he did was offer a chance to correct my priorities.

"I've got a plan..." Everybody leaned forward.

Chad hopped off the counter. "I'll put the coffee on."

The huddle had ended. Everybody had a job to do. Those with superpowers were going to scour every abandoned warehouse and shake down villains for information. Alejandro was already going through his phone, reaching out to every superhero booty call in search of intel. Griffin and Aiden acted as the 'man in the chair,' coordinating our efforts with the help of the HeroApp™.

We each had a mission leading to Jason's rescue.

The others were already out the door, all except for Chad. He had been silent for most of the discussion, a sign that something was not right with the man. In all the years I had known him, he never resisted a chance to jump into the conversation.

If we didn't have a pressing matter at hand, I'd sit down and have a cup of coffee with him while we laid everything on the table. I charged him, giving him a hug.

"Thank you," I said while squeezing his ribcage. "For all of this."

"You're going to find him," he squeaked out.

"I know." I put the barista down, ready to head out and scour the city for Damien.

"Can we talk?" I'd move Heaven and Hell for Chad. But his life wasn't on the line, at least not in any way I could sort.

"I need to find Jason."

"This is about Jason."

That caught my attention. It wouldn't shock me if he

had some insight about where he was being held. Chad had a knack for listening to the conversations happening in the HideOut. In one day, he knew more dirt about Vanguard's citizens than any news reporter did.

"Do you remember when the HideOut opened?"

"Yeah. Honestly, I barely remember it before you bought the shop. Just that my favorite barista worked there."

He blushed at the compliment.

"I took a risk. The coffee shop I bought was failing. I didn't know how I'd make my rent. Debt collectors were after me. Basically..." He let out a sigh. "My life felt like it was on the brink of falling apart."

"You turned it around. But I don't see how this—"

"Shhh." He put a finger to my lips. "I was a mess. If I couldn't keep the shop open, then I'd lose my apartment. Bernard, it's hard to admit, but I was prepared to live in my car." His tone shifted, almost somber. I knew it had been a difficult period, but I hadn't realized the extreme. "But then, this adorable brutish daddy bear offered to help."

I hadn't done much, not really. Chad was the heart of the coffee shop. I put my team to work rebranding the cafe. The community had rallied behind him, and the local shop owners did everything in their power to make sure his doors stayed open. It had been a wonderful grand re-opening.

"I'd do it again in a heartbeat. That's what friends are for."

"Exactly what I'm getting at. You've spent so long trying to split your life between Bernard and Sentinel. You've kept people at arm's length. Even Griffin, Alejandro, and Xander. There's always a wall in place. We want in, so stop trying to push us away."

Ouch. I hadn't expected a tough love speech from Chad. The more I thought about the three men who joined me every morning for coffee, the more I saw his point. Did we socialize beyond the confines of the HideOut? Rarely. They meant the world to me, but I had made sure they could only get so close.

"We care about you." He slapped me. I hardly felt it, but the act itself left my jaw hanging. "Stop pushing people away! Especially a cute guy who seems quite infatuated with you."

"Loving me got him kidnapped."

"There are a thousand things that could go wrong, Bernard. Tomorrow isn't a guarantee. All we have is today. Are you going to let fear rob him... rob *you* of that?"

"That's easy to say when you're dating a stud without powers."

Chad leaned back, resting his elbows on the counter. A smile spread across his face. "About that..."

My eyes went wide. Did everybody have an alter-ego

boyfriend? At this rate, I'd have to assume everybody I met on the street was either a superhero or dating one.

"I took a chance, Bernard." He stretched, his arm dangerously close to smacking me in the face again. "Look where it took me."

"He's a luck—"

"No, dammit!" Chad's eyes repeatedly darted from my face to his hand. It took a moment before I saw the silver band on his ring finger.

"Chad..." I took his hand, admiring the simplicity and elegance of the band. The silver held lines etched in a geometric pattern, simple at first glance but incredibly detailed upon further inspection. "I... Congratulations!"

He stood up, straightening his shirt. "Bernard Castle, the man who believed in me when I didn't believe in myself, will you be my best man?"

I wrapped my arms around him in a bear hug and started spinning. My feet lifted off the ground, hovering, while I squeezed the lucky man. I didn't have words to express how happy I was for him. It brought a renewed vigor to find Jason. If Chad could find his happily ever-after, then maybe it was possible this old man could do the same.

"Yes! I'd be honored."

He pushed away, dropping to the floor. I almost had to laugh. I wanted details. How did Reese propose? Where were they going to tie the knot? But it'd need to wait until Jason could be at my side.

"We'll finish this after I find Jason."

"Go," he barked, pointing at the door. "You're not allowed at my wedding without a date."

29

I HAD SCOURED THE CITY FOR THE LAST HOUR. EVERY EMPTY warehouse, a subterranean base belonging to the Lizard King, and any other lair I could remember. Each would be the perfect place for a villain to hide and hold hostages, but no luck. I was growing anxious, worried that as time passed, they'd eventually hurt Jason.

I needed x-ray vision or super hearing. Wielding lightning had its uses in battle, but it wasn't doing me any good right now. I needed somebody capable of locating—

My phone rang.

"Griffin?"

"WoofR!"

"I'm too busy to listen about creepy guys—"

"Jason's profile is on there. It's a geolocation app."

I stopped dead in my tracks. Hovering above an intersection, I opened the app and clicked on Jason's profile. Griffin was right, it showed his distance.

"Pick a direction. Fly."

I soared down Ventura St. 1.9 miles. I switched directions. 1.7 miles. "Griffin, you're a genius."

"Man in the chair!" He cheered. "Thanks goes to Aiden." I could hear Aiden in the background clapping.

I watched as the distance crept toward a half mile. When it increased, I changed course. Thankfully, it continued down. Before I knew it, it read less than five hundred feet.

"The audacity," I said. I stared up at Centurion headquarters. While we thought he had fled to a secret evil lair, he had only teleported down a few floors inside the building. The man had balls of steel, and I looked forward to punching them as much as his face.

"Griffin, call the others. He's in Centurion headquarters." He hung up, leaving me staring at the former home of Sentinel. It wasn't enough to hurt me. He wanted to destroy my reputation. The Deviants were about to create a public relations disaster. If he thought we'd shy away from a fight, he had another thing coming.

I didn't need to guess where he hid. The arrogance of the man left one option. As I rocketed up the side of the building, I reached the 99th floor, the home base of the

Centurions. Through the glass, I watched the pompous playboy laughing. The lightning poured out of my chest, vaporizing a row of windows as I entered.

"Damien!" I shouted.

Damien stood behind Jason, using him as a human shield. But he wasn't waiting alone. Wraith, Smoke, and Eclipse stood between me and my goal. His bastard Centurion replacements were about to find out why I earned my position on the world's strongest superhero team.

"We've been waiting," Damien said, brushing a hand along Jason's cheek. "It's a pity to see an innocent bystander suffer on your behalf."

"Vex!"

Rational thought deserted me. Flying forward, I narrowed my gaze and focused on Damien. The electricity gathered in my fist, ready to clobber with a supercharged punch. There was no point in focusing on his lackeys. Without their leader, they'd be nothing more than a nuisance.

Eclipse attempted to intercept, but with a roll to the side, I dodged the goon. I thought I'd make it. I might have if it weren't for Wraith and her liquid shadows. The ground was covered in black, tendrils shooting up, snaring my legs. They brought me to a dead halt no matter how hard I pushed myself.

"Your efforts don't seem to go according to plan." I'd pummel Damien before throwing his ass into jail.

Lightning shot from my hands, cutting through Wraith's smoke. As quickly as I severed one, another shot forward. My hands weren't the only outlet for the power. Lightning poured out of my skin, along my arms, legs, and then my eyes. Her smoke vaporized. The moment of surprise from the villainess provided the opportunity to hurl a bolt in her direction.

Pain spread through my body as something slammed into my back. The force knocked me to the floor, smashing tiles. I rolled over in time to see a heel speeding toward my face. I caught it and let the electricity jump from my hands to Smoke. He attempted to pull away, but I refused. I wanted the man electrocuted, smoking, so that he lived up to his name.

He staggered backward, but Eclipse had pulled at my legs. I tried to shake him. When that didn't work, I attempted to fly forward and pull myself free.

"Not this time," he said.

The black swallowed me until nothing of the real world remained. I had hoped to avoid being dragged into Eclipse's mental warfare. Out there, I could punch the bad guys. In this dark space, the only bad guy was myself.

"Do your worst!" I was prepared. As Jason appeared in the chair, I wanted to comment on Eclipse's predictability. He could only latch onto fears, and if he thought I hadn't already explored the darkness in my head, he was sorely mistaken.

"Is that all you've got, Eclipse?"

Damien's laughter filled the emptiness. While a phantom Damien stood behind Jason, I focused on my escape. I launched upward, seeking an exit. The longer he trapped me here, the more time his companions had to take advantage of my physical body.

There was no exit. At least none I could see in the darkness. For that matter, I didn't even know if I was truly flying or standing in place.

"Let me out!"

The chair returned, but there was no Jason in it. "What are you playing at?" Lightning poured out of my body, flying in every direction. The light vanished, swallowed by the darkness. If they trapped me here, what would happen to Jason? I couldn't save him from...

A grassy field with rolling hills faded into view. It'd be ideal if small gray objects didn't quickly follow. I couldn't fathom what Eclipse wanted me to see. The scene darkened as the small rectangles solidified. No, not rectangles, they were headstones.

"What?" As I approached, it became clear. I stood in a cemetery with thousands of headstones in neat and tidy rows. Standing on fresh brown dirt, I read the first name.

"Griffin Smith?"

As the wind picked up, I swore I heard his voice. The next stone, Alejandro Martinez, then Xander Bennett. I had to give credit to Eclipse. He struck at my biggest fear. Words materialized beneath the names. I leaned in, curious how Eclipse might take this further.

"Victim of Bernard Castle's Pride."

I raised an eyebrow. Cute, really it was, but this wasn't going to—

"You thought they wouldn't find me, Bernard." Behind the headstone, Griffin stepped forward. "Your arrogance killed me."

"We'd have been better off without you," Xander said.

"Papi, you could have protected us."

It wasn't a shock. But seeing the specters standing behind their respective stones, tugged at the question I had been grappling with for days. I thought Eclipse would try to slam me with a sense of terror, but his abilities had more nuance.

"Bernard…"

I closed my eyes, not wanting to turn and see another ghost, especially not this one. But I wouldn't let a villain have the satisfaction of winning. Pivoting on my heels, I spotted a translucent Jason. The scarlet line across his throat and red stains along his shirt were enough to tighten my gut.

"You put your needs before my safety."

I shook my head, trying to push the image of him away. Instead, I focused on the moment he stepped into Bottoms

Up and that smile, the one I never thought I'd see again. Eclipse could tug at my fears, but nothing could overcome the abundance of emotions as I realized fate offered me a second chance. I thought I failed Jason. He knew the risks, and he made it clear that he accepted them for the sake of us.

"Who gave you the right to decide—"

I laughed. Eclipse had overplayed his hand and made his first error. The argument between Jason and me replayed in my head. Making decisions without him, that had been *my* mistake. It wasn't one I'd repeat. Jason might not wield lightning, but that didn't mean he didn't have his own superpowers.

"Jason!" The lightning poured from my skin, obliterating the scene, blowing away tombstones and scorching earth. The darkness tore away, and for a second, I could see myself on the floor of Centurion headquarters.

"I'm coming for you." The electricity poured from every pore of my skin. It battered against an invisible barrier, shredding apart the darkness. I flew toward the exit. As I hit the tear, the world flashed. Once again, I was on the 99th floor, lying on my belly.

"Nice try," I growled. "Was that your best shot?"

"Oh dear, Bernard, that was only the beginning." Damien laughed as if he had the upper hand. "Jason needs to see his protector fall. That, for all your bravado, you can't keep him safe."

It was my turn to laugh. The chuckle turned into a deep roar in the belly as I pushed my way to my feet. I shook my head. Like Eclipse, Damien had made the same mistake. Jason didn't need a protector. He needed a boyfriend. Sentinel might be the one about to mop the floor with these fools, but it was Bernard who'd carry him home.

Wraith rushed forward as black spikes formed around her body. The woman's hands were replaced with blades. Usually, I'd charge into battle, axe in hand. We'd duke it out. But I didn't have time to suffer Damien's henchmen.

My foot broke through the floor as I slammed it down. Lightning jumped from my leg, rushing forward before leaping into her chest. If that wasn't enough voltage, I let the electricity pour from my body. I emptied my internal battery, but it was enough to throw her across the room, rolling next to her master.

"Who's next?" Bravado? I planned on making good on my threats.

"Worthless," Damien hissed as Wraith writhed on the ground. The black peeled away from her body, oozing along the floor until it wrapped around Damien's leg. "You don't deserve my grace."

It appeared he had recalled her powers. One less person to fight, but it couldn't be good that an egomaniac fortified himself.

"You've had it wrong, Damien. Hell, I had it wrong. Jason doesn't need a protector." I gave Jason a wink. He nodded his chin, the universal symbol for getting out of the way.

Jason slammed his head back, striking Damien in the gut. The villain swiped at Jason, knocking him and the chair across the room. With fists out, I summoned the lightning... or at least I tried.

"It seems you're out of juice, Sentinel."

If it wasn't for his goons preparing to strike, I'd have been embarrassed. Naked and standing with one of the most powerful men in Vanguard, it seemed the odds were against me. If I couldn't recharge, this would turn into a slugging match, and last time, that didn't go so well.

"I've been waiting for this day," Damien said as he stepped between Eclipse and Smoke. "The great Sentinel, once the greatest hero the world has ever seen. I've taken it all."

"Going to bore me with a lecture?" I started backing up to the window. I'd need a bolt or two of lightning to recharge.

"What do you have left, Bernard? The Centurions are no more. You're alone."

I reached the window.

"That's where you're wrong. I'm not alone."

Hellcat swung in, rolling along the floor, striking a pose. Okay, a little overkill, but she got points for panache. Lionheart and Hyperion hovered outside the window as EO teleported to my side.

"Did we hit our cue?" EO asked.

"Havoc, meet the Deviants."

Griffin better appreciate the dramatic entrance.

The watch dissolved. The nanites crawled along my naked arm, coating it in a shiny red. Eating away at the remnants of my jeans, it covered my body in a new suit. Red and white, not colors I'd choose, but they made a statement. They continued, draping a lengthy cape attached at the shoulders. Now I looked the part of a hero.

"About time you listened to me," Hellcat said.

"I dunno, was hot watching him fight naked," Lionheart said.

"Don't make me smack you," she said.

They bickered like a second Breakfast club. It had become a good ol' fashioned standoff. The three villains with shadow abilities and the Deviants, a hodgepodge of heroes that shouldn't function as a team. The more I thought about it, the more they reminded me of the group having morning coffee. Bernard had his found family. Now, so did Sentinel.

"Say the thing," Lionheart said. "Say it. You know you want to."

I rolled my eyes. "Fine." Sucking in air, I let out a roar. "Unleash the Deviants."

Like glorious warriors, Lionheart and Hyperion flew toward Smoke. EO vanished into a portal to appear behind Eclipse while Hellcat charged him from the front. They knew the plan—distract them until I got Jason out of harm's way. Then it'd be a flurry of powers and plowing one another through walls.

I didn't have time to summon lightning from the sky. It'd wait until I returned from stashing Jason at a safe distance. The only thing that mattered was getting to him and taking him far away from Damien.

Flying forward, I dipped under Hellcat as Eclipse threw her across the room. She vanished into a portal only to reappear behind him, driving a heel between his shoulder blades. I somersaulted over a wave of fire Lionheart used to separate Damien from Smoke. Like a well-oiled machine, they worked in tandem to bring down the bad guys. In a few short months, they'd achieved a synchronicity the Centurions had spent years perfecting.

"Howdy stranger," I said as I parked next to Jason. "Before you start in on me, I took your advice. I asked for help."

As I pulled the ropes off his hand, he didn't say a word. He lunged, wrapping his arms around my neck. "I'm so glad to see you." He held my face, and I could see tears running down his face.

"When this is over, can we revisit the worry about supervillain conversation? Together this time?"

"I appreciate the validation. But how about you kick his ass first? Then we'll talk boundaries."

"I was going to let him go." I smiled. I couldn't help it. Even in life-or-death situations, he remained cool and collected. "But for you, I'll pound the crap out of him."

The punch to my jaw sent me tumbling before I crushed the glass tubes used to house the Centurion's suits. Getting suckered punch while trying to have a moment. Classic supervillain. I'd be certain to pay him back for that. Thankfully, Damien seemed more interested in me than Jason.

"He can watch you die."

The shadows around his arms elongated until they transformed into blades. Good to know he had stolen Wraith's trademark. I thrust out a palm, hoping for a spark or two. It'd take days for my battery to recharge on its own.

"I guess we'll do this the old-fashioned way." As long as he focused on me, it meant the others could rescue Jason. But as I glanced across the room, Hellcat attacked Hyperion, cracking her staff over his head. Great, Smoke had gotten his hooks into the one person on our team without superpowers. We'd discuss this at the next staff meeting.

I pulled one of the metal studs from the wall, tearing it away from its rivets. I rushed Damien, putting muscle into the swing. As if it were nothing more than paper, his arms cut through the metal. I chucked the last of the beam at him, but the tendrils of black leaped from the floor, pulling it away.

I followed it with a punch. The impact shook the walls, cracking windows with a boom. The force did nothing to my opponent. While his face was hidden behind a mask of black. It curved enough to see the sadistic grin before he slammed his face into my forehead.

Damien blocked a right hook, sliding the blade across my forearm. It had been ages since something as mundane as a knife left a mark, let alone cut my skin. I hesitated. I barely had time to block a kick to the stomach. As I leaned back, dodging the tip of the knife across my throat, I realized he had me on the defense.

When the tendrils of black held my legs in place, the blades vanished, replaced by oversized fists. Damien seized the opportunity to land three blows, two to the face and the last to my kidney. I struggled to break free from the supernatural restraints, but they held fast. When another wrapped around my neck, he dragged me to my knees.

Damien stepped back as the shadows drew back from his face. He threw his hands in the air. "Victory. The great Sentinel thought a team of second-rate heroes would come to the rescue? Doesn't look like they're going to save you now."

His arm elongated, slimming until the tip touched the floor. Raising it over his head, it'd only be a few feet before it sliced me in half. I pulled, stretching the tendrils, but brute force wasn't doing the trick.

Damien charged. I wanted to say I stared down death, but I closed my eyes and gritted my teeth. Nobody wanted to see a lunatic get the last laugh. I bit down hard enough that the corners of my jaw ached, but...

Nothing?

"I'll save him."

30

Jason faced Damien with his arms spread out to protect me. The blade hovered in the arm, and despite his grunting, Damien couldn't move it. As he drew back and tried again, I shouted. It stopped short, striking an invisible barrier.

Jason had powers? I didn't have time to parse the information. The man I loved put his life on the line to save me. Pointing his hands at Damien, a blue globe of light hit Damien, sending him backward. Even if it wasn't enough to fall the man, the tendrils receded enough to pull free.

"Quick exit," Jason said.

A laser from Hyperion struck Damien, buying me time to grab Jason and barrel through a crumbling window. I could have set him down on a dozen rooftops, but then he'd be trapped. If Damien tried again, I wanted Jason somewhere he could hide from the psycho. I fell from the sky with Jason's arms wrapped around my neck.

"You have powers?"

We touched down, and Jason maintained his grip while he tested the sturdiness of the street. He stepped back, holding up his hands. They were covered in high-tech gauntlets... extremely *fashionable* gauntlets.

"There was a box on the bed at the hotel. The note said every hero's boyfriend should look just as stylish."

"Asher," I shook my head. "They'll do anything to get me in a kilt."

"I feel like I'm missing part of that conversation." He threw his arms around my neck again. "But the world deserves to see those calves." Jason had a knack for joking when he got nervous, even if he was right about my legs.

"I owe you an apology," I whispered in his ear. "I'm so sorry for being overbearing."

"I mean..." He stepped back while eyeing the skyscraper. "Maybe you weren't entirely wrong. But next time, try talking to me. We're in this together."

"Yes," I whispered, "we are."

"I did just save your life. Maybe you can be my sidekick."

"Whoa. Whoa. We don't throw around the 's-word' lightly in my line of work." I wrapped my hand around his waist and dipped him low. I'm sure the growing crowd of spectators was snapping photos. Let them. It'd give them something to put in the photo album. When the mask dissolved, I leaned in, kissing Jason.

Coming up for air, I couldn't help but smile. "I'd be your sidekick any day."

"We can be adorable later."

"I suppose I should save the day."

"Unless you want me to do it for you?"

I loved him. "Save one hero, and you're ready to take on the world."

"One studly hero."

"Fine." I laughed. "One studly hero."

"Make me a promise." His hands held my face, and in that moment, I would have promised Jason the world. Sure, there might be a supervillain threatening Vanguard, but the most important person in that city was in my arms.

"Come back to me," he said.

I'm sure he meant coming back to him after the fight. He wanted me to walk away unscathed so I could be Bernard. *His* Bernard. But I couldn't help but think of the night I walked away, leaving him without answers. I had spent years wallowing in regret. But I wouldn't make that mistake again.

"I'll always come back." The words were barely more than a whisper. As I tried to look away, he pulled my face back, locking eyes. He didn't need to speak. The tears forming in the corner of his eyes meant he understood the promise.

"Now go kick his ass."

"Yes, sir!"

If the tears measured my sincerity, the grin sprinkled in a dash of mischief. I'd need to make this a quick fight, so I could take that smirk back to the bedroom. We'd curl up in bed as we rehashed the night and celebrated our victory. It'd get sweaty and end with soft touches and nuzzling. We'd talk, and by the end, we'd be stronger for it. But first, I needed to stop Damien.

The skies turned dark as a storm settled over Centurion Tower. When I turned, ready to launch into the air, he slapped me on the ass.

"Go get 'em, Sentinel."

The skies opened and a deluge of rain as thunder shook the entire city. I passed the 99th floor, heading into the swirling storm above. The Deviants would need to hold on for another minute. With Jason safe, there wouldn't be any holding back.

The clouds grew dense, almost as if night consumed Vanguard early. Lightning lit up the darkness, tearing through the shadows in flashes of white. Asher's suit receded, pulling back into the watch, leaving me naked amongst the clouds.

Freedom.

The Deviants fought to protect Vanguard. My life had finally intertwined. Friends transformed into heroic colleagues. Those without power came to my aid. I didn't realize the weight of carrying the world's burdens. They shed away, distributed amongst the people I called friends. Family.

Thanks to Asher, even Jason proved he could handle himself. The tailor had gone behind my back, arming Jason. He might not be able to take on Havoc on his own, but then again, neither could I. The walls, the stone fortress I erected to keep the world at bay, didn't crumble. It exploded.

"Free," I whispered.

The lightning struck my chest and back, trying to burn me alive. I welcome the force of nature. The internal battery didn't recharge—it melted. Hundreds of bolts of light thrust into me, holding me in the sky. Never had I felt more in tune with the world. My hands glowed, electricity jumping between my fingers. The rest of those mental barriers I put in place vanished, and all that stood in their place... Sentinel.

As fast as the storm came, it vanished. I fell from the sky, plummeting toward Centurion headquarters. The suit spread across my body. It was time to end Damien's reign in Vanguard. But unlike before, this wouldn't be a solo venture.

I turned, blasting through the last of the 99th-floor's

windows. I'd need to leave an IOU for the next director. Instead of speeding toward Havoc, I had teammates that needed backup.

EO attempted to dodge Hellcat as she wailed on him with her staff. Shadow's abilities rendered her nothing more than a puppet. A dangerous puppet. He held back, not wanting to hurt a teammate. He fell through a portal, but her grappling hook snagged his ankle, dragging her right behind him.

I had assumed the field leader position on the Centurions because of my threat assessment abilities. New team, same threats. This was no different.

When EO reappeared, Hellcat attempted to knock him into Eclipse. "EO!"

I hurled a bolt of lightning in the wrong direction. EO caught my signal, opening a portal for the blast. He opened another behind Eclipse. The lightning hammered the villain in the back, knocking him away from the fight. It offered EO space to maneuver. Now to see to Hyperion and Lionheart.

Havoc rushed, hoping I didn't see him coming. I prepared for the impact, readying a lethal dosage of electricity. He vanished as a portal swallowed him. EO provided an opening. I took it, flying toward Hyperion.

Havoc came from a portal at full speed and slammed into a wall. I'd have to buy EO a drink for the assist. But right now, I needed Smoke out of commission to save Hellcat.

"Hyperion, power up!"

Lionheart ducked as I flew overhead, wrapping my arms around the villain. The electricity lit up the room, bright enough that even I had to close my eyes. If he had been anybody else, I'd have melted the skin from his body and left nothing but charred remains.

"Nice try, nightlight." Like his boss, it wasn't enough to render him unconscious. But that wasn't my goal.

"Lionheart, set up the pitch."

We hadn't trained. They didn't know the orders, and I didn't know how to relay them without giving away the plan. Instead, I trusted them. Smoke threw me aside, only to find Lionheart preparing a fiery uppercut.

The punch sent out a ring of fire, launching Smoke into the air. The goon thought I attempted to electrocute him. Nope. It was only a by-product of producing light for Hyperion to draw from. And by the glowing smoke pouring from his eyes, he had absorbed plenty.

"All yours," Lionheart shouted as he hurled balls of fire toward Havoc to keep him away.

Hyperion's entire body glowed, turning a blinding white. As he raised his fists, the blazing light narrowed until a laser slammed into Smoke's chest. Hyperion's power held him against the ceiling, and I was about to join the fray when Hyperion stepped forward with a grunt.

"Just. Stay. Down."

The shadows hugging Smoke ripped away until there was nothing but a man in a t-shirt and jeans. For a second, I thought the room turned dark, but it was just the absence of Hyperion's light. The villain fell from the ceiling, landing with a thud. One man down.

Spinning around, I was prepared to help EO, but it appeared Hellcat had some aggression she needed to work out. Jumping into a portal, she fell on top of Eclipse. Before he could grab her, she vanished into another portal. When we celebrated our victory, I'd be sure to award their teamwork with a gold star.

"I wouldn't get in the middle of that," Hyperion said. "She's likely to beat your ass."

"Yup. I'll wait my turn," Lionheart said.

I listened to Sebastian and Xander. I didn't need to make an enemy of Lydia, especially not as she growled with each punch. What she lacked in brute force, she made up for in grace. Eclipse swiped back and forth, trying to knock her aside. But the comic book store owner dodged without effort.

She yelled. "Are you just going to watch?" It was the closest thing we'd get to an invite.

Lionheart vanished through a portal, only to reappear behind Eclipse. His suit grew another set of arms, grappling with the villain. Fire poured out of his body, wrapping around Eclipse. It didn't seem to have any effect. It had been a diversion. EO fell out of a portal in the ceiling and drove his fits onto the man's head like a club.

"Sentinel!" I turned to see Hyperion stuck in the goopy shadows created by Havoc. They crawled along his legs despite his attempt to blast them with light. It seemed Havoc had more control of his powers than Wraith. It'd make it even more delicious as we slapped the cuffs on his wrist.

I slammed my foot on the floor, lightning shot out in a straight line. When it struck the shadows, they separated. Hyperion held out a hand, siphoning the light and redirecting it to the tendrils squeezing his calves. Before he was free, I flew forward, hand held out, ready to pull him free.

Havoc intercepted. Driving his fists into my chest. I went limp. The impact rattled the building, but he didn't stop as he drove me through the ceiling. Metal bent and tore as he continued flying upward. When we broke through, he drove his knuckles into my cheek, forcing me to fly backward along the roof.

"Do you think this changes anything?" Havoc lost his composure. The calm had vanished, replaced by rage. We might not have won, not yet. But we had upset his plans.

"You can't beat me, Sentinel. I'll build a new army, a stronger one. Vanguard will grovel before me."

I rubbed my jaw, checking to make sure he hadn't dislodged it. He packed a wallop. It hurt. There was no denying the strength he wielded. But after you banish an Olympian back to their mountain, strength didn't matter.

"You've already lost, Damien. Give up."

"You think this is the end of my story? Bernard, you can't stop me. When I'm done with you, I'll go after everybody you care about. Their blood will be on your hands."

My fingers tightened into a fist.

"That's your weakness, Bernard. You've made yourself vulnerable."

I brought my fists together overhead with a loud crack. The searing white light zoomed toward Damien. He raised a wall of shadows, swallowing the electricity. When that didn't work, I brought them down with a grunt. The next bolts came from the sky, hammering against the roof, blowing chunks of concrete in every direction. Damien hid in a bubble of shadows. They might not take him down, but they served as a perfect distraction.

Zipping toward him, the wall of black vanished, and he caught me around the neck. Redirecting my momentum, he swung me about, slamming me against the stairwell door. I stopped from flying off the roof.

"I admit, I thought pretty highly of you." He chuckled, not quite a laugh, but enough to know he thought I was a joke. "But it seems I was mistaken."

"Yeah? Why's that?"

"You can't stop me. You never could, and yet you won't quit. You're a fool, Bernard."

It was my turn to laugh. It might have been overkill, but I wanted him to see just how annoying that villain arrogance could be. I held up a finger, demanding he wait while I got it out of my system. Petty? Yes. Did it make me feel better after being thrown about like a rag doll? Absolutely.

"A fool? You've been threatening me like a B-rate villain. As Damien Vex, at least you were the head of a hate-filled tabloid. Now, you're just another villain."

"We'll see about that."

Damien's body nearly doubled in size, his limbs extending until he appeared more alien than human. Spikes protruded from his upper body and his hands turned into blades. At least he was willing to get his hands dirty to win.

"Oh." I laughed again. I wanted to make sure I landed the delivery. "One more thing."

"What's that?" Even the voice grew deeper, reverberating as if he spoke through a bullhorn.

"I'm not a fool." Pointing behind him, I smiled. "I'm the distraction."

Hellcat's grappling hook spun around his legs. She jumped back, falling through the hole in the roof so her weight tightened the rope. Hyperion lobbed a ball of light, the sparks showering around Damien as it struck his back. The man roared as he tried to turn, swinging his arms wildly, trying to keep his balance.

But it was Lionheart who flew forward, while flames

engulfed his body. Try as he might to stay upright, the ropes wouldn't give and he stumbled. I wished I could stay and continue watching the flailing. There's a chance I took a bit too much pleasure in Damien's literal fall from grace.

"EO, serve him up high!" With that command, EO opened a portal, swallowing Damien. I propelled myself upward into the middle of the storm. Damien fell out of EO's portal, high in the sky. For never training, we worked together like a true team. I'd owe everybody a drink after this.

I sped up, drawing back my fist, ready to clobber him if I got the chance. He reverted to his average muscular self, shaking off Hellcat's rope as he dodged out of the way.

"I knew it'd always come down to the two of us. One god against another."

"Who writes your dialogue?"

"Let's finish this."

"It's already done."

I couldn't defeat him with pure brawn. Part of being a hero is knowing my limitations and relying on the team to support me. Together, the Deviants had delivered Damien Vex into my domain. Amongst the turbulent winds and ionized air, I didn't need to raise a fist.

The first bolt of lightning smashed into his chest. He attempted to throw up a wall of darkness, but the next blasted through, striking him in the shoulder. The shadows he wielded like armor burned away, revealing flesh underneath. Here, amongst the storm, I only needed my powers to summon the forces of nature. Despite what Damien thought, not even his claim to godliness could resist.

"You can't—"

Two more bolts struck. Three. Four. His body spasmed before being consumed by the white light. The lightning might not hurt him, but thanks to Hyperion, Lionheart, and EO describing how they defeated Damien's henchmen, I suspected it'd do the trick.

I let it continue for almost a minute before I relinquished my control of the storm. Damien was no longer covered in shadows, and his body steamed as he fell from the sky. If I hadn't been a bigger man, I'd have let him splat against the street below. But I didn't want to risk a naked man landing on a little old lady.

"Morals," I growled, annoyed by my persistent code of conduct. I flew after him, grabbing the unconscious man under the armpits. His eyes shot open, and he drew his hand back. He poked me in the throat, barely hard enough to feel.

"What?"

"Somebody just an average criminal now?" He tried again. Damien was nothing more than a vile human. I didn't give him a second glance as I let go. It appeared whatever had given him his powers had vaporized in the storm. Good. He'd still go to the super ward for prisoners, but it'd be an extra victory knowing he was just average.

I raced down and grabbed him again.

"Before we lock you up, I need to grab the final issue of Revelations."

Was it catty? Yes. Did it make me feel good? Hells yes.

Half of Vanguard had arrived at the tower to see the aftermath of the fight. The streets were filled with police officers, fire trucks, ambulances, and hundreds of citizens. By the number of cellphones raised in the air, I'm certain the Deviants were going to be a hot topic on the HeroApp™.

Amidst the chaos, the only thing that mattered was finding Jason. I needed confirmation that he was all right. Damien might have been defeated, but I didn't trust him to not have a backup plan.

"We're with the Deviants! Bernard!"

I turned to see several police officers glancing in my direction as they held Griffin, Aiden, and Jason from rushing into the street. When I gave a nod, they stepped to the side, letting our unpowered counterparts through. I almost had to laugh at the situation. They might not have the ability to fly, but they were just as much Deviants as myself or Xander.

Jason leapt at me, arms wrapping around my neck as he showered me with kisses. I could get used to this. After a long day of saving the world, coming home to this sexy man? Yeah, this is the life I wanted.

"Are you okay?" he asked.

"I was going to ask you the same thing."

"You know..." He stepped back and flexed. "I beat up a bad guy. Basically, I'm a superhero." The cameras continued flashing as citizens yelled for our attention.

I should be nervous. Thousands of photos would put Jason next to not only Sentinel, but the Deviants. Villains everywhere were going to see the connection. As the worry crept into the back of my head, I shoved it away as I admired Jason's best strong-man pose. No, the worry wouldn't scare me away again, and if Vanguard wanted a photograph—

I snatched him by the shirt, pulling him close. Our faces were only inches apart. His arms wrapped around my neck as I held him by the waist. The universe had given me a second chance, the ability to make amends for a terrible decision. I wasn't going to ignore fate.

"Jason Jaynes," I whispered. "I love you."

"You're not so bad yourself," he whispered.

"We'll figure this out," I said.

"Bernard Castle..." He leaned in close enough I couldn't see his lips. "We could have figured it out then. I *know* we'll figure it out now."

His words weren't prying open an old wound so much as laying it to rest. He had been right. They all were. It took me time to come around. Each of them gave me space when I needed it, but not so much that I didn't know they were waiting should I need them. They started as friends, but now they were my family.

"One for the cameras?"

He raised his eyebrow. "Bernard, you exhibitionist, you."

Our toes rose off the ground and we turned with the breeze. The sound of cops shouting grew distant, and the crowds nearly vanished. I wanted to spend the rest of my life with Jason, proving I deserved him.

He kissed me. It started chaste, a peck, but our relationship was anything but chaste. I gently bit his lower lip. It served as a promise of what was to come later tonight, and every night after.

"He's getting away!"

Our romantic finale ended as we dropped to the ground. Damien had shaken off the cops, only one hand secured in cuffs. I had never seen somebody this angry. His master plan had failed, and by the sneer on his face, he wanted one last scuffle. Without his powers, he was nothing more than a disgruntled elitist with a grudge. It'd be sad dragging him back to the squad car.

Damien drew back his fist, ready to start another fight. Jason stood between us, and with a quick jab, he dropped Damien. Jason hissed as he cradled his knuckles. I stood still, blinking in disbelief. Jason Jaynes had dropped Damien Vex. The protector had become the protected.

The cops rushed over, grabbing Damien and securing the cuffs as they dragged him back to the car. Meanwhile, the crowds around the perimeter furiously snapped photos. I couldn't help but laugh as Jason held up his hands.

"Sidekick!"

I smacked my forehead. There was no point in fighting it. As the rest of the Deviants gathered around, we stood shoulder-to-shoulder behind Jason as he struck another pose.

"Man, he's going to be insufferable," Griffin said.

We all turned to stare at Griffin.

"What?"

I grabbed Jason around the waist, pulling him back against me. Now it made sense why they wanted me to join. They were a bunch of Deviants. They needed me to keep them in line.

For better or worse, this was my family.

— THE END—

EPILOGUE 1

"The rings."

I reached into my pocket and produced the black band with a single diamond. Handing one to Chad and the other to Reese, I couldn't help but daydream about the feeling of one around my finger. It was impossible not to think that someday this could be Jason and me.

Reese cleared his throat as he spun the ring in his hand. On the roof of the hotel, both grooms looked stunning in their Guild of Ash tuxedos. Even Mick, acting as the officiant, had taken the time to shave and make himself presentable. As the sun set behind the grooms, the scene bordered on majestic. The smell of flowers filled the air, adding to the romance of a beautiful wedding.

"I wrote this thing a hundred times, but I couldn't find the right words. How do you describe a feeling so complex that we hardly understand what it means? I love you. Three words, three *simple* words. But in the vast space between them are hopes, dreams, fears, excitement, and uncertainty. When you first spoke to me, I couldn't imagine our adventure would bring us here." He gestured to the crowd, to the people hanging on his every word. "But now, I can't see it happening any other way. Chad, I want to live with you in the space between those words. Forever."

Reese wiped away the tears on Chad's face before sliding the ring over his finger. As I rubbed the edge of my eye, I caught sight of Jason three rows back, sitting between Griffin and Xander. He mouthed, "I love you." And like Reese said, I hardly understood the meaning of the words. But with Jason, I wanted to find their definition, no matter how long it took.

"Reese," Chad said. Choked up, he feigned a cough to clear his throat. "I wish I could carry the weight of the world for you. But if you have to carry it on your shoulders, I'll be standing with you shoulder-to-shoulder. I wish I could promise you an eternity. But in this sliver of time we've been given, I'll spend it with you. I wish I could promise to never hurt you. But even when my intentions fall short, I'll set aside my pride to help you heal. I wish I could promise to always be the handsome man before you. But... you've seen my father, this one I *can* promise." The crowd laughed. "What I can promise you, Reese, is my heart. Without hesitation, I promise to love you more than I love coffee."

Those who knew Chad's addiction to coffee gasped before laughing. His words were the perfect blend of sentiment and humor, an accurate representation of their relationship. Chad's hands shook as he slid the ring on Reese's finger. He had plucked his heart from his chest and offered it to Reese. Dammit, now I was crying.

"Do you, Reese, take Chad to be your lawfully wedded husband?"

"I do."

"Do you, Chad—"

"I do!"

I, along with the rest of the audience, chuckled at Chad's eagerness.

There were easily a hundred people seated on either side of the aisle. When there was no more room, people stood in the back. All were eager to witness the next stage of this courtship. Amongst them were shop owners from the Ward, favorite customers, family, and, I suspected by the bulky men tugging at dress shirts, more than a few heroes.

"By the authority invested in me by the city of Vanguard, I now pronounce you husband and husband."

Reese wrapped his arm around Chad, spinning about and dipping him low. The crowd cheered as he went in for the kiss. As the groom's kiss went from chaste to vulgar, we clapped and cheered. They loved with reckless abandon, and the rest of us should only be so lucky.

I caught Jason smiling at me as he clapped. At a wedding with the man I loved, it was hard not to imagine us standing in front of Mick, saying our 'I do's.' At some point, would we be standing on a rooftop, surrounded by our friends and family crying, attempting to summarize our love with vows? I hoped so.

Chad and Reese came up for air, turning toward the aisle. Music filled the air as they linked arms. The happy couple walked through a shower of flower petals. The happy *husbands*. I followed, pausing as I reached the third row. I held out my arm, grinning from ear to ear. "If you'd be so kind."

Jason stepped over Alejandro and Theo, linking his arm with mine. Jason, my *boyfriend*, couldn't look any more handsome if he tried. The buttons of his suit jacket strained just enough to know there was a belly hidden away, and before the end of the night, I'd be resting my head on it.

We walked toward the doors, where tables of food awaited us.

"Someday," Jason whispered in my ear.

"Someday," I repeated.

"Mr. Bernard Jaynes."

"Mr. Jason Castle."

"We'll negotiate," he said as he planted a kiss on my cheek.

For the next two hours, we sat at our table, the Breakfast club, laughing and recounting humorous stories of our relationships. Sebastian gave Griffin grief over his obsession with comic books. Aiden revealed how Xander got emotional watching any movie with puppies. Even Theo admitted that Alejandro's insatiable appetite in the bedroom didn't compare to his newfound passion for cooking, and that he and Julian had been packing on the pounds.

These were my friends—my family. How did Alejandro put it? My ride-or-die crew? I would move Heaven or Hell for each of them. But more than the life-or-death situations, I'd host game nights, go on double dates, and heck, invite them to my house. Each of them had made it clear I'd compartmentalized my life and held back. They had been patient as I resolved my issues. It was time to move forward and stop hiding from these amazing men.

"He's making that face," Griffin said.

"What face?" Asked Sebastian.

"He does this thing when he's deep in thought," Xander added. "It eventually passes."

"Papi, are you okay? Do you remember where you are?"

My eyes narrowed as I glared at Alejandro.

"You know I can't protect you from him," Theo said.

"Papi would never hurt me. I'm his favorite."

"Hey!" Griffin said.

Xander waved at Griffin, dismissing his objections.

"Griffin, there's no point in denying the truth. We know Alejandro is Bernard's favorite." He picked up a champagne glass, taking a swig. "But I'm Sentinel's favorite."

"I hate you all," Griffin said with a laugh.

"Ahem." Jason cleared his throat. "You *were* his favorite."

The table froze. Jason had thrown down the gauntlet. I waited for a rapid string of cursing in Spanish from Alejandro. But instead, he grabbed a glass, raising it up in a toast.

"It's time to pass the baton. Papi, I hope Jason does for you all the things you refused to let me do."

"Questionable toast," Griffin said.

"Best we're going to get out of him," Xander said.

"Oh, I do." Jason raised a glass, locking eyes with me as it clanked against the others. "Don't I, sir?"

These might be my friends, and I wanted to spend the night laughing about our antics, but in one word, Jason made it clear the party needed to continue elsewhere. I couldn't down the champagne fast enough as my pants grew tight.

"We need to be going," I said. No explanation.

"Oh, I know that look, Papi."

Griffin laughed. "Going? He means coming."

"Go get 'em, big guy."

Yes, these were my friends. And I looked forward to seeing how the Breakfast club evolved beyond the confines of the HideOut. But as we waved to Chad and Reese, heading for the elevator that'd bring us to our room, only one man mattered.

Jason. My love.

––––––––––

Controlling lightning made for an impressive display of power in a fight. But as I watched Jason soap himself from the bed, I'd quickly give them up to be under the hot water with him. It didn't help that as he caught my spying, he gave his cock a few extra tugs. He knew exactly how to get my motor running.

It would have been easy enough to head back to my apartment, but I wanted to surprise Jason with one of the hotel's nicest suites. One side resembled a spacious living room and the other a bedroom with a king-sized bed. In the middle, a two-sided fireplace separated them.

I pushed a button on the mantle and flames illuminated the suite. I flipped off the lights, undressing in the warm flicker. Should I remove my briefs? Nah, I decided to let Jason be the one to unwrap his surprise.

Climbing into the bed, I had a direct line of sight to Jason as he toweled off. As he dried his belly, I admired the jiggle, and when he bent over to take care of his legs, I could see the wide curve of where his thighs turned into his ass. If he let me, I'd spend every night worshipping that beautiful body.

When he stepped out of the bathroom, it was hard to ignore the erection stretching the fabric of my underwear. Jason stood at the foot of the bed, the light from the fireplace casting him in shadow. It reminded me of his photo on WoofR, the one that caught my attention months ago.

He carelessly played with himself, and it wouldn't be long before I tore off my underwear and mounted him. Our game of chicken ended when he crawled onto the bed.

"Have I mentioned how sexy you are?"

"Once or twice," he said.

He slid between my legs, his head resting on my thigh. His breath warmed my underwear, causing my cock to jerk. Kissing the spot where my package pressed against my leg, he teased, keeping an eye on my bulge. For now, I let him, knowing full well that before I came, he'd be begging sir for mercy.

The kissing moved to my balls, and then along my shaft. By the time he reached the tip, a small wet circle had formed in the fabric. Despite repeating this routine every night for the last month, it hadn't lessened my body's reaction. Nobody knew how to taunt and tease like him. Despite years apart, he hadn't forgotten how to push every button.

"Take it out."

Jason followed orders, pulling my underwear half down my hips before freeing my cock. He repeated the kissing, but with his lips touching my skin, I closed my eyes and savored the sensation. He had explained that after a day of assisting teachers in training kids with powers, he didn't want to make decisions in the bedroom. By uttering the word, sir, he relinquished the reins.

With my eyes closed, I let out a long sigh, relaxing as Jason dragged his tongue along my balls. "Get it wet." He didn't question the command. He trusted me to satisfy his needs before the night was over.

I watched as his fingers circled the base of my cock, squeezing, trying to get his pointer and thumb to touch. The tiny gap shouldn't have made me smile. Every man likes to appreciate the size of their cock. Jason didn't seem to mind until I attempted to thrust the entirety of it into his ass. We'd see how well he followed orders before I decided how I'd mount him.

Angling it toward his mouth, he dragged his tongue over the head, the strand of precum hanging from his tongue. With a deep inhale, he descended, swallowing to the base. The wet warmth forced a moan from my lips. I reached down, holding the back of his head as I angled my hips, pushing the last against the bend of his throat. The moaning grew louder.

I held his head in place, savoring the sensation of his tongue flicking the underside of my cock. He attempted to pull away, but I held him in place, wanting a few extra seconds before he retreated. Instead of struggling, he reached under my hips, cupping my ass. I let my hand slide to the side of his face.

"Slow," I whispered.

Taking his time, he pulled away from my cock. He sucked in a ragged breath. He returned to a fast bobbing, his lips brushing that sensitive spot along the circumcision line. The sensation might have been exhilarating, but the gusto, that was the real turn-on. Jason was nothing short of a gentleman in public, but when the door closed, he let his freak flag fly.

"Ready to get fucked?"

He nodded with my cock in his mouth. "Yethsir." To stress his point, he got on his hands and knees, pushing his ass into the air. I froze, appreciating the sight of Jason. Beyond thinking with my cock, I claimed to be the luckiest man in the world.

The universe had granted me a second chance with this bear of a man. It had become equal parts picking up where we left off and learning about the men we had become over the last six years. From his new obsession with Korean tacos to him finally admitting he loved sappy rom-coms, I craved more. I reminded myself that I had been a fool leaving, but with that came a little voice saying I had the rest of my life to make up for my mistake.

He flicked my cock. "You're doing that thing."

I slapped his hand. "Give a guy a moment to appreciate the beautiful man in front of him."

He buried his face against my thigh. "Admire while you fuck."

He deftly moved between love and lust. When I called him handsome, his face turned red, but not when I said I wanted to fuck him. I loved... I loved everything about Jason.

Hovering off the bed, I zipped behind him. He had been apprehensive about powers in the bedroom, but he had grown to love a little extra spice. I wouldn't lie. It was fun showing off for him, especially when it made him moan.

Standing behind Jason, I admired the curves rounding from his hips to his ass. I had studied them, running my hand along his skin. I could feel him with my eyes. My hand hovered close enough to feel the heat, but only grazed his body. Tiny sparks jumped from my palm, crinkling and snapping against his ass.

"Fuck." He shoved his face into the comforter. It barely muted his moaning as he wiggled his backside. I continued, letting the sparks tickle along the underside of his balls. The moans turned to whimpers as he pushed his ass back. I knew exactly what he wanted, but I wanted to see how long I could tease him before he said it aloud.

The lightning stopped, but I used the energy to warm the palm of my hand. Reaching under his balls, I slowly wrapped my fingers around his cock. He was already leaking in anticipation. Perfect, just the way I wanted him.

I got down to my knees so I could admire his cock and the belly resting on the bed. The sight was enough to cause a gasp. His head came up, but before he could say anything, I buried my face between his cheeks. Whatever demands he was about to make were replaced with moaning as his fingers dug into the blanket.

Jason pushed back, wanting my tongue inside him. I resisted, continuing the teasing as I dragged the flat of my tongue across his ass. I stopped stroking as his hips thrust, fucking my hand in a slow, steady motion. With my free hand, I dug my fingers into his ass, parting his cheeks in preparation.

I drove my tongue inside Jason's hole. His head shot up, letting out an almost pornographic roar. His hips moved between fucking my hand and trying to get my tongue deeper. I could barely resist the temptation to make him come and use it as lube. But tonight, I wanted him to come while I was inside him.

"Fuck me." It bordered on begging, a command mixed with a whimper. "Please, sir." It was all the motivation I needed.

I let go of his cock and stood behind him, resting my length along the crack of his ass. Self-control had its limits, and as much as I wanted to make him beg, a man has needs. Right now, I *needed* to be inside my boyfriend, to feel his body underneath mine as I drove us to a climax.

"Good boy." I gave his ass a pat. He flinched, expecting the sharp sting of a slap. In good time.

Holding my cock, I rested the head against his ass and watched as it vanished. I couldn't hear Jason as I gasped. He was tight, and oh, so warm. I could have shoved my cock in him like a horny teenager, but I wanted to savor the sensation. Another inch and I bit my lip. Jason tried pushing back, but I grabbed his hips, holding him in place.

By the time I reached the halfway point, Jason had switched tactics, clenching his ass. If I held this position and let him continue, he'd make me come without a single thrust. But I had something a bit more flashy in store for the finale.

Pulling at his hips, I watched my cock disappear into Jason. I'm pretty sure we both moaned. Him from the width of my cock, me from the sense of satisfaction. Not from fucking Jason, but finally... my boyfriend. Goofy, I know, but there was something wonderful about Jason knowing me, all of me, and staying. If I thought about it for long, I'd get emotional, and right now, the bottom wrapped around my cock demanded his sir take care of him.

It started with a single thrust, all the way out, until just the head remained. Then the entire length. Slow. Steady. Each time my balls slapped against his taint, I grunted. As I held his hips, preventing him from pushing back, it felt like heaven. If I reached down, I'm sure I'd find Jason's cock rigid and dripping.

I slid out, waiting for the demands.

"Shove it in," he whimpered.

My hands slid from his hips, cupping his ass. I couldn't help but admire the softness, the way my hands sank into him. I gave him what he wanted. Without holding him in place, Jason moved back and forth, fucking himself on my cock.

Smack.

He hissed as my hand struck his left cheek. But he didn't miss a beat. Smack. The hiss turned into a whimper. On the third, he crumbled on the bed, leaving his ass in the air. In the morning, I'd admire the handprint. It'd be enough to get me worked up all over again.

I withdrew, grabbing Jason by the legs and rolling him onto his back. His eyes were wide with surprise. There were perks to having strength, especially in the bedroom.

His legs wrapped around my waist as I shoved in to the base. If it was hot seeing his ass in the air, waiting for me, this was indescribable. His heels dug into my ass, pulling me closer as I ran my hands along his belly. I had recommitted myself to learning every inch of his body. He was beautiful, so much so that I often wondered how I had gotten so lucky.

"I love you," I whispered.

"I know." He shot me a wink. Rascal.

I leaned forward, my face hovering inches above his.

With his cock trapped between our bellies, it'd only be a matter of minutes before the friction made him come.

With a kiss, I slid my hands behind his back. It wasn't the best angle for depth, but feeling his body pressed against mine was more important than my penis.

"Ready?"

His eyebrow raised. "For..."

I hoisted him upright, sliding a hand to his ass. Before superpowers, it'd be impossible to fuck Jason in this position. Big guys are hot as hell, but lifting them was challenging at best. He wrapped his arms around my neck as I pulled him close, savoring the sensation of his cock pressed against me.

"Show off," he whispered.

"Got to work to keep my man happy."

Cupping his ass, I raised and lowered him, letting my cock slide in and out. Hearing his breath in my ear took me to the edge. When he bit my earlobe, it became a struggle to resist the pleasure racing along my skin.

In a short, breathy voice, he said the magic words. "Come in me, sir."

I squeezed his ass, lowering him until my cock was buried. The orgasm started in my toes and I had to take a step back.

"I'm..."

I didn't have to finish the sentence as my cock jerked inside Jason. His heels dug in tight, and he moaned, a deep guttural sound from his belly. As I came inside my boyfriend, he coated my belly. His grip tightened, and with each pulse, he grunted, almost in time to my own orgasm.

Even as the bliss dwindled, I didn't want to put him down. I wanted to hold him until his muscles ached. When I softened, sliding from Jason, I decided it was time to call an end to the session, at least for tonight. But I wasn't letting him go.

I hovered off the floor, kissing along his neck to the base of his ear. I landed on the bed on my knees, laying him down. Rolling onto my back, I pulled him against me, his body on top of mine.

"You get a gold star," he panted.

"Keeping a tally?"

He laughed as he slid to my side, nuzzling against my chest. "There's an app for that."

I shook my head. "Of course there is."

"Don't worry. You're in the lead."

"Oh good, otherwise we'd have to try again."

He nodded. "I still have a cheek without your handprint."

Growl. I couldn't tell if he was teasing or if he wanted another round.

We had laid in bed for an hour, his head on my chest, playing with the trail of hair from my chest to my belly button. My phone shook along the table. Jason lifted his head, reaching over to pick it up. He rolled his eyes before showing me the screen.

Lydia: Deviants. Cthulhu is attacking the seaport.

"Nope," I said. "Let him destroy a few ships. I'm not moving from this spot."

Jason gave me a slight push toward the edge of the bed. When I protested, he pushed harder. "Go save the city. But you know the rule."

I couldn't hide the smile. We had taken time to put our insecurities on the table. He'd avoid the more dangerous parts of the city, and I'd stop treating him like a damsel in distress. He'd support my heroing, but Sunday nights were for us binging science fiction on the couch. The more we talked about our needs, the things that'd see us through the rocky times, the more I grasped why I loved him.

"Come home to my adorable boyfriend."

"Oh no, not that rule." His eyebrows waggled, forcing me to laugh.

"Fine." I hopped out of bed, naked, cock still at half-mast. With fists on my hips, I widened my shoulders, striking a classic superhero pose. As Jason's eyes fixated, the heat reached my face. Even my cock jumped from his admiration. The watch on my wrist dissolved, the red nanites coating my skin. As the suit spread across my body, I resisted the urge to giggle from the tickling.

Jason whistled. "I'll be peeling that off when you get back."

Thankfully, the suit hid my growing cock. If Jason wanted another round, he'd get exactly that. First, wrestle an eldritch god, then some wrestling with this sexy man. Damn.

I kissed him on the forehead before making for the balcony.

"Give 'em hell, Bernard."

"I always do." As I stepped onto the balcony, I watched Sebastian and Xander jump from their windows and take to the skies. My team, my family, we'd save the world... together. But we needed to make this quick, because I wanted to end the night nuzzling the back of Jason's neck. The thought of holding him while he slept was a reward that'd motivate. The man I love deserved nothing less.

My boyfriend. I'd never tire of that phrase. At least until he honored me with the privilege of being my husband. Eventually, I'd work up the courage to take the ring out of my nightstand and get down on one knee.

Forever. With Jason Jaynes, it would never be long enough.

EPILOGUE 2

Damien Vex. The only voice left in my head belonged to me. The whispers and smooth, seductive echo no longer pulled at my thoughts, controlling my body like a puppet. It had delivered on its promise of wealth, fame, and power.

But now? All that remained was emptiness.

I massaged the spot where the gem had been. Despite the dark hair on my chest, its former home remained bare.

The gentle snoring from the bunk above mine didn't hide the jingle of keys as a guard went about his rounds. It had only been a week since the judge's gavel ended my trial. Guilty. Murder, conspiracy, aggravated assault, disturbing the peace, all with a superpower enhancement. The jury hardly deliberated before announcing their verdict.

It might take the entirety of my sentence to sort out

which actions belonged to me and which belonged to the gem. Had it made me a villain? Or had it given me the opportunity to fulfill my desires? The mighty had fallen, and I smashed into the depths of rock bottom. There was nowhere to go but up. I prepared to claw my way to the top.

There was no room for pity or despair. Damien Vex's story wouldn't end up rotting inside a tiny cell. Already I had determined the power players within the prison. If I could access their power, I'd beat them into submission. Even if I still had my abilities, the collar around my neck prevented their use. I'd have to rely on my cunning, at first.

The echo of shoes walking along the patrol route differed from usual. The jingling had vanished, and the heavy fall of steel-toed boots was replaced with something more delicate. A shoe with a heel?

The figure stood in front of my cell, but I didn't want to give them the courtesy of being surprised. I held fast to staring at the worn-out springs of my cellmate's bunk. They cleared their throat. *She* cleared her throat. That's all it took for me to recognize my visitor.

"Carmen LaToya."

"Vex."

It surprised me the former director of the Centurions graced me with her presence. But I didn't let it show. I wouldn't allow her to have the upper hand.

"To what do I owe this pleasure?"

"Damien Vex." She spoke my name as if cursing. "I

caught the end of your trial. How many lifetimes did you receive?"

"Enough." Four lifetimes. But with parole, I'd be out when I was one hundred and two. It'd make for a wonderful birthday.

"How would you like to buy back your freedom?"

Curious. I sat up, sliding out of my bunk. The sunglasses were a nice touch. One might think she was attempting to be mysterious, but I recognized the technology. Carmen LaToya scrambled the cameras. There'd be no trace that she ever visited my cell.

I held onto the bars. Once upon a time, I'd be able to tear them apart like tin foil. Now I couldn't even make them rattle. The lack of power made her smirk. She took pleasure in knowing she had the upper hand. For now...

"What are you offering, LaToya?"

"Your freedom."

Clenching the bars tighter, I leaned against the metal, the coolness pressing into the sides of my face. Even with the court sentence, the bigger worry was my fellow inmates. I'd be an old man when they granted me freedom. That's if I survived a prison filled with powered villains.

"Not even you can convince the courts to—"

"What I'm offering is beyond the scope of the law."

Firing her from the Centurions had been a mistake. Carmen LaToya had a ruthlessness about her I hadn't previously noticed. If the courts did not condone her actions, I had to wonder which agency sent her. FBI? CIA? SHI?

She stepped close enough that I could reach out and grab her coat. LaToya held her position, and the smirk returned. She wanted it known that she didn't fear me. It'd be a mistake she'd regret. Eventually, in time, I'd wipe the smirk from her face. But for now, it appeared we needed one another.

"I'm listening."

"Damien Vex," she said, "this is the start of your story."

"Poetic."

"Heaven help us, but we need the villains of Vanguard."

The Men of Vanguard Universe
Continues In the Villains of Vanguard

WANT MORE BERNARD & JASON?

Scan For More Steamy Romance

AFTERWORD

I am a gay man obsessed with superheroes. As a kid, I had no role models, and that hasn't changed much as an adult. Because of this, I bringing my relationships, sex life, and love of comics to the forefront in the *Men of Vanguard Series*. The characters in these books reflect personal experiences and themes set against a fictional backdrop.

ABOUT THE AUTHOR

Superheroes stories are at core of Ryder O'Malley's origin story. Refusing to read as a child, everything changed with the first stack of comics. He has always been a fan of forbidden romances within the pages of comics. It should be expected that he'd turn around and start writing his own stories filled with sexy, super, man-on-man action. Ryder's novels draw on his own experiences as a gay man in search of love.

Ryder lives in Charlotte, North Carolina living his happily-ever-after. When he's not writing, he can be found working on book covers (which means he's admiring huskular bears with a little bit of chest hair.)

DISCORD
discord.gg/u4uc4362aC

PATREON
www.patreon.com/writeremyflagg

Ingram Content Group UK Ltd.
Milton Keynes UK
UKHW012253080523
421436UK00014B/352/J